Kenule Beeson Saro-Wiwa w   coast of Nigeria. He was born   with strong   bal links. He wa   Umuahia, where he later taught, and at the University of   adan. In the mid 1960s he became a graduate assistant at the University of Nigeria, and then an assistant lecturer at the University of Lagos.

Saro-Wiwa's interest in politics emerged during the late 1960s, when he was appointed administrator for Bonny, Rivers State. He had spells as Commissioner for Works, Land and Transport; Education; and Information and Home Affairs. In the early 1980s he turned to writing, and in 1983 he published his first novel. His very success-ful television series, *Basi & Co.*, ran from 1985 to 1990. His most highly respected work was *Sozaboy: A Novel in Rotten English*: an odd mixture of pidgin and idiomatic English and a satirical portrait of the corruption of Nigeria's military junta, with a bitingly humor-ous edge.

From 1990 his writing was ousted by his role as president of the Movement for the Survival of the Ogoni People (MOSOP), and he embarked on a campaign to bring their plight to the attention of the world. In 1993, after the election-day disturbances, Saro-Wiwa was imprisoned for a month and a day. The text of this book is a poignant account of his experience in prison. In May 1994 four Ogoni leaders were killed, suspected of collaborating with the military authorities, and Saro-Wiwa was again arrested, but this time the charge was murder – an accusation he always denied.

On 2 November 1995 Ken Saro-Wiwa was sentenced to death. Eight days later he was executed at Port Harcourt, Nigeria.

KEN SARO-WIWA

A MONTH AND
A DAY

A Detention Diary

INTRODUCTION BY WILLIAM BOYD

PENGUIN BOOKS

PENGUIN BOOKS

Published by the Penguin Group
Penguin Books Ltd, 27 Wrights Lane, London W8 5TZ, England
Penguin Books USA Inc., 375 Hudson Street, New York, New York 10014, USA
Penguin Books Australia Ltd, Ringwood, Victoria, Australia
Penguin Books Canada Ltd, 10 Alcorn Avenue, Toronto, Ontario, Canada M4V 3B2
Penguin Books (NZ) Ltd, 182–190 Wairau Road, Auckland 10, New Zealand

Penguin Books Ltd, Registered Offices: Harmondsworth, Middlesex, England

First published 1995
1 3 5 7 9 10 8 6 4 2

William Boyd's Introduction first appeared in
the 27 November 1995 issue of *The New Yorker*

Typeset by Datix International Limited, Bungay, Suffolk
Set in 11/13 pt Monophoto Sabon
Printed in England by Clays Ltd, St Ives plc

CONTENTS

INTRODUCTION

Ken Saro-Wiwa was a friend of mine. At eleven thirty in the morning on 10 November 1995, he was hanged in a prison in Port Harcourt, in eastern Nigeria, on the orders of General Sani Abacha, the military leader of Nigeria. Ken Saro-Wiwa was fifty-four years old, and an innocent man.

I first met Ken in the summer of 1986 at a British Council seminar at Cambridge University. He had come to England from Nigeria in his capacity as a publisher and had asked the British Council to arrange a meeting with me. He had read my first novel, *A Good Man in Africa*, and had recognized, despite fictional names and thin disguises, that it was set in Nigeria, the country that had been my home when I was in my teens and early twenties.

Ken had been a student at the University of Ibadan, in western Nigeria, in the mid sixties. My late father, Dr Alexander Boyd, had run the university health services there, and had treated Ken and come to know him. Ken recognized that the Dr Murray in my novel was a portrait of Dr Boyd and was curious to meet his son.

I remember that it was a sunny summer day, one of those days that are really too hot for England. In shirt-sleeves, we strolled about the immaculate quadrangle of a Cambridge college, talking about Nigeria. Ken was a small man, probably no more than five feet two or three. He was stocky and energetic – in fact, brim-full of energy – and had a big, wide smile. He smoked a pipe with a curved stem. I learnt later that the pipe was virtually a logo: in Nigeria people recognized him by it. In newsreel pictures that the Nigerian military released of the final days of Ken's show trial, there's a shot of him walking towards the courthouse, leaning on a stick, thinner and aged as a result of eighteen months' incarceration, the familiar pipe still clenched between his teeth.

Ken was not only a publisher but a businessman (in the grocery trade); a celebrated political journalist, with a particularly trenchant and swingeing style; and, I discovered, a prolific writer of novels, plays, poems and children's books (mostly published by him). He was, in addition, the highly successful writer and producer of Nigeria's most popular TV soap opera, *Basi & Co.*, which ran for 150-odd episodes in the mid eighties and was reputedly Africa's most watched soap opera, with an audience of up to thirty million. Basi and his cronies were a bunch of feckless Lagos wide-boys who, indigent and lazy, did nothing but hatch inept schemes for becoming rich. Although funny and wincingly accurate, the show was also unashamedly pedagogic. What was wrong with Basi and his chums was wrong with Nigeria: none of them wanted to work, and they all acted as though the world owed them a living; if that couldn't be acquired by fair means foul ones would do just as well. This was soap opera as a form of civic education.

Whenever Ken passed through London, we'd meet for lunch, usually in the Chelsea Arts Club. His wife and four children lived in England – the children attended school there – so he was a regular visitor. And, though I wrote a profile of him for the London *Times* (Ken was trying to get his books distributed in Britain), our encounters were mainly those of two writers with a lot in common, hanging out for a highly agreeable, bibulous hour or three.

Ken's writing was remarkably various, covering almost all

genres. *Sozaboy*, in my opinion his greatest work, is subtitled *A Novel in Rotten English* and is written in a unique combination of pidgin English, the lingua franca of the former West African British colonies, and an English that is, in its phrases and sentences, altogether more classical and lyrical. The language is a form of literary demotic, a benign hijacking of English, and a perfect vehicle for the story it tells, of a simple village boy recruited into the Biafran army during the Nigerian civil war. The boy has dreamed of being a soldier (a *soza*), but the harsh realities of this brutal conflict send him into a dizzying spiral of cruel disillusion. *Sozaboy* is not simply a great African novel but also a great antiwar novel – among the very best of the twentieth century.

Sozaboy was born of Ken's personal experience of the conflict – the Biafran War, as it came to be known – and, indeed, so were many of his other writings. Biafra was the name given to a loose ethnic grouping in eastern Nigeria, dominated by the Ibo tribe. The Ibo leader, Colonel Chukwuemeka Odumegwu Ojukwu, decided to secede from the Nigerian Federation, taking most of the country's oil reserves with him. In the war that was then waged against the secessionist state, perhaps a million people died, mainly of starvation in the shrinking heartland.

Not all the ethnic groups caught up in Ojukwu's secessionist dream were willing participants. Ken's tribe, the Ogoni, for one. When the war broke out, in 1967, Ken was on vacation and found himself trapped within the new borders of Biafra. He saw at once the absurdity of being forced to fight in another man's war, and he escaped through the front lines to the Federal side. He was appointed civilian administrator of the crucial oil port of Bonny on the Niger River Delta, and he served there until the final collapse of the Biafran forces in 1970. Ken wrote about his experiences of the civil war in his fine memoir, *On a Darkling Plain*.

Ken's later fight against the Nigerian military, as it turned out, was oddly prefigured in those years of the Biafran War: the helplessness of an ethnic minority in the face of an over-powering military dictatorship; oil and oil wealth as a destructive and corrupting catalyst in society, the need to be true to one's conscience.

This moral rigour was especially apparent in Ken's satirical political journalism (he was, over the years, a columnist on the Lagos daily newspapers *Punch*, *Vanguard* and *Daily Times*), much of which was charged with a Swiftian *saeva indignatio* at what he saw as the persistent ills of Nigerian life: tribalism, ignorance of the rights of minorities, rampant materialism, inefficiency and general graft. Apart from *Basi & Co.*, his journalism was what brought him his greatest renown among the population at large.

In the late eighties, I remember, Ken's conversations turned more and more frequently to the topic of his tribal homeland. The Ogoni are a small tribe (there are 250 tribes in Nigeria) of about half a million people living in a small area of the fertile Niger River Delta. The Ogoni's great misfortune is that their homeland happens to lie above a significant portion of Nigeria's oil reserves. Since the mid 1950s, Ogoniland has been devastated by the industrial pollution caused by the extraction of oil. What was once a placid rural community of prosperous farmers and fisher-men is now an ecological waste land reeking of sulphur, its creeks and water holes poisoned by indiscriminate oil spillage and ghoulishly lit at night by the orange flames of gas flares.

As Ken's concern for his homeland grew, he effectively abandoned his vocation and devoted himself to lobbying for the Ogoni cause at home and abroad. He was instrumental in setting up the Movement for the Survival of the Ogoni People (MOSOP) and soon became its figurehead. That struggle for survival was an ecological more than a political one: his people, he said, were being subjected to a 'slow genocide'. Ken protested the despoliation of his homeland and demanded compensation from the Nigerian government and from the international oil companies – Shell in particular. (He resented Shell profoundly and held the company responsible for the ecological calamity in Ogoniland.) But from the outset Ken made sure that the movement's protest was peaceful and non-violent. Nigeria today is a corrupt and dangerously violent nation: it was enormously to the credit of the Ogoni movement that it stayed true to its principles. Mass demonstrations were organized and passed off without incident. Abroad, Greenpeace and other environmental groups allied themselves with the Ogoni cause, but, ironically, the real measure of the success of Ken's agitation came when, in 1992, he was arrested by the Nigerian military and held in prison for some months without a trial. The next year, Shell Oil ceased its operations in the Ogoni region.

At that time, the Ogoni military was led by General Ibrahim Babangida. Ken was eventually released (after a campaign in the British media), and Babangida voluntarily yielded power to General Abacha, a crony, who was meant to supervise the transition of power to a civilian government after a general election, which was duly held in 1993. The nation went to the polls and democratically elected Chief Moshood Abiola as President. General Abacha then declared the election null and void and later imprisoned the victor. Nigeria entered a new era of near anarchy and despotism. Things looked bad for Nigeria, but they looked worse for the Ogoni and their leaders.

Over these years, Ken and I continued to meet for our Chelsea Arts Club lunches whenever he was in London. In 1992 he suffered a personal tragedy when his youngest son, aged fourteen, who was at Eton, died suddenly of heart failure during a rugby game. Strangely, Ken's awful grief gave a new force to his fight for his people's rights.

We met just before he returned to Nigeria. From my own experience of Nigeria, I knew of the uncompromising ruthlessness of political life there. Ken was not young, nor was he in the best of health (he too had a heart condition). As we said goodbye, I shook his hand and said, 'Be careful, Ken, OK?' And he laughed – his dry, delighted laugh – and replied, 'Oh, I'll be very careful, don't worry.' But I knew he wouldn't.

A succession of Nigerian military governments have survived as a result of the huge revenues generated by oil, and the military leaders themselves have routinely benefited from the oil revenues, making millions and millions of dollars. Any movement that threatened this flow of money was bound to be silenced – extinguished. With the ascendance of Abacha and his brazenly greedy junta, Ken was now squarely in harm's way. Even so, he returned to Nigeria to continue his protests. These protests were now conducted in a more sinister country than the one I had known – a country where rapes, murders and the burning of villages were being carried out as a deliberate policy of state terrorism. There have been 2,000 Ogoni deaths thus far.

In May of last year Ken was on his way to address a rally in an Ogoni town but was turned back at a military roadblock and headed, reluctantly, for home. The rally took place, a riot ensued, and in the general mayhem four Ogoni elders – believed to be sympathetic to the military – were killed.

Ken was arrested and, with fifteen others, was accused of incitement to murder. The fact that he was in a car some miles away and going in the opposite direction made no difference. He was imprisoned for more than a year and then was tried before a specially convened tribunal. There was no right of appeal. This 'judicial process' has been internationally condemned as a sham. It was a show trial in a kangaroo court designed to procure the verdict required by the government.

On Thursday, 2 November, Ken and eight co-defendants were found guilty and sentenced to death. Suddenly the world acknowledged the nature of Nigeria's degeneracy.

Things did not augur well. But, instinctively wanting to make the best of a bad situation, I hoped that the publicity surrounding Ken's case, along with the timely coincidence of the Commonwealth conference in New Zealand (the biennial gathering of the former members of the British Empire), would prevent the very worst from happening. Surely, I reasoned, the heads of state congregating in Auckland would not allow one of their members to flout their own human rights principles so callously and blatantly? General Abacha, however, did not dare leave his benighted country, which was represented by his Foreign Minister instead.

The presence of Nelson Mandela at the conference was especially encouraging, not only for me but also for all the people who had spent the last months fighting to free Ken. (We were a loosely knit organization, including International PEN, the Ogoni Foundation, Amnesty International, Greenpeace and others.) We felt that if anything could persuade the Nigerians to think again it would be Mandela's moral authority. We were baffled and confused, though, when Mandela did little more than persistently advocate that we should all be patient, that the problem would be resolved through an easy, low-key diplomacy.

Despite Mandela's advice, there was a clamorous condemnation in the media of the Nigerian military. In response, Abacha's junta released newsreel pictures of Ken's trial to establish the legality of the 'judicial process'. One saw a row of prisoners, still, faces drawn, heads bowed, confronting three stout officers, swagged with gold braid, ostentatiously passing pieces of paper to each other. In the background, a soldier strolled back and forth. Then Ken addressed the court. His voice was strong: he was redoubtably defiant; he seemed without fear, utterly convinced.

These images both defied belief and profoundly disturbed. If Abacha thought that this would make his tribunals look acceptable, then the level of naïvety, or blind ignorance, implied was astonishing. But a keening note of worry was also sounded: someone who could do something this damaging, I thought, was beyond the reach of reason. World opinion, international outrage, appeals for clemency seemed to me now to be nugatory. Abacha had painted himself into a corner. For him it had become a question of saving face, of loud bluster, of maintaining some sort of martial pride. I slept very badly that night.

The next day, 10 November, just after lunch, I received a call from the Writers in Prison Committee of International PEN. I was told that a source in Port Harcourt had seen the prisoners arrive at the gaol at dawn that day, in leg irons. Then the executioners had presented themselves, only to be turned away, because – it was a moment of grimmest, darkest farce – their papers were not in order. This source, however, was '110 per cent certain' that the executions had eventually occurred. Some hours later, this certainty was confirmed by the Nigerian military.

So now Ken was dead, along with eight co-defendants: hanged in a mass execution just as the Commonwealth Conference got under way.

I am bitter and I am dreadfully sad. Ken Saro-Wiwa, the bravest man I have known, is no more. From time to time, Ken managed to smuggle a letter out of prison. One of the last letters I received ended this way: 'I'm in good spirits . . . There's no doubt that my idea will succeed in time, but I'll have to bear the pain of the moment . . . the most important thing for me is that I've used my talents as a writer to enable the Ogoni people to confront their tormentors. I was not able to do it as a politician or a businessman. My writing did it. And it sure makes me feel good! I'm mentally prepared for the worst, but hopeful for the best. I think I have the moral victory.' You have, Ken. Rest in peace.

William Boyd
London
November 1995

First published in the 27 November 1995 issue of *The New Yorker*.

PREFACE

I had completed the first draft of this book when, on 21 May 1994, two of the men to whom I give a lot of attention, Mr Albert Badey and Chief Edward Kobani, were cruelly murdered along with two other prominent Ogoni men at Giokoo in Ogoni. That gruesome and sad event altered my original story somewhat but has not made material difference to it. My condolences go to the bereaved families.

It will be no surprise to my readers to know that the Movement for the Survival of the Ogoni People (MOSOP) was accused of the crime in which I suspect the Nigerian security agencies had a hand. I and the leadership of MOSOP were promptly arrested and I have since been in leg cuffs in a secret military camp outside Port Harcourt, where I have been held incommunicado and been tortured mentally and physically.

The ten months from 22 July 1993, when the incidents narrated in this book end, to 22 May 1994, when I was again arrested and detained, were very difficult for the Ogoni people and the events of that period would have enriched this book even more. However, given the fact that I am not certain what the immediate future may bring, I have thought it wise to get my original draft published and have therefore smuggled it into my detention cell and am correcting and redrafting it in very difficult circumstances. This may affect its quality somewhat, but should also not make material difference to it.

I have skipped some background material related to Ogoni, the Ogoni people and myself in this narration. This is because I have dealt with it in other books such as *On a Darkling Plain: An Account of the Nigerian Civil War* (Saros, London, 1989) and *Genocide in Nigeria: The Ogoni Tragedy* (Saros, London, 1992). Readers who require background material in order to further appreciate the story may consult these and my other books. However, this book can be ordinarily understood without reference to the others.

I should add that I have used the term 'Ogoni' in preference to 'Ogoniland', which is fast becoming current; this is because to the Ogoni, the land and the people are one and are expressed as such in our local languages. It emphasizes, to my mind, the close relationship between the Ogoni people and their environment.

Ken Saro-Wiwa
Port Harcourt
July 1994

CHAPTER ONE

Suddenly, my car screeched to a halt. I raised my head in surprise. Before me was an armed security man flagging the car down, his rifle pointing at my chauffeur's head. Then, just as suddenly, more security men in mufti headed for the rear door of the car, swung it open, and ordered me to get down. I refused to do so. They spoke more gruffly and I remained just as adamant. A superior officer whom I knew well ordered two of the men to get into the empty front seat of the car. They obeyed him. Then they ordered my chauffeur to do a U-turn against the traffic. He obeyed. The superior security officer had turned his own car around and ordered my chauffeur to follow him. Behind us was yet another car which I knew to be a security vehicle crammed with security men. We drove off in a convoy.

It was 21 June 1993. We were at a crossroads in Port Harcourt, at the busy UTC junction on the equally busy expressway linking the city with the town of Aba to the north. The drama took place in front of commuters, and I imagine that many would have guessed that I was being arrested. I, however, knew that for sure. It was my fourth arrest in three months.

As we drove towards the Port Harcourt Club Sports Ground, there was no doubt in my mind as to where we were going: the scrappy offices of the State Security Service (SSS), where I was already a well-known customer, as the saying goes in Nigeria. I chuckled to myself.

3

When we got to the walled-off compound of the dreaded SSS, I got out of my car and instructed my chauffeur to return to my office and let everyone know that I was under arrest. The security men did not impede his departure. They had more urgent matters on their minds.

There was a flurry of activity, a running up and down the crummy stairs by the most senior of my captors, and no one bothered much what I was doing with myself. On previous occasions, I would have engaged in a banter with the young security agents. This time around, I sensed that matters had become more serious and there was not much to joke about. There was an ominous air blowing through the building, once a beautiful place surrounded by a well-manicured lawn, but now generally run-down and definitely grubby. In a short while, the officer who had run upstairs returned, waving a piece of paper. I was ordered into the back of one of the waiting cars, between two gruff and unsmiling security men. We drove out of the SSS compound.

In ten minutes we were at the Central Police Station, a place with which I was not unfamiliar. It had been the state headquarters of the Nigerian Police force but when the force's new office buildings were complete, it got turned over to the State Intelligence and Investigation Bureau (SIIB). It was, as usual with public property in Nigeria, in disrepair. The lawn was littered with cars, in different colours and states. Some appeared to have been there for ages, waiting to be used as exhibits for cases that would never be tried.

I was ushered into a little cubicle which served as office for some investigating police officers, and asked to sit on a wooden bench. I sat there chewing on the stem of my pipe while one of the investigating police officers, who was taking down a statement from an accused person, stared incredulously at me. He might have been star-struck. I had been very much in the news lately, and, as often happens to those who have that misfortune, was considered more as a news item than as a living being with flesh and blood. Seeing me in the latter condition caused my friend's eternal surprise. I understood his agitation and smiled at it.

In another fifteen minutes a form was pushed in front of me and I was asked to write a statement about my activities on election day, 12 June 1993. The Ogoni, under leadership of the Movement for the Survival of the Ogoni People (MOSOP), had boycotted the election. I asked perfunctorily to be allowed to see my lawyer before committing myself to paper. The request, as I expected, was turned down. Without further ado, I whipped out my pen and wrote the required statement, knowing full well that it would never be used. I signed it with a flourish.

A beautiful young woman, a senior police officer, soon came in to examine the statement I had written. She read it, seemed satisfied, and then offered me a place on a rickety wooden chair in her curtained office next door. How sweet of her, I thought. She disappeared with the statement. I was left to my pipe. I stoked it, lit it, and drew deeply. My mind flew about like a bird on the wing.

The young lady returned and smilingly engaged me in conversation. We spoke about Nigeria, about the suffering of the peoples of Rivers State, of oil and the sorrows it had brought those on whose land it is found, of the social inequities in the country, of oppression and all such. She was an Izon, neighbours of the Ogoni and the fourth largest ethnic group of Nigeria's 200-odd groups; they lived in the main oil-producing area of the country. She fully understood all the arguments I had been making and certainly sympathized with them and with me for the travails I had suffered in recent months. She assured me, like many operatives I have met, and am yet to meet, that she did not mean any harm to me but that she was only doing her duty. I accepted her assertions graciously.

This conversation took the sting out of the waiting hour. She soon left the room and her place was taken by a middle-aged man who introduced himself as the husband of the young police officer. He also engaged me in a conversation similar to that of his wife. In this way did I spend another thirty minutes.

The lady returned to the room and asked me to accompany her to the main building. As we crossed the open courtyard with its litter of cars, a bird whispered to me that I was to be taken into detention in Lagos. Nothing that I did not expect. I was beginning to steel myself for any eventuality. It was only then that it occurred to me that I had not had a meal the whole day.

We climbed the dark, dingy steps of the main building to the first floor and I was led before another senior police officer in flowing cotton robes. He offered me a seat far from his work table and I sat there while there was a considerable toing and froing of other police officers, including the man who had played a leading role in my abduction on the express-way. They whispered conspiratorially to the senior police officer and he whispered orders back to them. I watched them with an amused look. Had I known exactly what they were planning, I doubt that I would have found it funny.

After what seemed an interminable wait, the senior police officer told me that on election day, 12 June 1993, policemen had been made to frog-march people in Ogoni and there had been disturbances. I let it be known to him that that was news to me, as I had been in Lagos, a thousand kilometres away and nowhere near Ogoni on the day in question. That did not impress him. He then told me that I was under arrest. I thanked him for the information.

A longish silence followed while I digested this. I looked round the room. It was large, big enough for a huge writing-desk and a full complement of cushioned chairs and two or three filing cabinets. The man at the desk, I noticed, was pencil-thin with aquiline features. He looked quite ungainly, his bearing undignified. I essayed to speak to him as a way of passing the time.

'Where do you come from?' I asked.

'Sokoto,' he replied.

As if I didn't know. Downstairs, you would meet men and women from the slave areas of the modern slave-state called Nigeria. Upstairs were the indigenous colonizers. They were not necessarily well spoken or well educated either. But they had power at their fingertips and knew it.

'How long have you been in Rivers State?' I asked. My mind was elsewhere.

'One year.' Or something to that effect. I was not listening. I did not care for his answer.

'Do you like it here?'

'Yes.'

You bet.

'I gather you're sending me to Lagos.'

'Who told you?'

'A bird.'

'What?'

'The wind.'

'I'm not sending you to Lagos.'

Liar. I wanted to hit him on his lying lips. I pulled out my pipe, struck a match and drew. The smoke danced into the air, upwards towards the ceiling.

'I haven't had anything to eat all day,' I said.

He drew a kola nut from the folds of his dress, broke it in two and offered me half. I declined. He bit into his half and crunched away. I blew more smoke into the air.

My stomach was grumbling like hell. 'I need to eat,' I said.
'We're making arrangements to get you your food,' he
replied.

He got up and walked slowly out of the room, his flowing
robes following after him on the dirty floor. And I was left to
my thoughts. Injustice stalks the land like a tiger on the
prowl. To be at the mercy of buffoons is the ultimate insult.
To find the instruments of state power reducing you to dust
is the injury.

Perforce, my mind went back to the events of that afternoon.
I had been at my 24 Aggrey Road office with the usual collection of Ogoni youths discussing the events of the election,
which the Ogoni people had decided to boycott. I had not
been present in Ogoni during the elections. On 11 June I was
on my way to the United Nations World Human Rights Conference, to be held the next week in Vienna, Austria. As I
completed immigration formalities at the international airport in Lagos, a security man impounded my passport – for
the third time in as many months – and ordered me to call at
the SSS office a week later. I cooled my heels in Lagos and
watched the Nigerian presidential elections of 12 June from
there. Now, Ogoni youths were filling me in on the details of
the boycott. As we talked, one of my security guards came to
inform me that a man he suspected to be from the SSS had
come calling and he had told him that I was not available.
The man had gone away, but he felt sure that he had not
gone far. He would, as was their wont, hang around till my
car showed up. He would then barge into my office. I
thanked the guard and continued to listen to the men in my
office.

A while afterwards my chauffeur returned, and, as the
security guard had informed me, five men walked into my
office behind him without bothering to knock on the door. I

recognized one of them as a security agent. They were all in mufti. I greeted the man whom I recognized cheerily and he smiled. We knew what it was all about, by routine.

'Oga wants to see you, sir,' he said, meaning that I was being summoned by his boss, the state director of the SSS.

'Sorry, I'm not available,' I reply.

'But, sir . . .'

'You know I have a high court injunction restraining you from infringing my fundamental human rights. It's not as it was in the past. Now, before you arrest me, you have to produce a warrant. You can't just barge into my office or tap me on the shoulder on the highway or at the airport and expect me to follow you. Do you have a warrant of arrest?'

'We haven't come to arrest you. We're only inviting you to the office.'

'To drink tea or have lunch?'

'Just come along with us,' pleaded a robust black man whom I hadn't seen before. He had perfect dentition, I observed.

'No, I'm sorry, I can't come with you.' This, with finality.

The altercation went on longer. And when they found that I was adamant, they trooped out of my office. The Ogoni youths advised me to leave. But I knew better and we continued our discussion.

Fifteen minutes later the security agents, all four or five of them, returned armed with a warrant of arrest. They presented me with it. I read it and noted that it was signed by a Mrs Aguma, Justice of the Peace. It stated expressly that the security agents were free to search my premises and if anything incriminating was found, I was to be brought before her court. I latched on to this and offered to go with them to Mrs Aguma's court and not to the SSS office.

The security agent had not read the warrant, and he took it from me and read it now before me. Then he pocketed it.

'You're making our work difficult for us,' said one of them. 'Just come with us to the office. There is nothing in it.'

'I have a court injunction. But if you like, I'll call in at your office later today. Say, six o'clock. Only as a matter of courtesy. I have a meeting at 2 pm.' I looked at my watch. It was already 2.15 pm. 'Oh dear, I'm late. And I don't like to go late to meetings!'

'All right, sir,' said one of them. 'We're leaving.' And they walked out of my office.

I tidied my desk, left my briefcase on my table and went downstairs into my car. As I opened my car door, a busload of policemen drove into the bus stop in front of my office. The fact that they drove against the normal flow of traffic, that the bus was new and did not bear the usual insignia of the Nigerian police force, made me suspicious. But I did not give further thought to it.

My office in Port Harcourt lies on the busy Aggrey Road in the centre of the old township, which had been very well laid out by the colonial government before the Nigerian military came to ruin it with their disorderliness and incompetence. No one wreaked more havoc on the layout of the old township than Governor Diete-Spiff, a navy officer who was appointed to office by the Gowon administration in 1967 upon the creation of Rivers State in that year. He proceeded to turn every open space created by the original planners of the town into a building lot. And by the time subsequent rulers of the state had stopped collecting garbage or cleaning the gutters, old Port Harcourt had become another slum. Because my office gave out on Aggrey Road, I did not get the full effect of the slum quality of the town. There was a bus stop pat in front of the office so I often found unsolicited entertainment of the street variety if I peeped through the window, or as I came in and went out.

But that afternoon I was not in search of entertainment. I

was, myself, providing much of it. So, driving out of the place was a welcome development. A large number of Ogoni youths, anxious to protect me from the security agents, had gathered, and some of them insisted they would come with me in the car, just in case. But I told them that I had no need for company. I did take a lawyer with me in the car, but that was to offer him a lift. As soon as we got to his chambers, I dropped him off and continued alone towards the venue of the meeting of Ogoni elders; they had been most affected by the boycott of the elections and were licking their wounds, threatening fire and brimstone against all who did not see eye to eye with them. I had hoped that the meeting would help assuage their fears and worries.

I had calculated that the meeting was going to last three to four hours and that at its conclusion I would report to the SSS at about 6 pm. So I planned.

What I did not know, and what I should have known, was that the security agents were not being sincere when they had said that they would be leaving me. I hardly thought that they would be waylaying me on a busy thoroughfare at 2.45 pm. And that by 6.30 I would be the guest of a fidgety, lying Assistant Commissioner of Police.

My host soon returned to his office, and this time he appeared a bit panicky. He picked up a walkie-talkie, put it back in its place, called his man Friday, asked for another walkie-talkie, found it impossible to operate the same, sat in his seat, looked out of the window, went back to the door, stepped out of the office, returned to the room and to his seat, and chewed on his kola nut.

At that point young Barry Kumbe from Ledum Mitee's chambers, my lawyers, asked to see the Assistant Commissioner of Police. The latter turned down the request. I pleaded with him to allow me speak to Barry. He would not allow it. I said I wanted at least to have someone tell my household of my whereabouts and possibly arrange a meal for me. My captor was unrelenting. I asked to use the gents. Permission granted.

On my way back from the hallowed ground, which was not kept neat at all, Barry Kumbe waylaid me. I informed him that I thought I might be taken to Lagos and asked him to make all the arrangements for my legal defence, if that was going to be of any use whatsoever.

I was still speaking with Barry when my captor arrived and ordered the former to go away. I returned to the room.

Night was already falling and I was roaring hungry.

'Have you really made arrangements for my dinner?' I asked.

He became rather impatient. 'Don't worry,' he said, 'we know our work.' The implication was that I was trying to teach him his job: a sin in Nigerian official circles punishable by great wickedness.

I watched him as he chewed on his kola nut. To stay the anger that was welling up in me, I had to have recourse to my pipe. There was continuous motion in the room as police officers came and went, conferring with their boss, as earlier on, in low conspiratorial tones. The slow minutes ticked by. I wondered what was in store for me.

At eight o'clock or thereabouts my medical doctor brother, Owens, was announced. This time, my captor had no hesitation in allowing him in. He then went out and allowed me and my brother to be alone. The Nigerian police hate lawyers. They do not mind doctors. Lesson learnt.

Owens and I share the same birthday, 10 October, fourteen years apart. He was always the most apolitical of men and seemed dedicated to himself. After qualifying from medical school at the University of Calabar, he had worked for a brief time in the Rivers State Ministry of Health, and when he found that constricting set up a clinic at Bori, the head-quarters of the Ogoni. Without electricity or telephone or pipe-borne water, Bori was nothing to write home about, and again Owens got bored with it. The practice was not satisfactory. The misery all around was virtually unbearable. And I believe that this was what turned him into a tireless political activist.

When we started the Movement for the Survival of the Ogoni People, it took him some time to assess the organiza-tion. But by 4 January 1993, when we had the mammoth protest march involving about 300,000 people which sig-nalled the commencement of the non-violent resistance to our denigration as a people, he had become a key factor in the movement. On the day of the march he was one of the few medical practitioners around, and the ambulance belong-ing to his clinic was the only vehicle available to take care of any emergency cases.

He walked into the room with a bundle of currency notes, a toothbrush and paste and some medicine. Most thoughtful of him, I noted gratefully.

'As I was coming upstairs, someone at the reception ad-vised me to give you enough medicine to last you a long time.'

We laughed.

'I understand I'm to be taken to Lagos. There's no aircraft tonight. So it's likely to be tomorrow. Meanwhile, I haven't had a bite all day. Can you arrange to get me something from my place?'

'I got some snacks on my way here.' And he offered me the meal.

It was inedible. Maybe it was not really that bad. But I am a fanatic for home-cooked food. All that mass-produced stuff never excites me. And as far as Nigeria is concerned, I remain doubtful of the level of hygiene in kitchens where junk food is prepared, and of the quality control of such food. Indeed, there is no control.

My brother soon departed and I waited anxiously for his return. I hardly thought that I was not to see him again that night.

A while after my brother left, the Assistant Commissioner of Police arrived and motioned to me to follow him. The dinner he had promised me had arrived. We went through the dimly lit corridor and the short staircase to the ground floor. There, stationed and waiting, was a vehicle I was to become more than familiar with over the next month and a day, a Peugeot J5 passenger bus.

I was ordered into the bus. As I climbed in, a gentleman in a lounge suit ordered me to put out my unlit pipe. I quickly pocketed it. Another police officer in a Yoruba-style caftan and trousers seized my packet of matches. My stomach roared.

The bus held several plastic jerry cans of petrol, there being a general shortage of petrol in the country at the time. The bus itself reeked of the smell of petrol and I felt like puking. I steeled myself courageously. The mere thought of driving in the vehicle to Lagos was enough to upset me. I hadn't travelled in that mode for over twenty-five years. Indeed, I hadn't travelled to Lagos by road for twenty years and more. Eight armed policemen climbed into the bus after me. In the front seat were the man in a lounge suit and another man whom I presumed to be a senior police officer. The man in the caftan sat next to me on one of the padded seats. I noticed that there was a pick-up van also full of armed policemen in front of the bus. And standing about were policemen armed with riot gear. In a few minutes, in a hail of tear gas, we were on our way out of the compound.

We drove into Aggrey Road, past my office. I noticed that

a small crowd had gathered in front, all of them wearing anxious faces. I looked at my watch. It was ten thirty. If we were going to Lagos, I thought, we would have to drive all night, arriving there the next morning at ten o'clock. My heart beat a wild tattoo. Why, I asked myself, would the police want to put me through such torture?

The bus sped through the heart of Port Harcourt, on to the Port Harcourt–Aba Expressway, and towards the Rumuo-kwuta junction. The normally busy road lay quiet, although a few vehicles still plied it. Once out of Port Harcourt, the lights of the houses disappeared from sight and the lights of the vehicle picked up the bushes as we rushed past.

The man in the lounge suit put me at considerable ease when he said, 'Mr Saro-Wiwa, I know you well by reputation. I have read a lot of your newspaper articles. But more than that, your wife and mine were together at Imaguero College in Benin in the seventies.'

'Really!' I exclaimed. 'Isn't it a small world? And what's your name?'

'Don't worry about that.'

'Where are we going to?'

'Don't worry. When we get there, you'll know.'

'Why do we have to drive at night? Am I safe?'

'Don't worry. At least you know you're in the hands of the police. You're safe.'

What comfort. The hands of the police offer safety and protection? The Nigerian police? Aren't they the ones who've shot people at check-points? Isn't it in their custody cells that accused persons regularly die? What protection could the police offer against a motor accident? What if armed robbers were to waylay the convoy and there was a shootout? A myriad uncomfortable thoughts crossed my mind.

I had in my hand only my black clutch-bag crammed with my tobacco, diary, address book, calculator, scissors for

15

cutting paper and pencil. I also had the 2,000 naira which my brother Owens had thoughtfully given me at the police station. He had, indeed offered me 5,000 naira, of which I had accepted only two. I had felt that I would not need the rest, and in any case, I did not have room in my clutch-bag for a bulky sum of money in currency notes. The thought of armed robbers made me hold my clutch-bag tightly. For a fleeting moment, I thought of the possibility of the policemen who were with me in the car pouncing on me and taking away the money. I dismissed the thought just as quickly.

The bus sped on through the night on the narrow tarmac road that led towards Warri in the west. In the brief conversation which I held with the man in the lounge suit, I gathered that he had attended the University of Ibadan, where he had read history, and the University of Lagos, where he had read law. He was, therefore, no ordinary police officer. Somehow, I felt a bit more comfortable knowing that I was in the hands of a man of some education.

Throughout that journey I did not sleep a wink. I knew the road to Warri well enough, having just done the trip early in April when I had been slated to give a lecture to the National Association of Itsekiri Students.

On that occasion I had driven in the comfort of my new air-conditioned car. The road through Izon country had been rough and so had the journey. I arrived in Warri to the welcoming hands of twenty police officers and men who had been detailed to arrest me on arrival. They promptly did so before I had had the opportunity of informing the students that I was in Warri. They took me to the police station, searched my bags and ordered me out of the town.

For good measure, they escorted me out of Delta State, in which Warri lies, stationing a senior police officer in my car to ensure that I did not escape, while another car full of police officers led the way. They dumped me on the other side of the Niger River in my home state, Rivers State, and bid me goodbye with a smile. I had been quite safe in the hands of the police.

Now, as we approached Warri towards one o'clock, I recalled that occasion and the furore it had raised in the Nigerian press. Thick-skinned as ever and versed in the ways of repression, the security agencies had not learnt to leave me alone.

Warri was as silent as a graveyard when we arrived there. My captors had meant, I understood from the conversation which followed, to stop at one of the police stations in the town in order to catch some sleep. In the event, they could not find their way to the particular police station and we had to stop at a petrol-filling station.

Everyone except myself went to sleep. I thought then of my youth and how I might have been tempted, in those heady days, to jump out of the bus, grab a rifle from one of the sleeping guards and shoot my way to safety or to adventure and death. I thought also, for a brief moment, of my family: father, mother, brothers and sisters and how they would be feeling. I thought of my children: he that was ill in my house in Port Harcourt; and of that other one, the elegant young boy, fourteen years old, who had been at Britain's premier school, Eton College, and whom I had buried only in March at Eton Wick.

But my main thought went to the Ogoni people and the travails they had been forced to endure for over a century, which travail I was as determined as iron to mitigate in my lifetime. I thought of the tremendous courage they had shown in the six months since I began to stir up things and to raise the questions which no one seemed willing to confront.

I wondered what they would do, faced as they were with my arrest.

They were unused to political activism and the dangers inherent in it. I had taken them on a hard journey and although I had prepared their minds for it in public speeches and in private, I was not quite sure how they would react in any particular circumstance. Some were used to the detention endured by mostly Yoruba activists in Nigeria. None of their kin had ever undergone such horrors. They had been sleepwalking their way towards extinction, not knowing what internal colonialism had done and was doing to them. It had fallen to me to wake them up from the sleep of the century and I had accepted in full the responsibility for doing so. Would they be able to stand up to the rigours of the struggle?

I was to learn later that Ogoni youths had shown far more solidarity, far more courage, than I had credited them with. Not knowing what had happened to me, they had gone in a group of 500 or more to the offices of the SSS and opened every single door in an effort to trace me. And when they had not found me there, they had gone to the Central Police Station in Port Harcourt, where they engaged the riot police in a struggle. They picked up canisters of tear gas shot by the police before they could explode and threw them back at their tormentors. They tore down a part of the brick wall which fenced off the police station from the rest of the town. And almost all night they lit bonfires along Aggrey Road to place a distance between the brutality of the police and themselves. They made sure that the town of Port Harcourt heard their protest at my arrest. And no one could stop them. My brother Owens, who tried to calm them, was openly accused of having received bribes from the police and he had to leave them to their devices!

*

Meanwhile, at four o'clock, my captors roused themselves from their sleep and we recommenced our journey. While we were stationary, the inside of the bus was quite stuffy. As we began to drive, fresh air streamed in and I felt refreshed, if not invigorated.

We drove on in silence, past sleepy little villages nestling close to the engulfing forest, over a bumpy tarmac road, towards Benin City.

The state of the road irked me. It was one of my over-riding concerns. Not the road itself, but the fact that in this rich, oil-bearing area, the roads should be so rickety, while in the north of Nigeria, in that arid part of the country, there were wide expressways constructed at great cost with the petrodollars which the delta belched forth. The injustice of it cried to the heavens. The fact that the victims of this injustice were too timid or ignorant to cry out against it was painful in the extreme. It was unacceptable. It had to be corrected at no matter what cost. To die fighting to right the wrong would be the greatest gift of life! Yes, the gift of life. And I felt better. What did a rough bus ride matter in the circumstances? It could be worse. May it be worse. The designers of the iniquitous system be shamed. My spirit would not be broken. Never!

Day had begun to break. From the east, daylight streamed in with a fresh breeze, and soon the electric lights of the houses of Benin City came into view. We drove through the town and soon reached the Benin–Lagos road.

Driving past the University of Benin which lies on the road, I was reminded of a life which I would have liked to live: that of an academic. This was what I had always wanted in life. I had had to forgo it more than twenty-five years earlier when I was faced with the possible break-up of Nigeria during the civil war of 1967. At that time, the thought of the possible continued enslavement of the Ogoni

19

people in the nascent, if still-born, Biafra, had forced me to take personal risks and to identify myself with the Federal government. And that had effectively ended what I have been told would have been a brilliant academic career.

I had not only given up my academic career; now, looking back on those twenty-five years, I began to feel that I had also failed to end the enslavement of the Ogoni. The condition of the Ogoni had got marginally better, but the future looked bleak unless something was done urgently.

Under the prevailing social and economic conditions of the country, however, my academic career might not have amounted to much and might not have been that fulfilling either. All the same, I continued to feel a nostalgia for academia, and each time I walked through a university campus felt an elation of spirit at the challenges which the place offered the intellect, if not the soul. I felt so now, even though the University of Benin appeared run down and I knew that it could not truly answer to the name of university.

An hour or so out of Benin, the bus developed a flat tyre. It proved then that the spare tyre was not properly inflated and that we would need the services of a vulcanizer for both tyres. There was no vulcanizer in sight at that time of the morning. We all had to get down from the bus. And for the first time in ten hours or so, I had the opportunity to stretch my legs.

The man in the lounge suit, whom I now knew to be in charge of the party, was predictably mad with the driver. He could not understand how any police driver worth his salt would leave home without assuring himself that his spare tyre was in good condition. He nattered and grumbled on and on and on. To calm himself, he now produced a sheet of paper from his pocket and began to peruse it. I drew nearer to him and engaged him in conversation, while I peeped over his shoulder to see what his notes contained. I observed that it was a list of Ogoni youths who worked with me in the MOSOP. I was certainly not the only one slated for arrest. My brother Owens was also on the list. And he was the only one running a medical clinic in Bori. I bit my lips ruefully and took a little walk to steel my nerves, while I lit my pipe.

Within the hour the vulcanizer arrived and work was completed on the two tyres. The driver filled the tank of the vehicle from the jerry cans of petrol in the bus and soon we were on our way again to Lagos.

CHAPTER TWO

We arrived in Lagos at about ten thirty in the morning, having travelled for roughly twelve hours. We drove to the notorious Alagbon Close, to the offices of the Federal Investigation and Intelligence Bureau (FIIB). There, I was asked to sit behind the reception desk.

The reception area, in consonance with the rest of the complex, was extremely dirty. The walls were grimy with the marks of the years. The place had not been painted for ages. Nor, I thought, had the floor been swept in years. There was, as might be expected, a continuous flow of human traffic through the area and, seated on a wooden chair, I became a sort of curious spectacle. One or two people who knew me by my pictures in the press were not sure whether they should greet me or not. Others who knew me well stopped to do so.

There was a telephone at the desk and I asked to be allowed to use it to contact my office. For a small consideration politely inferred, if not demanded, I was able to call Miss Joy Nunieh, a young Ogoni lawyer. I requested her to contact Dr Olu Onagoruwa, a well-known human rights lawyer, and inform him that I needed his services urgently. I also left word with my office to the effect that I was in Alagbon Close and in need of clothes, a transistor radio and food. This having been accomplished, I felt a little relieved.

Joy soon showed up to commiserate with me. Her office was close by and she arrived with sunshine smiles and best wishes. She had contacted Dr Onagoruwa's office and left word in his absence with one of his assistants. He had gone to court and she expected that once he returned to his chambers and got the message, he would be at Alagbon Close. Did I need anything? Yes, food. I had not eaten for eighteen hours or so. Joy bade me goodbye.

I was thirsty and ordered a Coke from a nearby kiosk. After I had had the Coke, I felt a whiff better and sat back in the wooden chair. The men who had brought me to Lagos were nowhere to be seen and I was left to wonder what would happen next.

At about three o'clock Dr Olu Onagoruwa's assuring presence came into the reception area. I leapt upon my feet and welcomed him effusively. He was equally expansive and demanded to know what had happened. I narrated it all to him. After hearing me out, he asked to see the investigating police officer and was directed to one of the low buildings across the road.

As soon as Olu was gone, I was invited to another office beyond the reception area by one of the officers who had brought me from Port Harcourt. He demanded that I make another statement in relation to the 12 June presidential elections.

'But I already made a statement in Port Harcourt,' I asserted.

'That was in Port Harcourt. You are now in Lagos.'

'Isn't it the same police force throughout the country?'

'It is. You have to make a statement in Lagos. Please fill in the form.'

He was quite softly spoken, but there was a firmness in his voice. I was later to know him as Mr Inah, a close relation of my classmate at the University of Ibadan, Wilfred Inah, an Ogoja man, who had risen to become Secretary to the Government of Cross River State with headquarters at Calabar, Nigeria's first capital.

Without further ado, I made the required statement quickly and gave the form back to Mr Inah. He read it and asked that I elaborate further on what had happened to Dr Bennet Birabi, Senate Minority Leader, on election day. I asked if that was particularly important. He confirmed that it was.

Bennet was something of a son or younger brother to me. He was the son of possibly the most famous Ogoni man in modern times, T.N. Paul Birabi, who died in 1953 within days of his wife, the elegant Victoria Maah, whom I had known at the Native Authority School, Bori, where I began my education. Orphaned at the early age of three, he was looked after by his uncle and grandmother until he completed his primary education. I was then a student at the University of Ibadan. When I learnt that Bennet was about to complete his primary school studies, I began to cast about for how he might further his education. At that time, I was working closely with the late Mr Edward Kobani, an educationist, in the Ogoni Divisional Union. He was president and I, secretary.

Together, we decided that for all Paul Birabi meant to the Ogoni people, his two children would certainly get a proper education. The first secondary school in Ogoni had been named after Birabi in recognition of his pioneering efforts in setting up the school; he was also the first graduate from Ogoni. He had studied at the famous Achimota College in Ghana and read mathematics at Southampton University. He subsequently became a master at Dennis Memorial Grammar School in Onitsha and vice-principal of the Okrika Grammar School. He later won an election to the Eastern Nigerian House of Assembly, from where he was nominated into the House of Representatives in Lagos. He attended the Nigerian Constitutional Conference in London in 1953 and it was upon his return from the conference that he met his untimely death. He was much beloved of the Ogoni people and they lost many years of political and social development through his death. His absence created a vacuum which was not filled for a long time.

Love of and admiration for Birabi was the reason the Ogoni Divisional Union decided to intervene in the education of young Bennet. Arrangement was made with the principal of Birabi Memorial Grammar School, who granted a concessional entry to the young boy. The payment of his fees became an immediate problem but we were able to ask for donations from several Ogoni people and so see him through his first year at school. Thereafter, arrangement was made with the Chairman of the Khana County Council, Mr William Nzidee, to award the boy a council bursary, although he belonged not to the Khana County Council but to the Gokana County Council.

Come the civil war, Bennet lost his grandmother in a refugee camp in the Igbo heartland. In 1969, as Commissioner for Education in Rivers State, I decided to send all the available senior secondary school boys in the state to the Baptist High School, Port Harcourt, as an emergency measure because of the lack of teachers and facilities. Bennet was one of the beneficiaries of the scheme.

He wrote me, outlining his difficulties, and I wrote back asking him to consider himself a member of my household henceforth. At that time, I had in my house a large number of brothers and sisters and other young Ogoni whom I was assisting through school. There was not much around, but we all shared what was available as one family, without discrimination. Many of those who benefited from that communion have since fulfilled themselves in various ways. I have been much rewarded in the knowledge that I was able to be of service to them when it mattered most in their lives.

Bennet was a part of my household, spending his holidays

with us and sharing in all we had until he graduated from medical school, married and established a practice in Port Harcourt.

I followed his career with very keen interest, but was somewhat disappointed when he threw in his lot in 1983 with the banned and subsequently disbanded National Party of Nigeria of the Second Republic. He seemed, like his father, destined for great things and even in the putrefaction of the Second Republic was able to win a seat in the House of Representatives and then to become a Federal Minister of State for twenty-one or so days.

Banned from politics after the military take-over at the end of 1983, he was available to partake in the activities of the MOSOP in 1990, but once the Babangida dictatorship lifted the ban, he joined the National Republican Convention and won a senatorial seat, becoming Senate Minority Leader.

Although I was thoroughly disenchanted with Babangida's quixotic political experiment, I was somewhat delighted with Bennet's position as it proved that Ogonis could rise to heights within the Nigerian system, weighted against them as it was.

Unfortunately for Bennet, the system was as corrupt as it could be. And it was responsible for the mistake which he had made and which had led to my being asked to make a statement about what happened to him on election day. I shall deal with this later in my narration.

To return to my story, I did say all I knew about what had happened to the Senate Minority Leader and, with the answers to one or two questions added to the statement, signed it. Thereafter, I was asked to return to the reception desk.

Shortly afterwards, the sergeant at the desk was called

away. Upon his return, he informed me that I was to go into the guardroom and instructed me to give him all my valuable property, including money, shoes, clutch-bag, watch and other things. I asked if I might keep my pen and some sheets of paper which were in my shirt pocket. He laughed. I believe that he knew well that in the guardroom I would find neither the time nor the opportunity to do any writing. I also asked him to allow me stay for a while, as I was expecting some clothes and particularly some underwear from my Lagos residence. I had been wearing the same clothes for two days and was feeling terribly uncomfortable. He agreed to let me be.

As I waited, word came that Dr Olu Onagoruwa wanted me at the office of the Assistant Commissioner of Police, to which he had gone earlier. I repaired there and met Olu with Assistant Commissioner of Police Kenneth Ogbeifun, the man in the lounge suit who had brought me from Port Harcourt. He appeared to be in charge of the team investigating my case.

Olu informed me that he had spoken with Mr Ogbeifun and that it appeared that he had not received specific instructions from his superiors as to what to do with me. I would have to stay in police custody for now but he would file a case against my arrest the next day.

'I have been asked to go into the guardroom,' I informed them. 'I've heard terrible stories as to what goes on in there. Can anything be done to save me the agony?'

Olu pleaded with Mr Ogbeifun to give me what special consideration he could offer. The latter apologized that he had failed to do so in the first instance. He then took me to the reception desk and informed the sergeant on duty that I was not to go into the guardroom for the night but was to remain at the reception desk.

Olu stood chatting with me for a while. While we were

thus, one of the detainees, a journalist from *News* magazine who knew both Olu and me well, came in from the guard-room beyond. He apparently had been a guest. He was in the special uniform which, I believe, all those in police custody have to wear. Behind him was another young man in similar attire whom he introduced to us simply as 'The President'.

I was later to come close to the system whereby suspects in police custody ordered their lives in a special hierarchical order, assuming titles and responsibility over the lives of in-mates. 'The President' was the boss of all the prisoners and he had responsibility for maintaining law and order in the guardroom! Quite a world of its own. And I was aware of it. Festus Iyayi, an award-winning Nigerian novelist, had lived in it in 1987 or thereabouts and had written about it in a Nigerian magazine. The journalist said he had been held in custody for a month. He had not been told what crime he had committed. Neither did his colleagues and employers know that he had been held.

Olu Onagoruwa soon left. Thanks to the order made by Kenneth Ogbeifun, I wasn't dumped into the guardroom, as might have been expected. The prospect of spending the night at the reception desk wasn't pleasant either. It was an open area, without doors and windows. Mosquitoes would make mincemeat of my beautiful body.

Joy Nunieh soon arrived, with a dish of rice and chicken, beer and ice-cold water. I was told that I couldn't have beer while in police custody and that I was to have my meal right there in the reception hall. I was hesitant so to do and asked if there was another room where I could have a measure of privacy.

The desk sergeant offered me a place in a low wooden building which must have been thought of as temporary when it was constructed. The building had since become permanent and now held a number of offices. The particular office into which I was led was most dreadful. Cobwebby, dusty, unswept, with broken cupboards and grimy desks lying in thorough disorder, I would rather not have had my meal there. But when I remembered that I had no alternative, I steeled myself and even convinced myself that it was as comfortable as the dining room in the Waldorf Astoria of New York City.

It was in that frame of mind that I fell to what was a very delicious meal indeed. Joy had stretched herself to offer me the best. How thoughtful of her! The daughter of the first Ogoni lawyer who was later to become a senator in the Second Republic, she was in the process of establishing herself as a successful lawyer in Lagos. And I have to confess that between herself and the meal she served, I might have preferred her if she had been equally available. Maybe that was why I didn't eat much, considering that I hadn't had a meal for almost forty-eight hours.

I washed the meal down with water and chatted at some length with Joy before she finally bade me goodnight. It was already getting on for seven o'clock. She would see me the following day, she said.

Soon after she left, my young friend, Hauwa, arrived with a bag containing some clothes, underwear, transistor radio and books, including my first novel, *Sozaboy*. And another meal which I was unable to eat. I had, in truth, lost my appetite for food in the face of the ordeal I was being put through.

Shortly afterwards, my brother Owens turned up in the company of my youngest brother of the same mother, Letam, a captain in the Nigerian army who had just completed his law studies at the University of Lagos. He had had to study on a part-time basis as a full-time student, taking in a stint in Liberia with the Nigerian contingent there before he eventually sat his examination. It was something of a surprise that he eventually got a degree. But then he was a bright chap, having come second in his class at the Nigerian Defence Academy in 1985. This was thought to be something of a record since he had not attended the Nigerian Military School at Zaria before going to the defence academy.

The presence of my brothers and Hauwa was comforting. We were family and my mind was taken off my ordeal. It was particularly nice of Owens to fly in from Port Harcourt, bringing with him my briefcase and a shoulder bag in which I often lodged the papers which my briefcase couldn't hold. Finally, Dr Broderick Ineneji, a civil rights lawyer and newly acquired friend, arrived. A highly experienced man who had worked for a long time in Britain and completed a doctoral thesis on ethnic minority problems, he was witty and engaging. Talking with him was quite a treat, and we had a bellyful of laughs, so much so that we didn't notice the heavy rain which came down that night.

When the rain eventually stopped, they all bade me goodnight and I was left alone to find some sleep in the only cushion chair in the room. It was well past one thirty in the morning.

No, I couldn't sleep that night. The stuffy room, the mosquitoes singing about my ears, the thought of what the next day would bring and my worries about the Ogoni people kept me wide awake. Owens had told me of the events which followed my departure from Port Harcourt the previous night and I was fearful that in my absence the violence which I feared most might erupt. I prayed that this should not be, as I was more than anxious to keep the struggle on a non-violent level.

Had I known that earlier that day the Ogoni people, provoked by the treatment I had received, poured on to the streets of Bori to demonstrate their anger, and that some hoodlums seized the opportunity to molest other citizens, I would have had a more troubled night.

As it was, I passed the night in doubt. I was not depressed, only apprehensive.

CHAPTER THREE

The dawning day met me in a state of preparedness for uncertainty. The real problem was how to perform my ablutions. There wasn't a toilet in sight. Outside of the office were several broken-down cars, much as in the police station in Port Harcourt. The ground was all soggy from the rain of the previous night and, indeed, it was still drizzling at about five thirty that morning.

I finally decided to ask the sergeant at the reception desk if there was a toilet that I could use. He chortled ominously. A toilet appeared to be a luxury in those parts. But he did offer to show me one, asking me, however, to wait while he found water which I would use to flush the hallowed place.

To cut a long story short, I did manage to find some peace with the aid of the fumes from my pipe. Isn't it amazing what service this pipe often renders me?

I returned to my place in the office to tune on the radio. I was listening to the BBC news at seven o'clock when Mr Inah came in. He asked me to follow him. I took up my bag and walked out. At the reception desk, I overheard him tell one of his subordinates to book him out as having travelled to Port Harcourt. I assumed then that I would be returning there with him. Accordingly, I asked if I could leave a message for subsequent callers who might wish to know where I had gone to. He agreed and I left a note saying that I had left for Port Harcourt.

Fearful of another road journey back to Port Harcourt, I asked if we would be flying.

'No,' came the prompt reply.

'Listen,' I pleaded, 'another road journey to Port Harcourt from Lagos will virtually kill me. I haven't travelled that much by road in a long time. Besides, I'm not in the best of health. I'm prepared to pay the air fare for everyone so that we fly to Port Harcourt.'

'You can tell the Assistant Commissioner so when you see him.'

'Is he travelling with us?'

'Yes. We're going to his house now to collect him.'

Outside, the J5 Peugeot bus in which we had travelled the previous day was waiting. This time, there were none of the armed guards of the previous day, which was some relief. Maybe I was no longer considered a dangerous criminal. The only other occupants of the bus were the driver and the third investigating police officer, the man in a caftan who had sat next to me on our journey out of Port Harcourt.

We drove out of Ikoyi through the Third Mainland Bridge towards Ikeja. The bridge connects Lagos Island and Ikoyi to the mainland of Lagos and is one of the measures taken to ease traffic flow in the Lagos metropolis. The population of Lagos had exploded once oil money from the delta had been cornered by the nation's rulers and transferred to Lagos from hapless communities like the Ogoni and the Ijaws who were too few to defend their inheritance. Most of that money was expended from and in Lagos, and it was to the latter city that the Dick Whittingtons and other carpetbaggers of Nigeria went to seek their fortune. Most of the money was also spent on foreign luxuries like cars, and soon the few roads in the city were clogged with cars, rendering movement well-nigh impossible. Overhead bridges became the norm in the city. These did not help much either. And so more bridges, such as the Third Mainland Bridge, had to be built. It had just opened to traffic and was predictably named after the dictator Babangida, who sat on the Nigerian throne at the time. Nor did it succeed in easing traffic.

That morning the bridge was as congested as ever, but since we were moving against the traffic we had a very smooth journey. We stopped to buy newspapers and I observed that my arrest two days earlier was in the news.

We drove into the government residential area in Ikeja towards Mr Ogbeifun's residence. I noted ruefully how over-grown with weeds the area had become. The road was all potholes. I recalled my early days in Lagos while I was at the University of Ibadan in the years shortly after independence. The area had been spick and span. Now it was virtually derelict. The houses occupied by civil servants were, of course, more run-down than others. The overall look of Ikeja was of general decline. And that was in spite of the huge amount of oil money transferred from the Niger River Delta to Lagos.

Mr Kenneth Ogbeifun was waiting for us when we arrived. He clambered into the bus after the morning's greetings. I immediately offered to fly all of us by air to Port Harcourt. Mr Ogbeifun said it was not possible. We had to pick up some other Ogoni detainees in Enugu or thereabouts. Could we then fly to Enugu? No, with finality. It was only then that I remembered that I had given the 2,000 naira which my brother had given me in Port Harcourt to Hauwa for safe keeping. I had thought that I would not need it. So that even if Mr Ogbeifun had decided to accept my offer, I wouldn't have been able to do as I had said. I resigned myself to another long road journey.

And who were those other Ogoni detainees about whom Mr Ogbeifun had spoken? If I remembered correctly, only Mr N. G. Dube, a member of the Steering Committee of

MOSOP had been held in Port Harcourt, and the information I had the morning of my arrest was that he had been released on bail. Mr Ogbeifun was not forthcoming on the matter and I decided not to press him further.

The journey that day was not very eventful. Mr Ogbeifun and his subordinates were quite relaxed and I engaged the former in a lively discussion on Nigerian politics. Of course, Mr Ogbeifun was very well informed and very engaging in his analysis of the subjects we discussed. He spoke English with an Edo (Benin) accent. He was not a handsome man by any standards, but he was well built, on the stocky side. He tended to sound cantankerous when he spoke, but had quite a sense of humour beneath his outwardly hard mien. I found him very interesting.

When I began to whine about breakfast, Mr Ogbeifun stopped the vehicle beside a roadside staIl, where he bought me corn and coconut. Ordinarily I would not have touched it for reasons of hygiene, but my standards were now being lowered, and I even found it tasty. By Jove! At the next petrol station, I bought bananas and groundnut from some hawkers and feasted on them. Yes, it was a feast. When you are on your way to becoming a beast, courtesy of the Nigerian security system, a wretched meal becomes a feast. It is a part of the dehumanization process.

At about one o'clock we arrived in Benin and I insisted on having lunch in a proper restaurant. We drove to the Palm Royal Motel and Mr Ogbeifun ordered the most junior of the three officers to accompany me to the restaurant. I barely had enough money for the meal and had to check my pocket and the menu before ordering.

I had been warned not to expect my captors to feed me. On such journeys they had to spend their own money and ask for reimbursement later. Such reimbursement often didn't appear. If it did, it could be a very long time coming.

The restaurant of the Palm Royal Motel was full when I entered and a few people there recognized me. One diner decided to share my table with me.

'I thought you were in detention?' he asked.

'So I am.'

'What are you doing here, then?'

'I came for lunch.'

'Why are you in Benin?'

'I'm travelling under police escort from Lagos to Port Harcourt.' I nodded in the direction of the police officer in mufti who sat at a point where he could see me clearly. 'He is guarding me,' I said.

'But you were supposed to have been arrested in Port Harcourt two days or so ago.'

'So I was. And then I was taken to Lagos and now I'm going back to Port Harcourt.'

He digested my words with his meal. I think he found it difficult taking in all I had said.

'What are you being detained for?'

'Election offences.'

'They should set you free soon.'

'Why?' I asked.

'CNN just announced the nullification of the election results.'

'You don't say!' I cried.

'It's true,' he said matter-of-factly. 'And all actions taken in regard of the elections are declared null and void.'

That put a new construction on my case. If, indeed, I was being held for an election offence, the nullification of the election negated the basis of my arrest. I ate the rest of my meal in silence.

The news soon went around that I was in the restaurant, and as I stood up to go several people came over to me, shook hands and expressed solidarity with me and my cause.

I returned to the bus, to the waiting arms of Mr Ogbeifun and his men, and we drove to the centre of Benin, where my captors had their lunch.

As we drove out of Benin towards Onitsha, I informed my captors of the nullification of the elections and asked them banteringly if they hadn't wasted their labour and government funds holding me the way they had.

We discussed the nullification of the election exhaustively. Mr Ogbeifun, a history graduate of the University of Ibadan, was impressive in his analysis. The only thing he wouldn't be drawn on was its effect on my detention and what he would do in the circumstances.

After we crossed the Onitsha Bridge, I came to know that we were headed for Awka, although I didn't know what Mr Ogbeifun would be doing there.

We arrived at Awka at about six o'clock in the evening and spent quite some time there while Mr Ogbeifun held discussions with his colleague. We had had a flat tyre at Onitsha and, it being late, didn't repair it. I had thought that the repair would be done at Awka but that didn't happen. The driver had told me that he thought we would be spending the night at Awka.

When Mr Ogbeifun finally emerged from his discussions, he gave orders that we were to move on.

'Where are we going?' I asked, and drew a blank.

I insisted.

'When we get there, you will know,' Mr Ogbeifun answered unhelpfully.

In his discussion with his assistant, Mr Inah, it became clear that certain formalities had to be observed in order to make possible what they were going to do next.

This was of some interest to me. It occurred to me that after my seizure on the expressway in Port Harcourt I had been taken to the SSS office and had then been formally transferred to the SIIB in Port Harcourt. They, in turn, had formally transferred me to the FIIB in Lagos. This must have explained the busy human traffic in the office of the Assistant Commissioner of Police in Port Harcourt. The way they set about it, you might have thought that they were engaged in legalities. Everything put together, I could only conclude that they were covering their tracks, just in case anything went wrong and they became accountable. All that formality was nothing but self-deception. And utter waste!

We arrived at Abagana Police Station about fifteen miles from Awka just past seven o'clock. A few minutes later Mr N. G. Dube and one other joined me in the bus. I was really delighted to see Dube. He was his normal cheerful self. There was a lot to talk about but I didn't want to talk just yet. I asked about the other gentleman. He introduced himself as Mr Kabari Nwiee, Executive Officer with the Rivers State Schools Board. He was Chairman of the National Youth Council of Ogoni People (NYCOP) in the village of Opuoko, in the eastern part of Ogoni.

It was utterly dark. A light rain had begun to fall and I was worried that the bus had no spare tyre. And that I didn't know exactly where we were going. Could we possibly be heading for Port Harcourt? It seemed rather dangerous to be going that far in the dark with the light rain that was falling.

I must have dozed off for some time. When I opened my eyes, we were close to Owerri. And I was rather relieved when the bus turned off the Onitsha–Port Harcourt road in the direction of Owerri township. We subsequently drove into the headquarters of the Imo State Police Command, Owerri. The time was ten o'clock. The rain was pouring down now in earnest.

We waited an interminably long time as Mr Ogbeifun

went into a long discussion with a tall, broad-shouldered senior police officer that desultory night. When he was done, he ordered us to get down from the bus with all our luggage. We obeyed his instruction. Then he led us to the reception desk where a police sergeant was on duty.

The reception area was the entrance to a long, two-storey building with rooms on both sides. Immediately to the right as you entered the building was a staircase leading to the upper floor. The ground floor had rooms for investigating police officers or, possibly, sergeants. From one of the rooms on the right came intermittent howls. I was to learn that this was the guardroom for suspects held in police custody.

We were led into a room next to the guardroom. There was no light in it, the only available light coming from a beam which fell from the fluorescent tube in the corridor. There was no door, the only door having fallen off its hinges. It was laid against the wall, and could be used to cover the opening in order to have some privacy. There were a few tables and chairs in the room. One particular chair was tied with a string to a table. Opposite the room was a bathroom from which came the stinking odour of human waste. This was to be our abode.

I took a look round and felt like throwing up. I placed my bag on one of the tables near what passed for a window giving out on to the courtyard. The smell of human waste came from that direction also. Much later, after I had been in Port Harcourt Prison, I realized that the smell was of the urine of the suspects in the guardroom who, at night, passed their urine into bottles and poured it through a chink in the wall to the ground outside. Good heavens!

Mr Ogbeifun was still with us, and I immediately complained about the conditions.

'I've done you a favour,' he replied stiffly. 'Would you rather be in the guardroom? That's where you should be. I've used my influence to secure you this special place. You should be thanking me, not complaining.'

And that was it. He informed me that he would be leaving for Port Harcourt and that we would have to remain there until his return.

I took counsel with myself and decided that the best I could expect from Mr Ogbeifun was that he contact my office in Port Harcourt so they would send me some money and make arrangements for my food. He agreed to oblige me, bade us goodnight and disappeared into the darkness. It was about midnight.

Our quarters were a great improvement on what my fellow detainees were used to. Both Dube and Nwiee had been arrested in Port Harcourt days before me and had received the full treatment normally given to those in police custody. They had been thrown into the guardroom at the Central Police Station in Port Harcourt. There, they met hardened criminals and petty thieves who held court and charged newcomers specific fees. If you had no money, you were subjected to brutality and condemned to stand up all night to fan the guardroom bosses with old newspapers. If you had money, you might be allowed to stay outside the toilet room in which some of the inmates were forced to sleep, so cramped was the available space.

Of course, there was no food. Inmates had to depend on food sent by their families. And whenever such food was sent, it had to be shared with the inmates, the bosses having the greater share thereof. Beatings were common in the guard-room and both Dube and Nwiee suffered a lot of indignities during their three-day stay there.

On the fourth day both were ordered to sign a release paper. But instead of being set free, they were bundled into a Peugeot pick-up van and, under the watchful eye of the Assistant Commissioner of Police, he of the undignified bearing whom I have mentioned earlier in this narration, were driven at night to the police station at Awka in Anambra State.

There, late at night, they were thrown into a cell worse than what they had had at Port Harcourt and infinitely more dehumanizing. It was more cramped and the inmates more vicious. Worse, they had no money to give the cell bosses and so had to endure the worst beatings.

They were subsequently moved to nearby Aguata, where they found the cell full to bursting. Their captors finally settled for Abagana, where we eventually found them.

So, happy to have escaped the brutality of the cell bosses, they were content with the accommodation we now found. Tired to the teeth, they found an old mattress in the office and laid it on the hard floor. They proposed that I sleep on it. I declined and asked both of them to use it. I did not think that I would sleep that night. They laid down and slept rather soundly, I thought.

I have spent some terrible nights in my life. But that night of Wednesday, 23 June 1993, must rank as one of the very worst in all of my experience. I slept no more than four hours, but most of the time was awake, always busy either writing or reading. Without light in the room, with the stench from the window next to me, the howls of the inmates of the guardroom next door, and the turmoil in my soul, I considered myself as being as close to hell as possible. I tuned to every conceivable station on my transistor radio and gathered every scrap of news I could get. And I prayed for daybreak, as my soul sang:

Prison Song
Bedbugs, fleas and insects
The howl of deranged suspects
The dark night bisect

Rudely breaking my nightmare
And now widely awake
I'm reminded of this crude place
Shared with unusual inmates

Strangely enough, and most uncharacteristically, I didn't give much thought to the nullification of the election on whose pretext I was being held. I had come to the conclusion long before then that nothing Babangida, the conman and dictator of Nigeria, did would surprise me. I considered him capable of just anything. In any case, I didn't think much of his so-called transition programme, which I had seen through earlier and pooh-poohed publicly in writing on every possible occasion. And yet I did feel that the nullification would become a significant turning point in the history of Nigeria.

When day finally broke, believe it or not, the first man I saw greeting me through the broken panes of the window was an Ogoni police constable who happened to be serving in Owerri. He was in mufti, being off-duty. Somehow, he had heard of our being at the station and had come calling. I gave him some money and the Port Harcourt telephone number of my assistant and friend, Apollos Onwuasoaku. He was to tell the latter that I was at Owerri, and to ask that he please make arrangements for my meals and send me some money. He returned to confirm that he had been able to deliver the message by telephone. This was a welcome surprise because telephones do not normally work in Nigeria. I thanked him profusely.

Daylight brought into full view the dilapidated and miserable condition of our abode. The outer courtyard was, as usual, littered with broken-down cars. Because the compound is rather large, these cars didn't appear as obtrusive as in Port Harcourt or Lagos. But if the outside of the building was sufferable, the inside was totally intolerable. It was all cobwebby and the walls were smudged.

The room in which we had passed the night had a number of lockers in which the policemen and officers stored their uniforms. They came to work in mufti and changed into their uniforms upon arrival. It also had 'exhibits' for cases which might never be heard: a ten-year-old dusty carpet, a broken-down fan and, of course, the old mattress on which Dube and Nwiee had slept at night. Then there were dusty files and sheets of paper piled up in one corner. Truly, no one could ever do meaningful work in such a messy, grimy surrounding.

The office was like some sort of market. It was the SIIB and there was no shortage of people who had come to sort out one thing or another. For all those who wished to deal with investigating police officers, a 'waiting room' was created in an open-sided corrugated-iron shed outside the main building, next to the broken-down cars in the open courtyard. Naturally, those waiting to transact 'business' had to be fed, so hawkers milled around the shed and there was quite some noise just next to the window where I had installed myself. Added to the stink from the suspects in the guardroom, I was having a horrible time indeed.

Also, earlier that morning, the inmates of the guardroom let forth a great howl, which I was to learn was their way of singing. The song, I was told, went something like 'Praise God, hallelujah! Praise God, amen!' The two lines were repeated over and over *ad nauseam*. This wild cacophony almost drove me round the bend that day when I first heard it.

Another problem that morning was the toilet facility. I know I do sound finicky about this, but the ability to dispose of waste properly distinguishes man from beast. I had had a problem in Lagos, which I got over somewhat, somehow. On the road to Owerri from Lagos, I had been well served at the Palm Royal Motel, Benin, after lunch. Now in Owerri, I could not see my way round the problem. From time to time gusts of wind wafted the stench of the toilet even to the room where we stayed. This was bad enough, but what if I had to go in there? I had to hold my system down by sheer will-power. I had been taught as a cadet at school that it could be done. I was not sure that it was good for me at my age, but do it I had to in the interests of, yes, my sanity.

The day dragged on interminably. I kept looking forward to the arrival of people from my office in Port Harcourt, and the sort of food I would have wanted to eat. Food was not forthcoming from the police, of course, and I had to provide for Dube and Nwiee.

Later, towards evening that day, my staff did arrive and with them my friend Mina, who brought me some food. At about the same moment Dr Garrick Leton and my cousin, Oxford-trained Simeon Idemyor, came calling. They were shocked by the sight of our abode. They didn't say it, but you could see it on their faces. We chatted for a while and, since it was getting late, they left with a promise to do something about our surroundings. Simeon had been in the Police Service Commission many years back and knew a number of the most senior officers. He hoped that he would be able to do something to make the Assistant Inspector-General of Police responsible for the area offer us fair treatment.

The next day, Thursday, 24 June, is absolutely dreary. We continue to share the cell with police officers, and the noise and stench are quite unbearable. Towards late evening, a fine man, Assistant Commissioner of Police Innocent Ilozuoke, comes into the cell and officially welcomes us as his guests. I complain about the conditions, particularly the absence of light. There is not much he can do, I perceive, and let him be.

The night is an absolute disaster. Since there is no light in the cell, I know that I am going to be miserable all night. Mosquitoes and the sounds from the overcrowded guard-room next door as well as the stench from the toilet and the human waste outside the paneless window, conjoin to aggravate my misery. When food arrives from Port Harcourt about a hundred kilometres away, I shove it aside.

I don't sleep all night. I sit by the table, tuning on the radio. I am relieved, though, to find Dube and Nwiee sleeping soundly. Our abode is, as I have indicated, a hundred times better than what they have had in the past.

Early on Friday I follow the routine of the men in police custody with keen interest. There is the usual movement as they file out to perform their morning ablutions. I notice that there is a very young boy among them. He cannot, surely, be more than twelve years old. And that worries me beyond telling. What sort of effect is his situation going to have on his psyche? Why should he be held in police custody with adults? He should be in a remand home. And when they get back to the cell and begin chanting their ghoulish song, 'Praise God, hallelujah!' I do not hear the wild cacophony; it is the young boy I see. And he is to assail my sensibilities all day.

Meanwhile, I notice that my health is deteriorating. At about ten o'clock I demand of Assistant Commissioner Ilozuoke to see a doctor who mercifully turns up at about 3.00 pm. He examines me, Dube and Nwiee and writes a prescription which he hands over to us. What are we expected to do with the prescription, we ask? We have no money and can buy no medicine. He leaves with a message that I need to see the cardiologist who has been managing me. He is a young doctor, Dr Idoko, an Igalaman from Kogi State in the middle of Nigeria.

By now I have had enough of police brutality. I storm into the office of Mr Ilozuoke's assistant, a Mr Chime, who is well dressed in mufti and looks elegant. On his table is a copy of Machiavelli's *The Prince* and also of Achebe's *Arrow of God*. I surmise quickly that he is either a reader or a mature student, most police officers being encouraged to take degrees in law if they do not already possess one. He is probably a man I can challenge.

I launch into a diatribe of the black man's inhumanity to his own kind, the trait responsible for the retardation of all blacks. It is inconceivable, I assert, that a man of my achievement and age can be subjected to the terrible indignities that have been meted out to me merely on suspicion and which I feel sure cannot be sustained in a court of law. In any case, even if I were on death row, I would be entitled to my favourite meal. I resent being starved to death, I declare, and being asked to buy my medicine. And there is no reason why I should be kept in a room without light, a bed or toilet facilities.

It works. Apologies, apologies. We have been dumped on the Imo State Police Command by the FIIB without preparation or instruction. He will exert himself on our behalf. Did I mind giving him an hour or so to hold discussions? He would get back to me.

A short while later, when Dr Leton and my cousin Simeon came again to see me, Mr Ilozuoke provided his personal funds, I later find out, to buy us food. He also ordered that we should be moved upstairs to his waiting room where conditions were marginally better. The stench was less, there was a fan, and although there was no bulb in the electrical connection on the ceiling, there were two dirty settees on which we could stretch. The Senior Police Officers' toilet is made available to us, thank God!

I arranged to have the toilet and waiting room cleared of

cobwebs and other detritus, the floor was swabbed and we could now live somewhat like human beings. The two-seater settee was useful. My famed shortness of frame meant that I could sleep on the settee.

Dr Idoko later turned up with some medicine, the cheapest available, no doubt, and I was assured of some relief from a running stomach, seven boils on my left posterior, and my swollen feet. Not quite. The medicines are not efficacious – they may well have been out of date! But mercifully, my brother Owens arrived the next day and after discussion with the doctor offered me something more potent which gave me faster relief. Owens spent a lot of time with us, day after day, trying to ensure that my health was properly taken care of and that I was moved to a hospital or clinic as soon as possible.

On Saturday, Sunday and Monday, we had to beg for the single meal a day which was offered. There was still no news of our captors and our hosts kept reminding us that we were 'in transit' and therefore not their responsibility.

Meanwhile, the news from Ogoni was of youths protesting against my detention. I sent notes through Dr Leton and Barry Kumbe, the young lawyer from Mr Ledum Mitee's chambers, advising that I was alive and well and warning against the destruction of property. The notes worked, I was later informed.

At the national level, citizens were responding to the humiliating insult which was the cancellation of the election. But leaderless or thoroughly misled, they did not develop a proper response to the situation. All were hurt but no one appeared to know what to do. It is through preying on the non-mobilization of the masses and the greed of the elite that Babangida has been able to assault the people of Nigeria and reduce them to intolerable levels of existence, dissipating all national assets in the process and plunging the nation deeper and deeper into debt. I felt sad that I couldn't contribute to this drama but had to watch it from the sidelines in illegal detention in a miserable cell.

CHAPTER FOUR

The days and nights passed slowly, considering the frenetic pace of activity to which I was accustomed. Travelling constantly between Port Harcourt and Lagos and then Europe, I never did have a dull moment. And there was always something new to do in each place I got to, all my efforts being bent to the improvement of the life of the Ogoni people and, by implication, the ethnic minorities and indigenous people of Nigeria, of Africa.

Now, as I lay idle in illegal detention, my thoughts went over my endeavours in this regard through the years.

My worry about the Ogoni has been an article of faith, conceived of in primary school, nurtured through secondary school, actualized in the Nigerian civil war in 1967–70 and during my tenure as a member of the Rivers State Executive Council, 1968–73.

My first thoughts on the matter were published in my pamphlet *The Ogoni Nationality Today and Tomorrow*, which was issued in April 1968 in the throes of the civil war. In that publication I outlined what may be regarded as the Ogoni agenda as I saw it.

It was essentially a young man's work, but it came straight from the heart. I had not crystallized my thoughts as philosophy, but it was clear enough to me what I wanted the Ogoni people to do and be within the context of Nigeria, and I believe that I did express myself accordingly.

I had been a young graduate assistant at the University of Nigeria, Nsukka, when the civil war broke out. That war was mostly about the control of the oil resources of the Ogoni and other ethnic groups in the Niger River Delta. I have dealt fully with my role in the war in my book *On a Darkling Plain*. Briefly put, when, as a young man, I was confronted with the possibility of the Ogoni existing as one of 200 or so ethnic groups in Nigeria or as one of 50 or so ethnic groups in secessionist Biafra, I had chosen the former. The reasons for that choice were complex and, as I say, I have narrated them in my civil war diary. Suffice it to say that to actualize my preference, I had undertaken what now looks like a crazy journey from my Ogoni home with a dug-out canoe, through the maze of rivers and creeks of the Niger Delta, to Lagos, where I identified with the Federal government, which was then trying to quell the Biafran secession. Within a month of my arrival in Lagos, I was pressed into service as a member of the Interim Advisory Council of the newly created Rivers State, of which Ogoni was a part. The Interim Advisory Council was a sort of Cabinet of a government-in-exile. As soon as a part of the new State was successfully invaded by the Federal forces in November 1967, I was appointed to administer it. And so I became Administrator for Bonny, the important export oil terminal in the Niger River Delta adjoining Ogoni territory. There, I worked among the civilian population and with the Federal forces as they advanced into my Ogoni home.

Once the Federal forces were in Ogoni, I followed them to bring succour and comfort to those Ogoni people who had remained behind to welcome the Federals instead of fleeing or being forcibly evacuated into the Igbo heartland further to the north.

Appointed as Commissioner (Minister) in a fully fledged Rivers State Cabinet at the end of 1968, I worked officially to rehabilitate the Ogoni and other ethnic groups who had been the main victims of the war.

Trudging over the one hundred rural villages in which the Ogoni lived, I was able to see for myself what the Ogoni as a people needed to resuscitate them, so to speak. Working tirelessly with the common people, I brought them education and hope. But, even more importantly, I was able to see that what they required most was the formation of a mass organization to press for their rights.

I found that the generality of the Ogoni people, the masses, were ready to follow dedicated leadership. However, that leadership had to be provided by educated people. Although I organized the masses and won their confidence, the problem was that educated Ogoni people were thin on the ground, and the few who were available were in the Igbo heartland while the war lasted. The mentality of the educated Ogoni was always to keep close to the government of the day in order to pick up crumbs from the master's table. Accordingly, although Ojukwu's rebel Biafran government was hostile to the Ogoni as a people, the educated few yet found pickings by grovelling at the feet of the administration.

When the Biafran rebellion collapsed, these men were forced to return to Ogoni and to Rivers State, of which Ogoni had become part following the break-up of former Eastern Nigeria into states. It fell to my lot, as the only Ogoni man who had identified openly with Rivers State from the beginning to the end of the war, to rehabilitate the returning Ogoni, and I did so without worrying about what role each had played in the Biafran débâcle.

I tried to reconcile one to each and each to the other and, when I judged it right, tried to set up a formalized structure in the Ogoni Development Association (ODA). Dr Garrick Leton, of whom more shall be heard hereafter, was elected President. That was in early 1971 or thereabouts. It was the last meeting of the Association to be held. I recall that two women, ordinary women, came up to me after the election to ask why I had spoilt the excellent work I had initiated. Bewildered, I asked them what I had done. I should, they said, have assumed the presidency and not declined it. I was to remember their opinion long afterwards.

I recall also the words of the late Dr Obi Wali, a man whose opinion I respected very much and to whom I grew quite close as the years passed. Looking over my work among the Ogoni in 1969, he had warned that all that I had done would be put in jeopardy once the educated Ogoni returned from the rebel area. The great unanimity I had achieved among the Ogoni, as I set their sights on a greater dawn, would be disputed and brought to a standstill, if I weren't careful. How right he proved to be!

Uniting the Ogoni masses proved an easier task than associating a handful of graduates with my vision for the Ogoni. The latter were all so desirous of finding a niche for themselves in the Rivers State government that they blindly undid all I was trying to do to put the Ogoni on a pedestal and secure for them some of the advantages I knew that they were entitled to, and which they had been denied in the past and might be denied again.

In the pamphlet *The Ogoni Nationality Today and Tomorrow* I had written, after tracing our communal failure in the past, as follows:

But we do ask that the disgrace of the past should be our armour against the future. We must each of us immediately resolve not to repeat the mistakes of the past. We have now been given an opportunity to reassert ourselves side by side with all other nationalities in the Nigerian federation. We cannot let this opportunity slip past us. If we do, posterity shall not forgive us, and we shall disappear as a people from the face of the earth. This must not happen.

The spirit of self-sacrifice which moved Birabi is still alive in our nationality today. The men who think as he did are not lacking. The present crisis will have served to bring such men to the fore. They will provide enlightened and dynamic leadership; they will, with active support, ensure that our nationality regains its lost dignity and honour, and transform our land for the betterment of our peoples. It is incumbent on us to entrust the future of our land to responsible persons who know what is going on in the world around them, and who will not succumb to petty inducements. This is important.

The Rivers State has been created, and a new Nigeria born. But we must remember that no matter the system of government, unless a people take their destiny into their own hands, no improvement will come to them. We cannot afford then to be complacent. We must begin immediately to organize ourselves enthusiastically for the difficult and turbulent days ahead. To start all over again is not going to be easy; the task will be made even more difficult by the uncertainty of the times and the hostility of some of our neighbours who have vowed to keep us as slaves for all time. But we must now bend to the labour. There is a great deal to be done and we must do it quickly and efficiently.

We reiterate that the task will not be easy. We shall be starting from a manifestly weak position. At the moment, the number of our people in the junior and senior cadre of the Federal public service and the corporations can be counted on the fingers of one hand. So also the number in the police and armed forces. Our children are largely out of school and university, many families have lost their bread-winners and our economy has collapsed completely. Our position is certainly not enviable, not even by comparison with other nationalities in Rivers State. But the measure of our success will be the way, manner and time in which we turn this position of weakness into strength. It is not an impossible task, and we urge that the sufferings of the past year should not dishearten our young men and women. We stand convinced that we shall rise.

We shall appeal to the Federal military government or whatever government succeeds it to continue to show concern for small nationalities such as ours – especially in constitution-making; that it take STRONG COGNIZANCE OF OUR DESIRES WITH REGARD TO THE COMPANIES PROSPECTING OR OPERATING ON OUR SOIL.

Our wish is that the Rivers State government so orders affairs in the state that all its component nationalities share in the prosperity and dignity which the state is expected to bring to the Rivers people as a whole. We must show that we have learnt from the mistakes of the past; and if there is a lesson to be learnt, it is that no group, however weak or small, can be taken for granted . . .

Looking back on these words now, I realize how pious my hopes were, and how much they failed. The first failure is attributable to the inability of the educated Ogoni to provide leadership. My efforts only engineered personal jealousies on the part of the elite who continued, as I have said, to scramble for personal advantages from the Rivers State Governor, who was an Ijaw, the major ethnic group in the state. In no time at all it was quite easy to replace me in the Rivers State Executive Council with another Ogoni man. I was sacked in March 1973. And this seemed perfectly all right by the Ogoni elite.

The Rivers State itself did not prove to be any better than the Eastern Region in reconciling the interests of its component ethnic groups. There was the usual bickering and the drive for supremacy on the part of the more numerous and the more powerful, and the Ogoni, unable, as I had predicted, to take care of their own interests, fell behind the others.

The Federal government, for its part, took on a unitary colour, thanks to the ruling military. In that unitarism, the resources of the Ogoni and other ethnic minorities in the Niger River Delta could be more easily purloined while paying lip-service to Nigerian federalism and unity.

As to constitution-making and provisions for protecting the ethnic minorities, when I tried to get into a constituent assembly which was to fashion a new Nigerian constitution in 1977, I was blocked first by some educated Ogoni people and then by the rulers of Nigeria. The Nigerian constitution which emerged offered a stronger central government and left the ethnic minorities totally unprotected in terms of their economic resources and their culture. For instance, it vested the entire mineral resources in the country in parliament to share as it pleased. In a situation where the ethnic minorities provided most of the mineral resources (oil) and yet were a minority in parliament, and where oil was the be-all and end-all of Nigerian politics and the economy, as well as the central focus of all budgetary ambitions, there was no way the ethnic minorities, including the Ogoni, could protect their great inheritance. Thus, by 1980 the Federal government had left the oil-bearing areas with only 1.5 per cent of the proceeds of oil production. Before the military seized power, the governments in the areas were entitled to at least 50 per cent of such proceeds, in addition to rent and royalties.

In 1977, after I failed, surprisingly, to get into the constituent assembly, I analysed why all my hopes for the Ogoni had failed to materialize. And I found that the task was a gargantuan one which would require an almost superhuman effort. My failure up to 1973 I could ascribe to my relative youth and inexperience. My failure in 1977 I could put down to my not having organized the Ogoni people properly. But I also knew that any such organization would require a lot of energy, patience and money. The first I had; the second I could cultivate; the last I lacked absolutely. It seemed proper to look for the last. I spent the next six years doing just that.

I wasn't looking for a lot of money: just enough to ensure that my children could go to school without pain if I were to dedicate myself to the interests of the Ogoni people, and that I had a roof over my head so that no one could throw me and my family into the rain. I already had four children and no property anywhere in the world. And the task to which I hoped to bend my steps would require the sort of devoted and single-minded attention which would not permit of diversions.

It was also important that in seeking limited financial security I should maintain my integrity and not go into deals Nigerian-style such as would make it impossible for me to look anyone in the eyes.

I had already been keeping a grocery store from 1973 when I was kicked out of the Rivers State government. I had also done some wholesale trading in locally manufactured and imported goods. But none of that was going to make me anything more than a marginally comfortable man. For all my effort, I had still not been able to own a house. The point was that I had not concentrated absolutely on trading. I had continued to show some interest in Ogoni politics, even contesting the local government elections in 1976. I won the election but declined to become Chairman of the Council which the Secretary to the government of Rivers State, Mr Francis Ellah, offered me. I wasn't a good councillor either, since I found the level of debate in the council not very high, and resigned after a while.

From October 1977, however, I gave my trading business

all I had. Shopkeeping and trading did teach me the virtues of saving the pennies and investing. It wasn't new to me. My mother and father had ensured that right from age seven I knew how to retail goods in the markets at Bori and neighbouring Ikot Abasi in present-day Akwa Ibom State.

One other lesson which my mother taught me but which I refused to learn was the importance of landed property. She dug at me perpetually, advising on the need to own land. I always told her that property owners were bourgeois and would be consumed by the revolution which I dreamt would happen; how, I did not say.

The lesson came in useful now, as I thought how to invest the profit I made from my trading activity. I began to invest in property – land and houses. Again, I was not looking for enormous investments, just enough to enable me to get by. I was able to buy a personal residence, a building for my office and shop and one or two other properties. By the end of 1983 I had satisfied my mother's yearning that I build myself a house in Bane, the Ogoni village where she lives. And, as far as I was concerned, my business career was over.

I then turned to writing and publishing. This, ostensibly, had nothing to do with the uplifting of the Ogoni. But a coup had taken place at the end of 1983, and even if I had had an interest in politics, I had learnt to studiously avoid military politics in Nigeria. It was bound to brutalize any civilian who took part. It seemed the right moment to turn to my first love. Writing fiction about the Ogoni and Nigeria seemed a worthwhile alternative to military politics or any politics for that matter. I threw myself into my new calling with all my enthusiasm and a sense of responsibility. I really took myself seriously, thinking that I had lost valuable time trading. I took down a number of old manuscripts which I had been writing either at university or during the civil war or while in government. I had shoved them into my drawer when I started trading in 1973. They were mostly incomplete.

Starting with my poetry volume, I brushed up a number of the poems and sent them off to my valued friend and fellow Ogoni, Theo Vincent, Professor of English at the University of Lagos. While I waited for him to evaluate the poetry collection, I wrote the second half of *Sozaboy*, my first novel, and sent it off to Longman Nigeria, which had published my children's books in 1973. And then I took up the short stories, writing eleven new stories to complete the volume of nineteen stories now titled *A Forest of Flowers*. All this in a whirlwind, of sorts.

Once Theo thought the poems were publishable, I went ahead to make plans to publish them myself, having ascertained from an editor at Longman that Nigerian publishers were hesitant to publish poetry and drama. I sent off the typescript to Richard Clay, the printers, in London. They came back to me with a quotation, using terms which I did not understand. I hated to be so baffled and decided that I would some day have to take courses in publishing.

But before then I had got involved in television production, not through any design of mine but by sheer accident. I have narrated elsewhere how I was pressed into it by a friend from my University of Ibadan days, Dr Victoria Ezeokoli, who happened to be Director of Programmes, Nigerian Television Authority, at the time. It began as a joke, but once I got into it, I gave it my all, as usual. I created, wrote, produced, financed and marketed a comedy series which ran for five years (October 1985–October 1990) on Nigerian network television, receiving much praise locally and internationally.

Television production sharpened my writing skills and the flying success of the series, *Basi & Co.*, established my reputation as a creative writer. But above all, I learnt how to deal with the press and how to promote an idea, publicity being very central to the success of a television series. That was the importance of my television work to the Ogoni question.

Once the television programme got on the screen, I began to wonder why Longman had not indicated if they would publish *Sozaboy* or not. I got tired of waiting and decided to publish it myself. I followed all the motions of a publisher without knowing what I was doing. I was merely using the knowledge I had acquired at government college, Umuahia, and the University of Ibadan where I had edited student magazines. The singular mistake I made was to proofread the book alone. I needed four different pairs of eyes! Consequently, when the book came out in hard cover, there were at least fifty typos in it! Since then, proofreading has become the most interesting part of publishing for me. Will I ever publish an error-free book?

Several books followed in quick succession, but none was more important to me than my diary of the Nigerian civil war, *On a Darkling Plain*. Like *Sozaboy*, it came from a very impressionable time of my life, a time of great drama and even greater challenges. I had written quite some part of the book before 1973. But to complete it, I had to do further research and to consider the direction in which Nigeria as a country was going in the 1980s.

I was nearing the end of my research when, out of the blue, I was appointed a full-time Executive Director of the Federal government's Directorate of Mass Mobilization for Self-reliance, Social Justice and Economic Recovery (MAMSER). The appointment, in September 1987, took me entirely by surprise. I didn't see how I could be appointed, as a businessman, to a full-time government job. But a few of my friends thought I had been so critical of the government that someone had decided to find out if I meant well or merely delighted in being negative.

It was going to be a very expensive venture for me, I thought. Abandoning all the things I was doing to take on a regular job – something I hadn't done almost all of my life – didn't appeal at all. However, once I read the inaugural address given by the man next to Babangida, the military dictator who had seized power in a palace coup in 1985, and noting that in conception the directorate was supposed to revolutionize the country, I decided to give it a shot. I would do it for one year, no more. The directorate was asked to:

– awaken the consciousness of all categories of Nigerians to their rights and obligations as citizens;

– sensitize, induct and equip all Nigerians to fight against internal and external domination of our resources by a few individuals and groups;

– reorientate Nigerians to shun waste and vanity and to shed all pretences of affluence in their life-styles;

– create consciousness about power and its use, and about the proper role of the government in serving the collective interests of Nigerians;

– propagate the need to eschew all vices in public life, including corruption, dishonesty, electoral and census malpractice, ethnic and religious bigotry;

– propagate the virtues of hard work, honesty, self-reliance, commitment to, and promotion of, national integration; and

– inculcate in Nigerians the virtues of patriotism and positive participation in national affairs.

I assumed responsibility for research in the directorate. The year proved useful. For all the money the government was spending on the project, it would not succeed, I noticed early. You couldn't mobilize people in the absence of an ideology. And mobilizing the people would be to ask them to question seriously the military government itself. So there were certain things we would not, as executives, be able to do. There were also some rather serious management deficiencies in the organization, deficiencies in common with government departments in Nigeria. Together, these two factors rendered the directorate still-born. I resigned my position in October 1988.

However, in one year of thinking and living social mobilization and social justice, I came to certain conclusions which have since conditioned my attitude to change and society in Nigeria.

As soon as I left MAMSER, I got down to completing my research for my civil war diary, *On a Darkling Plain*. By this time, I had completed publishing arrangements for *Prisoners of Jebs*, which I had serialized in *Vanguard* newspaper in 1985/6. I was writing short stories and children's books furiously, and *Basi & Co.* was still on screen and taking up a lot of my time and money.

I had expected to publish six books, including *On a Darkling Plain*, in 1989. All sorts of problems reared their heads in that year, including the death of my beloved friend, and mother of two of my children, the angelic Nomsy, to whom be peace eternal. I published five of the books, less 'the dark plain', which finally got a public launch at the Nigerian Institute of International Affairs in Lagos on 22 March 1990.

The launch was well attended by the Nigerian academia, journalists, diplomats and the literati, including wives of diplomats and expatriate staff of various organizations – members of the African Literature Club – to whom I had read some of my works on previous occasions.

I used the opportunity of the launch to speak about the obligations of the country to the oil-bearing delta and to make certain pronouncements about the future of Nigeria:

Mr Chairman, Honourable Minister, Your Excellencies, Ladies and Gentlemen,

It is a pleasure to present to you, *On a Darkling Plain: An Account of the Nigerian Civil War*. Although I wrote most of the book as soon as the civil war ended in 1970, it has taken some time to convince myself of the right moment to make it public. I thank Kole Omotoso for encouraging its publication.

A civil war is a very divisive event; writing about it cannot be easy, especially when one is seeking to present the truth and that truth has as many sides to it as there are protagonists and interests. A civil war in a country with as many ethnic groups, religious sects, social classes and conflicts as Nigeria has serious repercussions for individuals, families and communities. Writing about it is equivalent to walking a minefield. It places a dire responsibility upon the writer.

This responsibility I accepted long ago and have treated with due seriousness and diligence. I do not claim to be infallible but I do assert that I have written from as objective a viewpoint as is possible in the circumstances.

I do not expect the book to please anyone. I expect it to provoke debate and thought, to add to the corpus of viewpoints on the civil war, and to help chart a new path in the political thinking and social behaviour of Nigerians.

In spite of my hesitations about all that surrounded the last civil war, I wish to pay tribute to the men and women on both sides who fought against injustice, against hypocrisy and humbug as they saw it. We must ensure that those who died fighting, shall not have died in vain.

Many of those who participated in the war in one form or the other and survived it will readily agree that the country we fought for is not the country we have today. There is still more fighting to be done, in the minds of Nigerians, and for the minds of Nigerians, if the country we dream of is to emerge.

I do not mean to review the book; Professor Theo Vincent has already done so in his inimitable style. However, I wish to draw attention to two broad areas which my story and my study of Nigerian society have highlighted: the ethnic question and oil.

The ethnic nature of Nigerian society is a real one. It cannot be prayed or wished away and those who try to do so, at least in public, only have to turn to the example of the Soviet Union, Yugoslavia and Romania to disabuse their minds. I therefore suggest that the make-up of the country as a federation of 300 ethnic groups be taken into full account in formulating policies of governance. The present division of the country into a federation in which some ethnic groups are split into several states, whereas other ethnic groups are forced to remain together in a difficult, unitary system inimical to the federal culture of the country, is a recipe for dissension and future wars. Chief Awolowo put it most succinctly: 'Under a true Federal constitution, each group, however small, is entitled to the same treatment as any other group, however large. Opportunity must be afforded to each to evolve its own peculiar political institution. The present structure reinforces indigenous colonialism – a crude, harsh, unscientific and illogical system.'

Oil was very much at the centre of the war. The people who live on oil-bearing land were the main victims of the war. Twenty years after the war, the system of revenue allocation, the development policies of successive Federal administrations and the insensitivity of the Nigerian elite have turned the delta and its environs into an ecological disaster and dehumanized its inhabitants. The notion that the oil-bearing areas can provide the revenue of the country and yet be denied a proper share of that revenue because it is perceived that the inhabitants of the area are few in number is unjust, immoral, unnatural and ungodly. Why should the people on oil-bearing land be tortured? Why are they entitled to but 1.5 per cent of their resources? Why has this money not been paid as and when due? Where is the interest the money has generated over the last ten years? The peoples of Rivers and Bendel States, in particular, sit very heavy on the conscience of Nigeria.

The silence of Nigeria's social reformers, writers and legal men over this issue is deafening. Therefore, the affected peoples must immediately gird their loins and demand without equivocation their rightful patrimony. They must not be frightened by the enormity of the task, by the immorality of the present. History and world opinion are on their side.

I call upon the Babangida administration to extend its human rights dispensation, its social justice claims to the minorities throughout Nigeria and, particularly, to the minorities of the delta and its environs. I call upon the administration to pay up all monies owed to the communities with interest and to radically increase the percentage of oil revenue payable to them.

I call upon the Nigerian elite to play fair by all Nigerian communities, to allow scientific methodology to replace sleight-of-hand as an instrument of social engineering and to show compassion to the less privileged of our society so that we can achieve a better Nigeria and hand over a meaningful legacy and a beautiful country to the future.

It was a controversial book. I had put my views on the rights of the ethnic minorities very strongly, and expected to take a rap on the knuckles from ethnic hegemonists in Nigeria. They didn't disappoint me. Some Igbos found the book particularly challenging and, even without reading it, began to savage me, not the book.

In a way, it was fortuitous that I was writing a column in the government-owned weekly *Sunday Times* at the time. Dr Yemi Ogunbiyi, an academic, had recently assumed the managing directorship of the Federal government-owned *Daily Times* outfit and was in search of good freelance writers. (In Nigeria, a freelance writer is one who writes for free, without financial compensation.) He offered me an opportunity and I wrote a column called 'Similia'. I used the column to answer the critics of my new book, and to develop further the ideas which I had expressed in it, quite apart from my other concerns.

The newspaper column widened my reading audience and spread my ideas to a considerable extent. Week after week, I made sure that the name Ogoni appeared before the eyes of readers. It was a television technique, designed to leave the name indelibly in their minds. Sometimes I would deliberately provoke readers or fly a kite in the acerbic and polemical column. And I invariably got the sort of reaction I expected.

By the time the controversy over 'the darkling plain' died down, I had stopped producing *Basi & Co.*, the 'Similia' column was on its way out (it was becoming too anti-establishment and was duly axed), and the Ogoni question had begun increasingly to occupy my detailed attention.

Even as the controversy over 'the darkling plain' raged, I had begun the process of mobilizing the Ogoni people. First, I organized a seminar under the auspices of the newly formed Ogoni Central Union, of which I had been elected President. The best Ogoni brains presented papers on aspects of Ogoni life; culture and education, the disorganization of the Ogoni, their traumatic existence, agriculture, the economy, women. The seminar conclusions pointed to the need for the Ogoni people to organize themselves better and to take responsibility for their political existence.

I canvassed the idea of forming a mass organization with Kagote, a club for the Ogoni elite, and the Ogoni Klub, another club for young Ogoni professionals. I attended meeting after meeting with them and pressed my views hard all the time. I found a ready response.

In a way, it was fortunate that, at that time, most Ogoni politicians had been banned from the political process which the cunning dictator, Babangida, had put into motion. The politicians were bitter over their ban and were looking for some relevance, something to keep them in the limelight. And they had none of the constraints which belonging to a political party would have put on them. Thus, when I proposed the signing of an Ogoni Bill of Rights under the auspices of the Ogoni Central Union, no one demurred. On 26 August 1990, when we met at Bori (the headquarters of the Ogoni people) to approve the bill which I had written, the atmosphere was that of a carnival. Everyone approved of it and wanted to put their signature to it. We proposed five signatories in each of the six Ogoni kingdoms (hitherto called 'clans' – a misnomer in my view) of Babbe, Eleme, Gokana, Ken-Khana, Nyo-Khana and Tai, but to satisfy everyone we had to increase the signatories to six per kingdom.

The final document was later passed round and all signed except for the Eleme kingdom, whose government-appointed ruler, Ngei O. Ngei, had chaired our meeting. In the end, he raised questions about the bill which would have delayed our work. We therefore decided to leave Eleme out and to call upon them later when we would have identified a leadership in the Eleme kingdom truly committed to the progress of the area.

Presented to the government and people of Nigeria

We, the people of Ogoni (Babbe, Gokana, Ken-Khana, Nyo-Khana and Tai) numbering about 500,000, being a separate and distinct ethnic nationality within the Federal Republic of Nigeria, wish to draw the attention of the government and people of Nigeria to the undermentioned facts:

1. That the Ogoni people, before the advent of British colonialism, were not conquered or colonized by any other ethnic group in present-day Nigeria.

2. That British colonization forced us into the administrative division of Opobo from 1908 to 1947.

3. That we protested against this forced union until the Ogoni Native Authority was created in 1947 and placed under the then Rivers Province.

4. That in 1951 we were forcibly included in the Eastern Region of Nigeria, where we suffered utter neglect.

5. That we protested against the neglect by voting against the party in power in the region in 1957, and against the forced union by testimony, before the Willink Commission of Inquiry into Minority Fears in 1958.

6. That this protest led to the inclusion of our nationality in Rivers State in 1967, which state consists of several ethnic nationalities with differing cultures, languages and aspirations.

7. That oil was struck and produced in commercial quantities on our land in 1958 at K. Dere (Bomu oilfield).

8. That oil has been mined on our land since 1958 to this day from the following oilfields: (i) Bomu (ii) Bodo West (iii) Tai (iv) Korokoro (v) Yorla (vi) Lubara Creek and (vii) Afam by Shell Petroleum Development Company (Nigeria) Limited.

9. That in over 30 years of oil mining, the Ogoni nationality have provided the Nigerian nation with a total revenue
estimated at over forty billion naira, thirty billion dollars.

10. That in return for the above contribution, the Ogoni
people have received NOTHING.

11. That today, the Ogoni people have:

    (i)   No representation whatsoever in ALL institu-
        tions of the Federal government of Nigeria.

    (ii) No pipe-borne water.

    (iii) No electricity.

    (iv) No job opportunities for the citizens in Federal,
        state, public sector or private sector companies.

    (v)   No social or economic project of the Federal
        government.

12. That the Ogoni languages of Gokana and Khana are
undeveloped and are about to disappear, whereas other Nigerian languages are being forced on us.

13. That the ethnic politics of successive Federal and state
governments are gradually pushing the Ogoni people to slavery and possible extinction.

14. That the Shell Petroleum Development Company of
Nigeria Limited does not employ Ogoni people at a meaningful or any level at all, in defiance of the Federal government's
regulations.

15. That the search for oil has caused severe land and food
shortages in Ogoni, one of the most densely populated areas
of Africa (average 1,500 per square mile; national average
300 per square mile).

16. That neglectful environmental pollution laws and sub-
standard inspection techniques of the Federal authorities
have led to the complete degradation of the Ogoni environment, turning our homeland into an ecological disaster.

17. That the Ogoni people lack education, health and
other social facilities.

18. That it is intolerable that one of the richest areas of Nigeria should wallow in abject poverty and destitution.

19. That successive Federal administrations have trampled on every minority right enshrined in the Nigerian constitution to the detriment of the Ogoni and have, by administrative structuring and other noxious acts transferred Ogoni wealth exclusively to other parts of the republic.

20. That the Ogoni people wish to manage their own affairs.

Now, therefore, while reaffirming our wish to remain a part of the Federal Republic of Nigeria, we make demand upon the Republic as follows:

That the Ogoni people be granted Political Autonomy to participate in the affairs of the republic as a distinct and separate unit by whatever name called, provided that this autonomy guarantees the following:

(a) political control of Ogoni affairs by Ogoni people;
(b) the right to the control and use of a fair proportion of Ogoni economic resources for Ogoni development;
(c) adequate and direct representation as of right in all Nigerian national institutions;
(d) the use and development of Ogoni languages in Ogoni territory;
(e) the full development of Ogoni culture;
(f) the right to religious freedom;
(g) the right to protect the Ogoni environment and ecology from further degradation.

We make the above demand in the knowledge that it does not deny any other ethnic group in the Nigerian Federation their rights and that it can only be conducive to peace, justice and fairplay and hence stability and progress in the Nigerian nation.

We make the above demand in the belief that, as Obafemi Awolowo has written: in a true Federation, each ethnic group no matter how small, is entitled to the same treatment as any other ethnic group, no matter how large.

We demand these rights as equal members of the Nigerian Federation who contribute and have contributed to the growth of the Federation and have a right to expect full returns from that Federation.

Adopted by general acclaim of the Ogoni people on the 26th day of August, 1990 at Bori, Rivers State, and signed by:

BABBE: HRH Mark Tsaro-Igbara, Gbenemene Babbe; HRH F. M. K. Noryaa, Menebua, Ka-Babbe; Chief M. A. M. Tornwe III, JP; Prince J. S. Sangha; Dr Israel Kue; Chief A. M. N. Gua.

GOKANA: HRH James P. Bagia, Gberesako XI, Gbenemene Gokana; Chief E. N. Kobani, JP, Tonsimene Gokana; Dr B. N. Birabi; Chief Kemte Giadom, JP; Chief S. N. Orage.

KEN-KHANA: HRH M. H. S. Eguru, Gbenemene Ken-Khana; HRH C. B. S. Nwikina, Emah III, Menebua Bom; Mr M. C. Daanwii; Chief T. N. Nwieke; Mr Ken Saro-Wiwa; Mr Simeon Idemyor.

NYO-KHANA: HRH W. Z. P. Nzidee, Gbenemene Baa I of Nyo-Khana; Dr G. B. Leton, OON, JP; Mr Lekue Lah-Loolo; Mr L. E. Mwara; Chief E. A. Apenu; Pastor M. P. Maeba.

TAI: HRH B. A. Mballey, Gbenemene Tai; HRH G. N. Gininwa, Menebua Tua-Tua; Chief J. S. Agbara; Chief D. J. K. Kumbe; Chief Fred Gwezia; HRH A. Demor-Kanni, Menebua Nonwa.

The document was despatched to Babangida's Armed Forces Ruling Council by me as President of the Ogoni Central Union. As I expected, we only got an acknowledgement from the bureaucrats in the residency (Babangida being the only unelected President, perhaps, in the whole world). But the die had been cast.

We had decided to publish the bill in a national newspaper, and I insisted that its signatories would have to contribute towards the cost of buying newspaper space. This was a way of committing the signatories to the sacrifice that the struggle would need.

We then organized a launch of the Bill of Rights in all the six Ogoni kingdoms. The idea was to present and explain the document to the Ogoni masses. Written in English, it had to be presented to them in the Ogoni tongues. Mr Ledum Mitee, a brilliant young Ogoni lawyer, was one of those entrusted with the task. This form of public education was one we were to rely on increasingly in the course of the struggle.

By the end of the year, there was considerable excitement in Ogoni over the Ogoni Bill of Rights. I continued to press the case for non-violent struggle at every available forum. On 26 December 1990, I was invited to deliver the keynote address to the Kagote Club at its annual luncheon. I spoke as follows:

Chiefs, Elders, Compatriots, Ladies and Gentlemen,

It gives me great pleasure to be with you this afternoon and I thank you for inviting me to give this keynote address.

Let me begin by congratulating you on keeping this organization going all through this year. I am sure that should you keep this habit, Kagote will be able, in time, to influence events in Ogoni for the better.

71

I am sure that you all know the very serious circumstances in which Ogoni finds itself today. Never before in the history of our nationality have we been faced collectively by such terrible challenges. Never before has there been need for unity, unanimity and consensus. Even at the risk of being tiresome, since I have dealt with this elsewhere, I would like to delineate the dire peril which the Ogoni people face.

Historically, the Ogoni people have always been fierce and independent. This is the reason they have never been colonized by other people, were not taken as slaves in the course of the notorious trans-atlantic slave trade, were known to their neighbours as 'cannibals' and were able to preserve for themselves the most fertile and most healthy part of the coastal plains terraces north of the Niger River Delta. Additional to this was the law passed by our ancestors forbidding intermarriage with our neighbours with the exception of the Ibibio, whose women Ogoni men were permitted to marry. This served to preserve the purity of the Ogoni, to preserve their language and culture and to stop their absorption or dilution by any of the neighbouring larger groups.

At the same time, the Ogoni have been known to 'display an exceptional achievement in their original, abstract masks'. I would like you to note the words 'exceptional' and 'original'. These are marks of the distinction of the Ogoni people which we must not forget.

It is also relevant to note that as storytellers and in other art forms the Ogoni are gifted and hold their own quite easily. The Ogoni have made contributions of the first order to modern African literature in English. And Ogoni was, before the advent of British colonialism, a very orderly society.

The advent of British colonialism was to shatter Ogoni society and inflict on us a backwardness from which we are still struggling to escape. It was British colonialism which forced alien administrative structures on us and herded us into the domestic colonialism of Nigeria. Right from 1908 when Ogoni was administered as a part of Opobo Division, through the creation of Rivers Province in 1947, Eastern Region in 1951 and Rivers State in 1967, the Ogoni people have struggled to resist colonialism and return to their much cherished autonomy and self-determination. I am encouraged to think that this heroic struggle by our people is beginning to see the light at the end of a very dark tunnel.

Some of you here have taken part in this struggle from the very early days. Most of you must be aware of the struggles in the thirties through the fifties of Birabi and others in the Ogoni Central Union and the Ogoni State Representative Assembly.

I have to state without equivocation that this struggle has been made doubly difficult by what I have characterized as the crude and harsh nature of Nigerian domestic colonialism, a colonialism which is cruel, unfeeling and monstrous. Its method has been an outrageous denial of rights, a usurpation of our economic resources, a dehumanization which has sought to demoralize our people by characterizing them as meek, obscure and foolish. All these fly in the face of the facts, of history. Because the Ogoni people are hardworking, talented and intelligent. If we have been able to achieve what we have in our dire circumstance, can anyone imagine what we would have done had we benefited from equal opportunities?

As a result of domestic colonialism, the Ogoni people have virtually lost pride in themselves and their ability, have voted for a multiplicity of parties in elections, have regarded themselves as perpetual clients of other ethnic groups and have come to think that there is nowhere else to go but down.

When you consider the census cheating, the administrative

malstructuring, the unfair revenue allocation formulations, the lack of protection of minority rights in the Nigerian constitution, we must regard it as something of a miracle that Ogoni still exists at all. Yes, we merely exist; barely exist. Most of our children are not at school, while those who have secured an education do not find jobs. Those who have jobs do not find promotion, as progress in Nigeria is not by merit but by preferment. Our languages are dying, our culture is disappearing. For a people who proved themselves as providers of food to those who live in the inhospitable delta, the fact that we are buying food today is an absolute disgrace. Land is in very short supply in Ogoni and what is available is no longer enough to feed our teeming population. Where will our children live and farm twenty years hence? The Ogoni do not have a share in the economic life of Nigeria.

And all this is happening to a people whose home is one of the richest in Africa. Over the past thirty-two years Ogoni has offered Nigeria an estimated US thirty billion dollars and received NOTHING in return, except a blighted countryside, and atmosphere full of carbon dioxide, carbon monoxide and hydrocarbons; a land in which wildlife is unknown; a land of polluted streams and creeks, of rivers without fish, a land which is, in every sense of the term, an ecological disaster. This is not acceptable.

What to do? Hopeless as the situation is, bleak as the picture is, we can and must do something to save Ogoni. The responsibility is yours and mine, and we must all co-operate to redeem our nationality, to save our progeny.

As clearly enunciated in the Ogoni Bill of Rights presented to the government and people of Nigeria in October 1990, the only thing that will save the Ogoni people is the achievement of political autonomy accompanied by, among others, the right to use a fair proportion of Ogoni resources for the development of Ogoni – its education, health, agriculture and culture. This is the great task before us in this last decade of the twentieth century.

Some, looking at the enormity of the task, must ask, 'Can we do it?' The answer, unequivocally, is, YES. For where there is a will, there is a way. Ogoni must be saved.

We have taken the first important step in clearing our minds, in achieving unity of leadership, in projecting our case before Nigeria and, I must tell you, before some international organizations interested in the matter. The next task is to mobilize every Ogoni man, woman and child on the nature and necessity of our cause so that everyone knows and believes in that cause and holds it as a religion, refusing to be bullied or bribed therefrom. And finally, we must begin to build up action to transform our current advantages into political scores.

This is not, I repeat, NOT a call to violent action. We have a moral claim over Nigeria. This moral claim arises as much from the murder of 30,000 Ogoni people during the civil war by Ojukwu's followers as the usurpation of US thirty billion dollars' worth of our oil and the destruction of our ecology amounting to the same sum. Our strength derives from this moral advantage and that is what we have to press home.

You will, therefore, find that the Ogoni people have an agenda and everyone, as I have said, has a role in actualizing that agenda. This is no time to feast and make merry like sheep being led unwittingly to the slaughterhouse. This is a time to think and act. Brothers and sisters, be courageous in asking for Ogoni rights. Morality, time and world opinion are on our side.

Wherever an Ogoni man or woman may be, he must not forget our agenda to save our nationality, our language, our culture, our heritage. Ogoni people must co-operate with one another, as individuals, as groups, because that is the only way we can survive. Wherever they may be, they must proclaim their Ogoniness, from the rooftop if possible. There is absolutely no shame and little restraint in doing so. The Ogoni are so far down in the well that only shouting loudly can they be heard by those on the surface of the soil.

In the ongoing political exercise, I think it is well to understand, as I have said on several other occasions, that no matter which of the parties wins, no difference will be made to the generality of the Ogoni people. Both parties are built on fundaments inimical to Ogoni progress. Therefore, the Ogoni people and their politicians must not break their heads over which of the parties wins, can win, does not win, should win.

However, we must support the progression to democratic rule, as it is only through democratic action that we can re-establish our rights. The duty of the party politicians among us is to represent Ogoni, their constituencies; to push the Ogoni agenda within their parties. I believe that the Ogoni agenda is the only one that can save Nigeria from future destruction. This agenda postulates the equality of all ethnic groups, big or small, within the Nigerian federation as well as the evolution of proper, undiluted federalism in the nation. In this way Nigerians will not be oppressed, their creative spirit will be freed and their productivity and self-reliance promoted. Cheating will end in the nation, corruption will be minimized and justice will prevail.

As we go into 1991, I must tell you that I have been very encouraged by one particular event. I spent four weeks in November/December in the United States as a Distinguished Visiting Fellow of the United States Information Agency. I found there a small number of Ogoni professionals, all of them properly employed, some of them self-employed and doing well. There is an Ogoni attorney with his own private chambers in Houston, and an Ogoni pharmacist with a chain of stores, Ogoni doctors with their own private clinics and there are Ogoni university professors. This shows what Ogoni people can do, even in the toughest competition, when there is some equality of opportunity.

Therefore, my final plea to you all is work hard, think, embrace education for your family, friends and associates and co-operate with one another in the achievement of the Ogoni agenda. And since the Ogoni must have their full share of Nigerian life, Ogoni people must participate in all aspects of Nigerian life – in sports, the arts, debates, celebrations, in everything Nigerian. We have contributed so much to the country, we cannot afford to be denied anything in it.

Members of your organization have a most important role to play in actualizing the Ogoni agenda. As I see it, the generation to which I belong is about to leave the scene. There is a need for the next generation to prepare itself to continue where we shall have left off. I therefore call upon the youth of Ogoni to prepare themselves for leadership through study, self-denial, participation in community development and, faithful interest in Nigerian, African and current world affairs.

I will end by thanking you for giving me the opportunity of proclaiming, before this distinguished audience, the Ogoni agenda. I hope that you will leave here determined to contribute to the realization of a new order in the Nigerian polity – an order which will enable Nigeria take its place among the civilized nations of the world and help the black man wipe the shame of the centuries from his brows.

God bless you all.

It took quite some time to get the funds for a full-page advertorial for the Bill of Rights in a national newspaper. In the intervening period, we held meetings to determine under what organization we were going to operate, since all the signatories were not members of the Ogoni Central Union.

At a meeting in Bodo, at the residence of late Edward Kobani, the name of the organization, Movement for the Survival of the Ogoni People (MOSOP) was chosen, someone reminding us of its similarity to the Israeli secret service organization, Mossad. Choosing the officials was not difficult; the places were open and there was work to do. I had made up my mind that I would not head the organization; I thought that I would best serve it and the Ogoni people by writing and propagating its ideology as well as doing the press work. And in any case, there was need to associate as many of the elite as possible with the organization. If they did not have a visible role, knowing them as I did, they would happily scuttle the movement.

In the end, Dr Garrick Leton agreed to be President, and Mr L.L. Lah-Loolo was made Vice-President. The position of Secretary was given to a young lawyer, Mr Saanakaa, who was also President of the Ogoni Klub. Chief Titus Nwieke was named Treasurer.

I have to stress that there was no election as such. We were a steering committee formed to set up MOSOP, and I was made 'spokesman', a role which allowed me to speak not only on behalf of the movement but also for the Ogoni people.

At that time I still had all my balls in the air. I was about to end the production of *Basi & Co.*, and the 'Similia' column in the *Sunday Times* was also about to end. It had been a busy year for me all right. Apart from my usual routine, I was also able to visit the Soviet Union at the invitation of the African Institute of that country, and later in the year I was, as stated previously, a Distinguished Visiting Fellow of the United States Information Agency, touring the

United States and talking to and meeting with anyone whom I pleased over a six-week period.

The two visits were important in the development of the Ogoni cause, which had, at that time, become the greatest of my concerns. In the Soviet Union I was able to see the beginnings of the death of a multi-ethnic state where the ethnic groups had been held together by force and violence. The rumbles of disintegration had already started and after I compared notes with Edwin Madunagu, a self-confessed Marxist on the *Guardian* newspaper who was also touring the Soviet Union at the time, there was no doubt in my mind that the Union was on the verge of collapse. My interpreters and guides, who were all young, confirmed as much.

The visit to the United States sharpened my awareness of the need to organize the Ogoni people to struggle for their environment. One visit to a group in Denver, Colorado, interested in the trees in the wilderness of the Colorado state, showed what could be done by an environment group to press demands on government and companies.

A bit of research and thinking of my childhood days showed me how conscious of their environment the Ogoni have always been and how far they went in an effort to protect it. I had shown that consciousness myself all along. In my pamphlet *The Ogoni Nationality Today and Tomorrow*, published during the Nigerian civil war in 1968, I had pointedly stated *inter alia*: 'We refuse to accept that the only responsibility which Shell–BP owes our nation is the spoliation of our lands . . .' And I had written the poetic lines:

> The flares of Shell are flames of hell
> We bake beneath their light
> Nought for us save the blight
> Of cursèd neglect and cursèd Shell.

I had also played a major role in attempting to get Shell to pay reparation to the Ogoni landlords after the blow-out on Shell's Bomu Oilwell 11 in 1971.

What I had neglected to do was to organize the people to protect their environment. The Ogoni Bill of Rights which I had written and presented to the chiefs and leaders for adoption in August 1990 before I left for the United States was strong on environmental protection. What the trip did was to convince me that the environment would have to be a strong plank on which to base the burgeoning Movement for the Survival of the Ogoni People.

I returned to Nigeria knowing that my career as a businessman was effectively over; so also my television production work. Dr Yemi Ogunbiyi, after my article 'The Coming War in the Delta', axed the 'Similia' column, thus serving notice that my arguments for the Ogoni and the humiliation of the people of the oil-bearing areas of the delta were not acceptable to the Babangida administration. Dr Ogunbiyi was himself under pressure for not turning the newspaper into a megaphone of the government, and was soon dismissed unceremoniously, bringing to an end a very exciting period in the life of the *Daily Times* Group.

From that moment onwards, I dedicated myself in full to the Ogoni cause. I sorted out at the back of my mind the two facets of the case: the complete devastation of the environment by the oil companies prospecting for and mining oil in Ogoni, notably Shell and Chevron; the political marginalization and economic strangulation of the Ogoni, which was the responsibility of succeeding administrations in the country. And I began to cast about for ways of confronting both institutions.

The year 1991 marked my fiftieth on earth and I had an important project to commemorate it. I had proposed to publish no less than eight books, seven of them mine, the eighth a volume of stories by a budding Nigerian writer, Maxwell Nwagboso. I wrote furiously and published speedily and was able by 10 October, my birthday, to organize a launch of the eight books at the J. K. Randle Hall in Lagos. At the launch I made certain proposals on the Nigerian condition, it being my credo that literature in a critical situation such as Nigeria's cannot be divorced from politics. Indeed, literature must serve society by steeping itself in politics, by intervention, and writers must not merely write to amuse or to take a bemused, critical look at society. They must play an interventionist role. My experience has been that African governments can ignore writers, taking comfort in the fact that only few can read and write, and that those who read find little time for the luxury of literary consumption beyond the need to pass examinations based on set texts. Therefore, the writer must be *l'homme engagé*: the intellectual man of action.

He must take part in mass organizations. He must establish direct contact with the people and resort to the strength of African literature – oratory in the tongue. For the word is power and more powerful is it when expressed in common currency. That is why a writer who takes part in mass organizations will deliver his message more effectively than one who only writes waiting for time to work its literary wonders. The only problem I see is that such a writer must strive to maintain his authenticity, which stands a chance of being corrupted by the demands of politics. A struggle will necessarily ensue, but that should conduce to making the writer even better. For we write best of the things we directly experience, better of what we hear, and well of what we imagine.

This is probably the reason why the best Nigerian writers have involved themselves actively in 'politics'. Wole Soyinka, Nigeria's Nobel Laureate, is an outstanding example. Even the normally placid and wise Chinua Achebe was forced to work within one of the political parties to buttress his call on all Nigerians to 'proselytize for civilized values'. Chris Okigbo died fighting on the side of the Biafran secessionists. And Festus Iyayi has been involved in labour unions and recently in the Campaign for Democracy organization. Which only goes to prove what I have said elsewhere, that in a situation as critical as Nigeria's, it is idle merely to sit by and watch or record goons and bumpkins run the nation aground and dehumanize the people.

This is not to say that I discount the value of those who only write, stand and wait. I am only reacting to my social situation, as every writer of my value must.

Accordingly, my address at the well-attended launch was long on politics, short on literature. I spoke as follows:

Before the Curtain Falls

Mr Chairman, Your Excellencies, Ladies and Gentlemen, Dear Friends,

I wish to thank you all for the kind sentiments you have expressed here either in words or by your mere presence. It is gratifying to know that there are people who care for your ideas while you are still alive.

A writer is his cause. At fifty, he may still dream dreams and see visions, but he must also wither into the truth. So today, I re-dedicate myself to what has always been my primary concern as a man and a writer: the development of a stable, modern Nigeria which embraces civilized values; a Nigeria where no ethnic group or individual is oppressed, a democratic nation where minority rights are protected, education is a right, freedom of speech and association are guaranteed, and where merit and competence are held as beacons. Convinced that most Nigerians share this concern, I will stand for it at all times and in all places.

If there was ever any doubt that the Nigeria of our dreams is far away, the recent World Bank Report on Nigeria has put paid to such doubts. What we have today is the rump of a country, illiterate, lacking in moral fibre, financially bankrupt and tottering dangerously on the brink of disaster. This should shake us out of all complacency.

The great issues of today are the structure of the Federation, our environment, an economy laden with debts which we must pay and not merely reschedule to the detriment of our children, education and the future of our youth. I have raised these issues in the books which have been presented here today.

So long as the structure of the Federation is weak, so long shall we continue to stumble from military dictatorships to civilian chaos with the same result: anarchy. Nigeria is a federation of ethnic groups. Since 1966 the military have sought to turn this federation into a unitary system with the same dismal results. Historical forces at work in the world dictate that all multi-ethnic states become confederations of independent ethnic groups. The Soviet Union and Yugoslavia are cases in point. Nigeria cannot waltz in an opposite direction. Current attempts to do so, if not immediately reversed, could lead to the total collapse of the nation.

We must end immediately the oppression of minority ethnic groups and free all Nigerians to express themselves and develop their cultures, their languages and their political systems using their resources as best they may. The late Chief Obafemi Awolowo said so almost fifty years ago. The nation has degenerated by the same measure as we have failed to pay heed to his thoughts.

Oil pollution is a great menace to the Nigerian environment. I wish to warn that the harm being done to the environment of the Niger River Delta must be ameliorated by the oil companies which prospect for oil there; the degradation of the ecosystem must end and the dehumanization of the inhabitants of the areas must cease and restitution be made for past wrong.

The two tasks I have outlined above are fundamental to the health of the nation and to the improvement of all other facets of our national life.

It has been said that the way to the future is the current transition programme, which is expected to lead to democratic civilian rule. This second attempt is basically no different from the 1979 experiment. And it is headed in a more disastrous direction. The transition has been described as a train, and is said to be on course. I disagree. The train is rusty and stands in the station; its route is strewn with danger, the passengers in the train are suffering and hungry, the larger majority of passengers and their goods are not on board. I do not believe that in the space of one year, given our deficiencies, we can peacefully hold six elections and a census. Besides, the constitution which is meant to usher in democracy is faulty; it does not protect minority rights, a basic requirement for democracy; it has been doctored by the military; the recent creation of new states and local governments has vitiated most of its tenets.

Over the past thirty years, a few military men have tried to dictate what course the nation should take. The results have been uniformly unedifying, as the military themselves have acknowledged recently. The look of a democratic Nigeria cannot, should not, be decided by military decree; it must be the collective decision of all Nigerians operating in a democratic context without coercion. The military are dedicated Nigerians but they should now honourably retire without equivocation from the political process and take their proper place within the nation so that Nigerians can resume the search for good government without fear of intimidation.

I am not by this bashing the military. No. Quite clearly, what we are faced with is a massive failure of vision and intellect on the part of the Nigerian elite – that failure which led to the easy enslavement of Africa, which has made Africans the playthings of other peoples and races, which made African rulers persist in the slave trade long after Europe had tired of it.

Anyone who witnessed the killings, looting and burnings engineered during civilian rule in 1964 and 1965, anyone who witnessed the massive electoral fraud and the treasury looting of the civilians of 1979–83 that drove Nigeria into debt peonage and reduced all Nigerians into Sap-induced slavery, must tremble at the thought that this country is about to return to civilian rule.

Anyone who thinks that splitting Nigeria into 50 states (ensuring that the majority ethnic groups have forty or so of them) and 600 local governments, and then sharing oil money according to a formula of 50:25:25 or whatever, between Federal, state and local governments respectively, is about to solve the problems of ethnic oppression, competitive ethnicity, economic mismanagement, moral ineptitude and other evils is applying a simplistic solution to a complex problem.

Any Yoruba person who believes in the split of Yorubaland into six states to increase the Yoruba share of oil money must ask himself or herself why Chief Obafemi Awolowo was able to administer Western Nigeria successfully with far less money than is available today to the six states put together.

Any Nigerian who places trust in sharing oil money must ask why Korea and Japan, who have little or no natural resources are today leading industrial nations.

Nigerians of the majority ethnic groups must ask themselves if they must mindlessly grind the minority ethnic groups to the dust, cheat and rob them openly, drive them to extinction, all in the name of what.

In 1958 it was obvious that the federating ethnic groups of Nigeria needed to establish the fundament of their co-operation. The British opined that if that was to be done, independence would have to be postponed. Nigerian leaders decided to have independence first and talk later. They only got to talk in 1966 after several murders of political leaders and massacres of common people. But the Ad-hoc Conference of 1966 called by Gowon was scuttled by Ojukwu when the discussions did not appear to be going in the direction the latter wanted. We plunged into civil war.

Many of the issues raised by Ojukwu and which led to war are as valid today as they were then. The untidy end of the war, the scampering of the ideologues of Biafra who have failed to sustain their arguments, greed for the oil of the delta, and the impatience of the Nigerian military with philosophy have conjoined to stop Nigerians from seeking a rational solution to their collective dilemma.

Our ship of state is today sinking! A few are manipulating the system to their advantage, but our intellectuals, our women, our youth, the masses are being flushed down the drain. All our systems, educational, economic, health, are in a shambles. Yet we persist in our national obtuseness. Sycophancy and self-deceit lie to the public and try to convince us that all is well or will soon be so. No. As I say in *Basi & Co.*, to be, we have to think.

The words of Descartes, *Cogito ergo sum*. Nigerians must think deeply. We must shun the simplistic solutions now being proffered.

I cast no blame on individuals or groups. I only want to mitigate that disaster which superficial thinking or even lack of thought has visited on Africa in the last 700 or so years. Nigeria deserves better than what we now have.

I therefore suggest that elected representatives of all ethnic groups in Nigeria should gather at a National Conference to select an interim government consisting of twenty reputable Nigerian men and women including retired judges of proven integrity, religious leaders, retired diplomats, intellectuals and elder statesmen from all parts of the country. The interim government will remain in office for one year while the National Conference discusses a more durable political structure and other extra-constitutional issues that will conduce to a more progressive, stable and democratic country.

I call upon all the minority ethnic groups in Nigeria to follow the example of the Ogoni people and demand their rights to political autonomy and freedom in Nigeria. In times past, such minority commitment has saved Nigeria. It can be so even now as the nation stands on the crossroads once again.

I appeal to those friends of our country whose endeavours brought the country together in the first place and whose investment and technology keep it going today to assist in this search for a rational solution to the Nigerian dilemma without placing too much of a burden on our severely distressed populace. Before the curtain falls.

I also appeal to the Nigerian press to continue to stand courageously for a democratic Nigeria according to the wishes of all Nigerians, to crusade for social justice and for the rights and liberties of the oppressed masses, oppressed ethnic groups and the disadvantaged of our country. Else the curtain will fall.

Thank you.

The launch, chaired by Professor Claude Ake (of whom more later), was a success, as far as I could judge it. It was well attended. Miss Joy Nunieh read one of the Ogoni folktales from my newly published collection, *The Singing Anthill: Ogoni Folktales*, and my eldest son, Kenule Jr. arrived from his London base to give a vote of thanks at the end of the day.

Even as I wrote, edited and published the books, I continued to search for assistance in my major project of confronting the denigrators of the Ogoni.

But I was essentially knocking on closed doors. I had met William Boyd, the celebrated British writer, in England at the academically popular British Council-organized 'Cambridge Seminar' in the summer of 1988. Having read his award-winning book, *A Good Man in Africa*, I was delighted when he turned up to do a reading of his work in progress. At the end of the reading, I asked him privately why he had set *A Good Man in Africa* in Ibadan.

'My father was a doctor at the University of Ibadan,' he replied.

And it all came together. I remembered the Dr Boyd of our days in Ibadan University. A good, funny doctor he was, much beloved by students. He had a fund of stories about his reaction to their favourite illness: the clap. I introduced myself to William, and he recognized the author of *Sozaboy*, a book which he told me he had enjoyed very much. And from that moment there developed a friendship which I have found most useful.

It was to William that I turned whenever I hit a brick wall in my solicitation on behalf of the Ogoni. I remember his asking me, some time in 1991, to contact both Amnesty International and Greenpeace. I telephoned Greenpeace. 'We don't work in Africa,' was the chilling reply I got. And when I called up Amnesty, I was asked, 'Is anyone dead? Is anyone in gaol?' And when I replied in the negative, I was told nothing could be done. Was I upset? The Ogoni people were being killed all right, but in an unconventional way. Amnesty was only interested in conventional killings. And as to Greenpeace, why would it not show concern for Africa? For Ogoni? It did seem that the Ogoni were destined for extinction.

I returned from London, that particular trip, in cavernous despair. The knowledge I had acquired on my trips went into preparing an addendum to the Ogoni Bill of Rights, which was presented to the MOSOP Steering Committee and approved by them. 'An Appeal to the International Community' was advertised in a Nigerian national daily; this time I paid for the advert myself without waiting for other Ogoni contributors.

Addendum to the Ogoni Bill of Rights

We, the people of Ogoni, being a separate and distinct ethnic nationality within the Federal Republic of Nigeria, hereby state as follows:

A. That on 2 October 1990 we addressed an 'Ogoni Bill of Rights' to the President of the Federal Republic of Nigeria, General Ibrahim Babangida, and members of the Armed Forces Ruling Council;

B. That after a one-year wait, the President has been unable to grant us the audience which we sought to have with him in order to discuss the legitimate demands contained in the Ogoni Bill of Rights;

C. That our demands as outlined in the Ogoni Bill of Rights are legitimate, just and our inalienable rights and in accord with civilized values worldwide;

D. That the government of the Federal Republic of Nigeria has continued, since 2 October 1990, to decree measures and implement policies which further marginalize the Ogoni people, denying us political autonomy, our rights to our resources, to the development of our languages and culture, to adequate representation as of right in all Nigerian national institutions and to the protection of our environment and ecology from further degradation.

E. That we cannot sit idly by while we are, as a people, dehumanized and slowly exterminated and driven to extinction even as our rich resources are siphoned off to the exclusive comfort and improvement of other Nigerian communities, and the shareholders of multinational oil companies.

Now, therefore, while reaffirming our wish to remain a part of the Federal Republic of Nigeria, we hereby authorize the Movement for the Survival of the Ogoni People (MOSOP) to make representation, for as long as these injustices continue, to the United Nations Commission on Human Rights, the Commonwealth Secretariat, the African Commission on Human and Peoples' Rights, the European Community and all international bodies which have a role to play in the preservation of our nationality, as follows:

1. That the government of the Federal Republic of Nigeria has, in utter disregard and contempt for human rights, since independence in 1960 till date, denied us our political rights to self-determination, economic rights to our resources, cultural rights to the development of our languages and culture, and social rights to education, health and adequate housing and to representation as of right in national institutions;

2. That, in particular, the Federal Republic of Nigeria has refused to pay us oil royalties and mining rents amounting to an estimated US twenty billion dollars for petroleum mined from our soil for over thirty-three years;

3. That the constitution of the Federal Republic of Nigeria does not protect any of our rights whatsoever as an ethnic minority of 500,000 in a nation of about a hundred million people and that the voting power and military might

of the majority ethnic groups have been used remorselessly against us at every point in time;

4. That multi-national oil companies, namely Shell (Dutch/British) and Chevron (American) have severally and jointly devastated our environment and ecology, having flared gas in our villages for thirty-three years and caused oil spillages, blow-outs, etc., and have dehumanized our people, denying them employment and those benefits which industrial organizations in Europe and America routinely contribute to their areas of operation;

5. That the Nigerian elite (bureaucratic, military, industrial and academic) have turned a blind eye and a deaf ear to these acts of dehumanization by the ethnic majority and have colluded with all the agents of destruction aimed at us;

6. That we cannot seek restitution in the courts of law in Nigeria, as the act of expropriation of our rights and resources has been institutionalized in the 1979 and 1989 constitutions of the Federal Republic of Nigeria, which constitutions were acts of a constituent assembly imposed by a military regime and do not, in any way, protect minority rights or bear resemblance to the tacit agreement made at Nigerian independence;

7. That the Ogoni people abjure violence in their just struggle for their rights within the Federal Republic of Nigeria but will, through every lawful means, and for as long as is necessary, fight for social justice and equity for themselves and their progeny, and in particular demand political autonomy as a distinct and separate unit within the Nigerian nation with full right to (i) control Ogoni political affairs, (ii) use at least 50 per cent of Ogoni economic resources for Ogoni development; (iii) protect the Ogoni environment and ecology from further degradation; (iv) ensure the full restitution of the harm done to the health of our people by the flaring of gas, oil spillages, oil blow-outs, etc., by the

following oil companies: Shell, Chevron and their Nigerian accomplices.

8. That without the intervention of the international community, the government of the Federal Republic of Nigeria and the ethnic majority will continue these noxious policies until the Ogoni people are obliterated from the face of the earth.

Adopted by the general acclaim of the Ogoni people on the 26th day of August 1991 at Bori, Rivers State of Nigeria.

I did recognize that other groups were suffering the same fate as the Ogoni. To tackle the wider problem, I thought of establishing organizations which would deal with the environmental and political problems of threatened peoples. And so were born the Ethnic Minority Rights Organization of Nigeria and the Nigerian Society for the Protection of the Environment, both of which later merged into the Ethnic Minority Rights Organization of Africa (EMIROAF).

But there was a silver lining in the clouds. In October 1990, just before I went on my trip to the United States, a few youths in the Etche community of Rivers State, neighbours of the Ogoni, had gone protesting against the destructive actions of Shell in the area. As usual, they were visited with high-handed brutality by the authorities. About 80 people were brutally murdered and almost 500 houses razed to the ground. It made the headlines, and some news magazines devoted considerable space to it. The news filtered through to England, where two filmmakers, Glen Ellis and Kay Bishop, were already examining the activities of Shell in the Third World. That report brought them to Port Harcourt and, inevitably, to my doorstep.

Thus did it happen that the Ogoni case came to be reported in the documentary film *The Heat of the Moment*, which was shown on Channel 4 in the United Kingdom in October of 1992.

The arrival of Glen and Kay was more important in another respect. When they interviewed me for the film, I told them of my frustrations in campaigning for the Ogoni cause. They promised to assist me in subsequent visits to the United Kingdom. And they were as good as their word.

At my next visit, we went knocking on several doors: Friends of the Earth, Survival International, and others. Again, we drew a blank, but I was receiving a much valued education.

In June of 1992 I found myself on a sponsored trip to Germany. I was expected to take part in a summer literature seminar at the University of Bayreuth, but as part of that I had to do a tour of Germany with other Africans who were taking part in the seminar. The group consisted of Dr Femi Osofisan, a great Nigerian playwright, poet and well-known academic, and Afem Akeh, the literary editor of the *Daily Times*. Also on the trip were a South African poet, a Ugandan civil servant, and a Zimbabwean folklorist. Touring Germany, I asked to be permitted to visit Göttingen, to meet with a non-governmental organization, the Association of Threatened Peoples of Germany. There, it was impressed on me that going to Geneva to participate in the United Nations Working Group on Indigenous Populations would be helpful. For one, I would be able to present the Ogoni case before a world audience, and for another, I would meet several non-governmental organizations interested in human rights.

And so to Geneva I went that summer of 1992. I had earlier been in contact with the Unrepresented Nations and Peoples Organization (UNPO), which also sent an invitation to EMIROAF to come to Geneva, offering to hold workshops which would enable us to learn how to work with the United Nations.

The UNPO was a real find. The organization had been set up two years earlier by a young Dutch lawyer, Michael van Walt van der Praag, the polyglot son of a Dutch diplomat who had represented the legal interests of the Dalai Lama. His contact with the Tibetan question led him to the conclusion that there were several peoples all over the world who needed to be heard, whose interests needed to be represented in international forums, and who needed to be guided to struggle non-violently for their rights. The organization had grown rapidly and was already making an impact on peoples in the former Soviet Union, in Asia and even in Europe. Other Africans would soon be joining the organization: in the summer of 1992 only the Batwa of Rwanda and the Ogoni had known of the UNPO.

I learnt a lot from Michael about the ways of the United Nations and its Human Rights Commission, and he patiently guided me on this first contact with the UN. The great appeal of the UNPO for me was its insistence that its members forswear violence in their struggle for local autonomy, self-determination or independence.

UNPO had a small outfit based at The Hague and staffed almost entirely by volunteers who had more than the normal share of dedication. The organization was later to play a very prominent, vital role in the Ogoni struggle as, indeed, in the struggles of Abkhazia, Chechenya, Bourgainville, etc.

That summer, I was able to make a presentation to the Working Group on Indigenous Populations in the following terms:

Madam Chairperson,

I wish to thank you for offering me the opportunity of addressing the 10th session of the Working Group on Indigenous Populations ... I speak on behalf of the Ogoni people, a distinct ethnic nation within the Federal Republic of Nigeria. You will forgive me if I am somewhat emotional about this matter. I am an Ogoni.

Ogoni territory lies on 404 square miles of the coastal plains terraces to the north-east of the Niger River Delta. Inhabited by 500,000 people, its population density of about 1,500 per square mile is among the highest in any rural area of the world and compares with the Nigerian national average of 300.

The Ogoni people have settled in this area as farmers and fishermen since remembered time and had established a well-organized social system before the British colonialist invaded them in 1901. Within thirteen years, the British had destroyed the fabric of Ogoni society. British rule of the area was 'haphazard' and no treaties were signed with the Ogoni. By 1960, when colonial rule ended, the British had consigned the Ogoni willy-nilly to a new nation, Nigeria, consisting of 350 or so other peoples previously held together by force, violence and much argument in Britain's commercial and imperial interest.

The nation which the British left behind was supposed to be a federal democracy, but the federating ethnic nations were bound by few agreements and the peoples were so disparate, so culturally different, so varied in size, that force and violence seemed to be the only way of maintaining the nation. In the circumstances, the interests of the few and weak such as the Ogoni were bound to suffer and have suffered.

Petroleum was discovered in Ogoni in 1958 and since then an estimated US hundred billion dollars' worth of oil and gas has been carted away from Ogoni land. In return for this, the Ogoni people have received nothing.

Oil exploration has turned Ogoni into a waste land: lands, streams, and creeks are totally and continually polluted; the atmosphere has been poisoned, charged as it is with hydrocarbon vapours, methane, carbon monoxide, carbon dioxide and soot emitted by gas which has been flared twenty-four hours a day for thirty-three years in very close proximity to human habitation. Acid rain, oil spillages and oil blow-outs have devastated Ogoni territory. High-pressure oil pipe-lines crisscross the surface of Ogoni farmlands and villages dangerously.

The results of such unchecked environmental pollution and degradation include the complete destruction of the eco-system. Mangrove forests have fallen to the toxicity of oil and are being replaced by noxious nypa palms; the rain forest has fallen to the axe of the multinational oil companies, all wildlife is dead, marine life is gone, the farmlands have been rendered infertile by acid rain and the once beautiful Ogoni countryside is no longer a source of fresh air and green vegetation. All one sees and feels around is death. Environmental degradation has been a lethal weapon in the war against the indigenous Ogoni people.

Incidental to and indeed compounding this ecological devastation is the political marginalization and complete oppression of the Ogoni and especially the denial of their rights, including land rights. At independence Nigeria consisted of three regions. Since then, thirty states have been created largely for the ethnic majorities who rule the country. Most of the states so created are unviable and depend entirely on Ogoni resources for their survival. The demands of the Ogoni for autonomy and self-determination even within the Nigerian nation have been ignored. The Ogoni have been corralled into a multi-ethnic administrative state in which they remain a minority and therefore suffer several disabilities. Mining rents and royalties for Ogoni oil are not being paid to Ogoni people. In spite of the enormous wealth of their land the Ogoni people continue to live in pristine conditions in the absence of electricity, pipe-borne water,

hospitals, housing and schools. The Ogoni are being consigned to slavery and extinction.

Madam Chairperson, faced by these terrible odds, the
Ogoni people have continued courageously to demand social
justice and equity. In October 1990 the Chiefs and leaders of
Ogoni submitted a Bill of Rights to the Nigerian President
and his council. The Bill called for (a) political control of
Ogoni affairs by Ogoni people (b) the right to control and
use a fair proportion of Ogoni economic resources for Ogoni
development (c) adequate and direct representation as of
right in all Nigerian national institutions (d) the use and
development of Ogoni languages in Ogoni territory and (e)
the right to protect the Ogoni environment and ecology from
further degradation. The Ogoni are yet to receive a reply to
these minimum demands.

Copies of the Ogoni Bill of Rights and of a book, *Genocide in Nigeria: The Ogoni Tragedy*, authored by me and
which explains the Ogoni case fully, have been submitted to
the Secretariat of the Working Group.

The extermination of the Ogoni people appears to be
policy. The Ogoni have suffered at the hands of the military
dictatorships which have ruled Nigeria over the past decades.
The new constitution, which is supposed to usher in a democratic government in 1993, does not protect the rights of the
Ogoni. Indeed, it institutionalizes the expropriation of their
land. A recently concluded national census omits all refer-
ences to the ethnic origins of all citizens, which in a multi-
ethnic state is a violation of community rights.

Nigeria has an external debt of over thirty billion dollars.
None of that debt was incurred on any project in the Ogoni
area or on any project remotely beneficial to the Ogoni. The
International Monetary Fund and the World Bank, keen on
the payment of the debt, are encouraging intensified exploitation of oil and gas, which constitute 94 per cent of Nigeria's

Gross Domestic Product. Such exploitation is against the wishes of the Ogoni people as it only worsens the degradation of the Ogoni environment and the decimation of the Ogoni people. Studies have indicated that more Ogoni people are dying now than are being born. The Ogoni are faced by a powerful combination of titanic forces from far and near, driven by greed and cold statistics. Only the international community, acting with compassion and a sense of responsibility to the human race, can avert the catastrophe which is about to overtake the Ogoni. The Ogoni people are now appealing to that Community . . .

National ideas of national independence, the fact of Africans ruling Africans in nations conceived by and for European economic interests have intensified, not destroyed, the propensity of man to subject weak peoples by force, violence and legal quibbling to slavery and extinction. I respectfully invite you to visit Nigeria, so that you can see for yourself that indigenous peoples abound there and that they suffer incredibly at the hands of rulers and the economic interests of other nations.

I spent ten to twelve days in Geneva that summer. I had holidayed there in the early eighties with my sons, taking them on a tour of the United Nations buildings. I was then ignorant of its very important work. Now I saw for myself how backward Nigeria is in regard to the setting-up of non-governmental organizations and working through them for the protection of rights.

I also made valuable contact with individuals and groups from other parts of the world. I came to know that the UN had busied itself for more than a decade with the problems of such peoples as the Ogoni (indigenous people) or national minorities in various countries. I ought to have been in Geneva much sooner.

One thing which struck me was the extent of misery among indigenous peoples throughout the world. Every case was very important to those who argued it, and it was possible to put one's concerns in a global perspective. But I'm afraid that I left Geneva after two weeks convinced that the exploitation of the Ogoni was the most criminal of the cases I had heard, and that it was the more tragic because its victims weren't aware of it or, if they were, didn't know how to extricate themselves.

Perhaps the most important result of my trip to Geneva was that my address to the Working Group on Indigenous Populations got published in Nigerian newspapers. And this, I believe, is what may have convinced the Ogoni elite that there was some value in what I was doing. I wasn't told, but there may well have been many skeptics who would have wondered what chance we had prosecuting our case against a powerful company like Shell and a fascist government like Babangida's which was bent on spending every single cent that came from oil; or, indeed, against the entire Nigerian elite, who didn't want to work but were living happily off the lottery which they had won in oil revenues, without worrying about the cost of earning such revenues.

Ever since the Steering Committee of MOSOP was formally set up in early 1991, I had found an unwillingness to attend the meetings of the committee. And try as much as we would, we could not form a quorum at meetings. It was as if all the signatories to the Bill of Rights had gone to sleep after having signed the document in 1990. Even when Babangida and his military colleagues showed their hands at their most insensitive and most bandit-like in creating additional states and local governments from which the Ogoni and others in Rivers State were excluded, few seemed to worry.

And yet it was this act alone which so outraged me that I decided that, come life or death, the brutalization of the peoples in the oil-bearing delta of the Niger would have to be questioned, exposed and brought to a stop. The way and manner in which the states and local governments were created were an affront to truth and civility, a slap in the face of modern history; it was robbery with violence. What Babangida was doing was transferring the resources of the delta, of the Ogoni and other ethnic minorities to the ethnic majorities – the Hausa-Fulani, the Igbo and the Yoruba – since most of the new states and local governments were created in the homes of these three. None of the local governments or states so created was viable: they all depended on oil revenues which were to be shared by the states and local governments according to the most outrageous of criteria such as expanse of land, equality, underdevelopment and all such stupidities. The brazen injustice of it hurt my sensibilities beyond description.

Ruminating over the development, and watching Nigeria literally go down the drain through the incompetence and banditry of the ruling military and civilian politicians, I became stronger in my conviction that the only thing that could save Nigeria was the political restructuring of the country. I had written and said as much in my various works and public pronouncements since 1990 but my words had obviously fallen on deaf ears. Something else had to be done to bring the urgency of the matter home.

After November 1990, however, Ogoni youth had seized the gauntlet. They formed the Committee for Ogoni Autonomy (COA) and met regularly in Port Harcourt. My nephew, Barika Idamkue, a political science graduate of the University of Port Harcourt, was the moving spirit of the committee. All they did was to educate themselves on the Ogoni problem and help form a core of knowledgeable activists around which our youths would later rally. I spoke to this group whenever I was available in Port Harcourt and they were meeting. It gave me an opportunity to keep them abreast of my activities on behalf of the Ogoni people. When my nephew relocated to Bori later in 1991, I lost touch with them. They continued to meet in Bori, but the group now had a different membership.

My contact with UNPO in Geneva and other organizations and activists had introduced me to the nature of non-violent struggle for rights. And I already knew how successful the mobilization movements in Nigeria had been once they were based on the ethnic group. Awolowo, Azikiwe and Ahmadu Bello had successfully mobilized their kinsmen, the Yoruba, the Igbo and the Hausa-Fulani respectively. I thought I could do the same for the Ogoni.

I quickly wrote and published a book, *Genocide in Nigeria: The Ogoni Tragedy*, which told the Ogoni story in urgent terms and called attention to its environmental and political problems.

Perhaps one reason the MOSOP Steering Committee had not worked effectively was the return of partisan politics. When we had signed the Bill of Rights in 1990, most Ogoni politicians, as I have said, had been banned from participation in politics. By 1991 the ban on a few of them had been lifted and this had seduced them away from the efforts of the MOSOP.

By 1992 Babangida's trickery and unpredictability, as he manoeuvred and fooled the Nigerian people, had lifted the ban on most politicians, but some of the older Ogoni politicians were still working with us in the MOSOP. However, their commitment to the hard work that was essential in promoting the cause had become questionable. Mainstream politicians work for immediate reward. A movement like the MOSOP is involved in alternative politics, with a more long-term perspective.

One result of this, for instance, is that in my absences

abroad, meetings were hardly held, and when they were held in the residence of the President, Dr Garrick Leton, achieved little or nothing.

After the publication of the report on my United Nations trip and reports of the airing of the film *Heat of the Moment*, a few younger men began to attend the meetings of the Steering Committee. We, however, recognized the need to broaden the base of our support beyond the signatories to the Bill of Rights and the few youths who had begun to attend meetings with us. So we organized a two-day tour of the Ogoni kingdoms, on 14 and 28 November 1992.

The results we got took me entirely by surprise. I hadn't mixed much with the youth of Ogoni over the years, since there was no organization which took care of all Ogoni people. On that tour, I found that there was a large number of youth angry with a society that had cheated them and who were therefore eager to hear us, to learn. I have to explain that the term 'youth' is used here to describe people who are below the age of forty.

Generally on our tour Dr Leton as President would make an introductory speech, and then call on me as 'Spokesman of the Ogoni People' (a sort of ideologue and prime mover) to address the audience. I would then outline the Ogoni case without embroidery and suggest that we do something to extricate ourselves from our cruel fate. Other speakers, including those on the floor, might follow, and, based on the decision of the assembled, we would introduce the motion which I had prepared in advance.

The motion called upon Shell, Chevron and the Nigerian National Petroleum Corporation (NNPC), the three oil companies operating in Ogoni, to pay damages of US four billion dollars for destroying the environment, six billion dollars in unpaid rents and royalties, and all within thirty days or it would be assumed that they had decided to quit the land. The resolution was unanimously carried in the six kingdoms of Ogoni.

Two scenes will remain indelible in my memory because they gave me so much comfort and encouragement: the first was on 14 November 1992 at Bori, when we met at the Suanu Finimale Nwika Conference Centre, which was to become the scene of many a stirring meeting. There, I found a very ready response and also highly intelligent questions from a very knowledgeable audience.

The second was at the secondary school in Kpor in the Gokana kingdom. The late Edward Kobani had done a good job. Stung by the charge that the Gokana had not been attending meetings and that they were betraying the Ogoni cause, he went all out between 14 November when we held the first series of meetings and the 28th of the same month when we got to Gokana kingdom and invited the people to come forward. They responded fully.

The hall into which we were crammed proved too small and we had perforce to go into the open air. I spoke in one of the four Ogoni languages from the balcony of the upper floor of the secondary school building at Kpor in Gokana. And the response was immediate and overwhelming. From the reaction of the sea of faces down below, you would have thought that I had been lecturing them for years. Indeed, on reflection, I now realize what happened. I was not telling these people anything they had not known. I had only given voice to the facts and fears they had harboured in their hearts for years but which they dared not express for fear of the expected reprisals which they knew the Nigerian state would not hesitate to visit on them.

The usual resolutions were adopted by acclamation and Chief E.B. Nyone of Lewe said one of the funniest closing prayers I have ever heard, or will ever, hear. It was not a prayer as such. It was a political speech, witty in the Ogoni tradition, satirical and sarcastic by turns, punctuated at intervals with 'in the name of Jesus', to which the crowd answered 'amen' in loud voice. It sent us all away in very cheerful spirit.

As I drove off, the crowd ran after my car, waving and screaming with delight. Was I satisfied? The burden of the expectations I had stirred in the minds of the Ogoni people sat heavily on me.

Mr B.M. Wifa, one-time Attorney-General of Rivers State, an Ogoni man from Kono, has been a friend from our primary school days. I have always held him in highest regard. He was extremely bright in our days at the Native Authority School, Bori, and confirmed his class at the Methodist College, Uzuakoli, where he excelled in mathematics. He might have been an engineer had he wanted to. He chose the law, and since he could not find a bursary, and no one in Ogoni was able to sponsor him, had to work and study in the United Kingdom for a long time before he finally became a lawyer. I relied a lot on his legal opinions; he had become a solicitor to my firm, Saros International Limited, and I always gave him my non-fiction work to read to ensure that there was nothing libellous therein. I discussed my ideas on the Ogoni people with him regularly and, although he did not wish to play any prominent role in the struggle, held himself ready to assist quietly.

It was to him I turned in writing the 'Demand Notice' to the three oil companies. After he had vetted my draft, I sent off the letter on 3 December 1992, knowing full well that they would ignore it.

The four days prior to that I had spent with Ogoni youths preparing the ground for the massive protest march which we had planned for 4 January 1993.

The 4th of January was significant in a way and it was carefully chosen. The disgraced dictator, Babangida, was expected to hand over power on 2 January 1993. If he did so, we would be serving notice to the new administration that the Ogoni people would no longer accept exploitation and a slave status in Nigeria. If Babangida failed to hand over, we would be confronting him directly and daring him to do his worst.

This was a decision which I had taken on my own. I didn't present it directly to the Ogoni people. I would merely guide them to the action, checking on the way if it was acceptable by their collective reaction. The only man I took into confidence was the historian, Dr Ben Naanen, a young academic at the University of Port Harcourt, whose analytical powers I respect. He did not appreciate the finer points on first presentation as we sat over dinner on the anniversary of my fifty-first birthday, 10 October 1992, at a Chinese restaurant in Central London, but it did not take long to convince him.

I travelled to London after submitting the 'Demand Notice' to the oil companies. My purpose was to attend the inauguration of the United Nations International Year for the World's Indigenous Populations in New York. On arrival in London, I found that it was not going to be possible to get to New York because of visa problems. I therefore spent the time convincing Greenpeace to send a team to watch the protest march for the environment planned for 4 January 1993 in Ogoni.

At first they wouldn't hear of it. But when I affirmed that I was expecting no less than 300,000 people to take part in the march, they finally agreed to send a cameraman. Shelley Braithwaite, an Australian lady of the London-based Rainforest Action Group, also agreed to travel as my guest to Ogoni to participate in the march.

I returned to Nigeria shortly before Christmas. I stopped

in Lagos to invite the press to Ogoni on 4 January before proceeding to Port Harcourt.

When I arrived there, I found considerable ferment in security circles over the planned demonstration. Dr Leton and Edward Kobani had earned the attention of the operatives of the notorious repressive SSS. On Christmas day itself, early in the morning, Dr Leton rang me up.

'The SSS have invited me once again,' he moaned.

'On Christmas day?' I asked in astonishment.

'Yes.'

'What could they possibly want that couldn't wait until tomorrow or the day after?'

'God alone knows.'

'I'll come with you, if you don't mind,' I said.

I put on a shirt and headed for Dr Leton's. From there, we drove to the offices of the dreaded SSS. At the gate we inquired if the State Director was available. On being told that he was at his residence, we headed there. We had decided earlier not to deal with his subordinates as they were likely to mess around with us.

We met Mr Terebor, State Director of the SSS, on arrival. A small man with an inhuman face, he spoke English with a Yoruba accent. As is usual with me, I asked where he came from and found out that he was of Ondo State (one of the six Yoruba states) origin. He had studied physics at the University of Ife and I could not, for the life of me, understand what he was doing in the notorious SSS when the country was crying out for teachers of physics in secondary schools. I believe that he said something about teaching not being rewarding.

We chatted generally and when we asked why we were being invited on Christmas day to a security chat and were not allowed to enjoy the festival with our family, he apologized and offered us drinks. Then he telephoned his subordinates and two of them showed up. His immediate assistant was a Mr Egwi from Delta State and there was another operative from Enugu State. Mr Egwi was rather upset that we had called on his boss instead of reporting to him as he had ordered. We spoke generally and I assured them that the Ogoni people and their leaders were not up to mischief but were celebrating the end of the year in their usual way. We offered to co-operate fully with them to ensure that there was no breach of the peace, and I placed in the hands of all three of them my complimentary card, complete with my office and home addresses and telephone numbers. I was baiting them all right. The important thing was for them not to molest Dr Leton, who I thought didn't have the resilience for the harassment of the security hounds. In any case, I had decided that I would take the flak that came from the decision to mobilize the Ogoni people.

We parted on friendly terms. And I headed home. Shortly after arrival there, the telephone rang and the voice of Rufus Ada George, Governor of Rivers State, came over the wire. He was inviting me to lunch in Government House. I was preparing to answer the invitation when he rang again to ask where he could reach Dr Leton. I provided him with the required telephone number.

Dr Leton and I arrived at Government House within minutes of each other. We found there almost the full complement of the Cabinet of Rivers State. I did not know many of them beyond the Deputy Governor, Dr Odili, and my friend and fellow Ogoni, Dr Israel Kue, one of the most brilliant boys in our days at the Native Authority School, Bori, who had confirmed his class at the Methodist Boys High School, Oron, and gone on to meet me at Government College, Umuahia where he did his 'A' levels. He subsequently came to Ibadan University to read medicine, ending his studies in the United States. In another society he might have ended up as a great cardiologist. In Nigeria he was condemned to a position in the Cabinet of Rivers State. He was one of the oldest members of the Cabinet, most of whom sat meekly before their Governor like houseboys.

Also present was Dr Nwifa Ndegwe, another Ogoni man of whom I was decidedly not fond. He had studied at Okrika Grammar School where he was a classmate of Governor Ada George. He subsequently earned a doctorate at Makerere University in Uganda. At the height of the Nigerian civil war, when I was casting about for Ogoni people to help develop Rivers State, I encouraged him to return home and found him several positions in the government. When the Gowon regime collapsed, and inquiries were made into Rivers State institutions, he was severely criticized by the board of inquiry set up to investigate the affair, headed by Cyrus Nunieh, the first Ogoni lawyer.

Dr Ndegwe returned to a teaching position at the College of Science and Technology in Port Harcourt. The quirks and quackery of the Babangida regime, and the winning of the gubernatorial election by his friend Rufus Ada George enabled him to re-emerge in public life. When the Oil Minerals Producing Areas Commission (OMPADEC), a body meant to disburse the peanuts set aside by those who had seized the oil resources of the delta to the unfortunate inhabitants thereof, was set up, he was nominated by Ada George to represent Rivers State on it.

Governor Rufus Ada George's company spoke for him. I did not know him before he became Governor. I did hear that he had served in the Second Republic as Secretary to the Rivers State government of Melford Okilo – a useless government if ever there was one. I came to know later that when that government was dismissed in a military coup in 1984, he took up a position as Finance Director in a firm owned by Gilbert Chagoury, a Lebanese businessman whom I had known intimately in my business days and for whom I held a healthy regard. Gilbert knew his onions around Nigeria and Nigerian leaders! And he is a jolly good businessman with a nose for money.

Ada George's connection with Gilbert helped him to the position of Governor. A big, bespectacled man, perpetually dressed in big white Victorian pyjama-type shirts on top of white trousers to give an impression of superstitious sanctity, he laid claim to being a born-again Christian, regularly proclaiming his membership of one of the funny Pentecostal churches set up by a little-known fellow in Port Harcourt.

At first meeting he cut a deceptively friendly look, with an engaging gap-toothed smile. In the early days when I was casting about for assistance in my struggle for the Niger River Delta environment, he gave me some support. It proved that all he wanted me to do was to make noises abroad and not educate the victims of the degradation of the delta to their rights to a healthy environment.

On Christmas day 1992 he was in his usual element, allowing me a place next to him at the Christmas dinner table, while his commissioners huddled silently together like rain-beaten hens at the far end of the table. It was a sumptuous meal too, complete with wines and champagne, all at the public expense. Unused to such luxuries, I indulged myself fully. When I raised the matter of the invitation to the security office on Christmas day of all days, he claimed to know nothing about it. Vile politician!

Two days later the Kagote Club honoured me with its first Ogoni National Merit Award. At the award ceremony which was held at the Suanu Finimale Nwika Conference Centre in Bori, I said as follows:

Chiefs, Elders, Compatriots, Ladies and Gentlemen,

I wish to thank the Executive and members of Kagote for the honour done me today. Although I had disavowed all Nigerian honours for the reason that I consider most Nigerian decisions inimical to good sense and propriety, I could not resist your invitation because if there is anything an Ogoni man should honour, it is the respect of another Ogoni man. For, as the Bible says, a prophet is not without honour, save in his own country, and in his own house. Therefore, to be the first man to be honoured by the elite club of the Ogoni people is definitely something to be treasured. I am grateful and I gladly dedicate this honour to the thirty wise men who signed that historic document, the Ogoni Bill of Rights, on 26 August 1990.

The honour you have done me today quite humbles me, but it also gives me hope. You have, by your action, accepted my thesis that the Ogoni nation and people face terrible odds, but that relying on our age-old traditions, our genius, we can extricate ourselves from the quagmire in which our abundant wealth has paradoxically placed us.

The lives and achievements of modern Ogoni men like T. N. Paul Birabi, S. F. Wika, the Reverends Wiko and Badey and Bishop Vincent, to mention the departed of blessed memory, only convince me that Ogoni people can claim for themselves a rightful place in Africa and in human civilization.

The modest contribution which I have made and for which I presume you have honoured me has been to restore to the Ogoni people the self-identity, that self-respect which almost one hundred years of British colonialism and indigenous Nigerian colonialism sought to take away from them. Yet, this is but the very first step on a journey of a thousand miles. Which is one reason I would have wished that your decision to honour me had been delayed.

The road ahead remains quite perilous, and treading it will require the total energies, the total faith, the total endurance and the total commitment of all Ogoni people, no matter their calling or their abilities. Just as I have been able to use my literary abilities to re-establish the identity of the Ogoni in national and international circles, so can any other Ogoni person, determined to place himself or herself in the service of our nation, succeed in mapping out and prosecuting a course of action for the benefit of us all.

We have taken the first important step in clearing our minds, in achieving unity of leadership, in projecting our case before Nigeria. The next task is to mobilize every Ogoni man, woman and child on the nature and necessity of our cause so that everyone knows and believes in that cause and holds it as a religion, refusing to be bullied or bribed therefrom. And finally, we must begin to build up action to transform our current advantages into political scores.

We have been faithful to this agenda which we set up for ourselves. We have established the Ogoni identity and placed Ogoni on the national agenda; we have mobilized all Ogoni people. We must now move on to the next item on our list: to establish a government of Ogoni people by Ogoni people for Ogoni people in Ogoni within a confederal Nigeria. This is very important because we cannot and should not tolerate a situation where our best men and women are exiled from our land; a situation where our genius is not being placed at the disposal of our land.

I make the above statement advisedly. All successful Ogoni men and women are in Port Harcourt, Lagos, or some such centre in Nigeria or overseas. To be in Ogoni means that you are not successful. Out in the diaspora, the Ogoni man is insignificant and is forced to bring up his children outside of Ogoni culture. It is not surprising that a new generation of highly trained Ogoni men and women

111

are growing up, marrying outside the tribe and raising another generation who are further alienated from the nation because they have not grown up within Ogoni culture and traditions. This is surely the path to the extinction of our nation.

I am not opposed to people going out in search of greener pastures, all I am saying is that they should do so by choice and not by necessity. I am quite sure that were there a level of government capable of engaging the energies and intellect of our best people for all areas of human endeavour – academic, industrial and administrative – most of those who live and work in Port Harcourt and Lagos would certainly not do so. I am, for one, impatient to return to Bori to live permanently. Because Ogoni is extremely wealthy, there should be no difficulty in operating that level of government which will enable me to do so. The end of our enforced exile must be our immediate concern.

When I gave the address at Kono on 26 December 1990 it is possible that some may not have taken me seriously. Yet, within two years, the central tenets of the Ogoni Bill of Rights have formed the basis of the alternative to Babangida's botched democracy programme.

I refer to Chief Anthony Enahoro's Movement for National Reformation, which has adopted almost wholesale the position of the Ogoni nation on a very loose federalism or confederalism as the only possible future for Nigeria. I believe that this movement will find international support and that it will gain favour with all Nigerians in the very near future and so end our nightmare.

This will be most welcome as, with due respect, General Babangida's kabukabu presidency, his kakistocracy, has been a complete failure and has spelt the death of the Ogoni and other delta peoples. His touted transition truck is completely rusty, without a roadworthiness certificate or an insurance policy; its licence has expired. Yet its driver insists on taking it out on an endless journey. The driver's licence needs renewal, but he insists on proceeding without it, depending on his ability to bribe the traffic policemen along the way. Loaded with touts, the truck stops at odd places to pick up stranded passengers. If an unwitting passenger complains later about the state of the truck, the touts shout him down, shut him up and threaten to offload him and leave him at the mercy of armed robbers. The touts, dependent on the driver for their 'chop' money, chant his praise even as he drives recklessly without a spare tyre or head lamps towards the precipice. I fear the truck, the driver and the touts, and I fear for the passengers. God grant that they do not involve innocent by-standers in a fatal accident. I advise everyone to stand far away from the possible paths of the deadly truck.

We must renew our faith in the Ogoni Bill of Rights and pursue the attainment of our rights in a non-violent manner. And we must get absolutely ready for the achievement of our desires because the challenges which that achievement will pose are as tough as any that have gone before. I dare to predict that we will be at our goal post before the end of this decade.

I have personally dedicated myself to the Ogoni nation. For me, the struggle is my first priority, taking precedence over all other interests. For I believe that the achievement of the Ogoni will serve as an example to other ethnic minorities and oppressed peoples throughout Africa. Therefore, what you have done today is very great encouragement to me and to others on the continent who wish to serve their peoples honestly and sincerely.

I have tried to emulate T. N. Paul Birabi, the late father of your outgoing President, Dr Bennet Birabi, who I see is following in the footsteps of his famous forebear and doing us honour in the process. I still consider myself at the very middle of my career; given life, I hope to do more. But on a day like this, I recall the words of Longfellow's famous poem:

> Lives of great men all remind us
> We can make our lives sublime
> And departing leave behind us
> Footprints on the sands of time.
>
> Let us, then, be up and doing,
> With a heart for any fate;
> Still achieving, still pursuing,
> Learn to labour and to wait.

Once again, I thank you and wish you God's abundant blessing.

I spent the following week in constant communication with Governor Ada George and the security agents. They didn't want the Ogoni protest march to go on. I didn't understand their doubts. The march was billed as a peaceful one. They argued that it would be violent. I didn't see how it would be. I asked that they monitor it closely and nip any tendency to violence in the bud. But they were as jittery as I was adamant.

In spite of Ada George (who, by virtue of his position, was Chairman of the Rivers State Security Council, which consisted of the heads of the army, navy, air force, police and SSS) we continued to plan the demonstration. The Greenpeace photographer Tim Lambon soon arrived and set to work filming the devastated Ogoni environment. He was not impeded in his work in any way.

As noted earlier, I was not quite aware of the level of expertise available among the young of Ogoni. But as they clustered round me in my office and we planned the day, I began to learn one or two things about them. They were quite high on enthusiasm and dedicated to the cause we had outlined.

Then the usual doubts came from the usual quarters. Dr Leton began to plead that we call off the demonstration. Ogoni had been ringed round by the military. Babangida had decided not to hand over power which was his birthright and had given orders that there be no processions throughout the country. Anyone found in a march carrying placards would be shot. He claimed even to have had a dream in which he was shot while carrying a placard.

This manner of reasoning from a man who was supposed to be leading the movement chilled me. I feared that it might infect the younger men and destroy the work of a whole year. I laid great store by the protest march: it was a psychological break point. If we could defy the authorities and successfully protest our denigration, the Ogoni would be on their way to a proper future.

As of Saturday, 2 January 1993, the debate was still going on. The planning committee, consisting of myself and some youths, was still at work, placards had been written and stored, loud-speaker equipment procured, and procedures laid down – all at my expense. But would we march? I called a meeting at Dr Leton's residence in Beeri, a few miles from the Bori headquarters of the Ogoni nation. And then God dropped from the skies.

He arrived in the person of a close family relation who informed us that he had, on his own, investigated the disposition of the troops in the area. Police and army were around all right, but they would not shoot unless they had given three warnings. In any case, they would shoot into the air before shooting into the crowd.

Right or wrong, it served to dispel all fears. From that moment onwards, no one spoke of not marching for fear of the army or the police. We concluded the meeting on a high note of optimism and dispersed to our various homes.

I checked with the co-ordinators we had appointed in each of the kingdoms to ensure that all was well. They confirmed that it was so. Four men and, where possible, a woman had been assigned the task of forming committees in each village, and the village committees in turn had been given the responsibility of ensuring that everyone turned out for the protest march along with dance troupes, masquerades and all such.

One word about the festival aspect of the march. Joy should not have been a part of so serious and monumental a protest. But I was very worried about a number of things. True, we had told everyone that we were not going to be violent; that not a stone would be thrown. But how could we be sure that this would be carried out? Crowd control was another problem. If we could not keep the men, women and children who would turn out busy, then the devil would find them an occupation. Hence the decision to keep them entertained with spectacle and song. The other problem is what we would do if people were wounded or hurt. The hospital in Bori was no use at all. There was a fine Ogoni doctor there all right, John Nwidaada of Kpean, a gracious young man trained in Moscow. But he had no equipment. The hospital had been opened with fanfare in 1952. I was in our school's musical band at Bori, which was in attendance on the occasion. T. N. Paul Birabi had spoken on the day, outlining his hopes that the hospital would help provide medical care to all Ogoni people. His hopes were not borne out. Although the hospital started out well, it degenerated to the point where, by January 1993, it was no better than the dispensaries which each kingdom of the Ogoni had had in my childhood days.

There was not much we could do as far as medical problems were concerned. My brother Owens' clinic had an ambulance and he, of course, volunteered it along with all his staff and his services. I had to hope for the best.

That Saturday, we did not quite succeed in checking out all the arrangements. We scheduled another meeting for the next day, after the Sunday service of 3 January.

CHAPTER FIVE

We had not initially thought of presaging the protest march of 4 January with an inter-denominational service and a visit to the tomb of T. N. Paul Birabi. The inspiration for that came from Goodluck Diigbo, a journalist from Kaani who turned up at my office regularly and voluntarily to render invaluable advice on the public relations aspects of our endeavour. He was quite a godsend, being a good organizer and far more knowledgeable about the psyche of the Ogoni people at that time than I was. He lived among them; I did not. He knew the power of the Christian churches over the people; I was not aware of it. He also knew well the influence of radio as a mobilizer, working as he did in the state radio broadcasting station, Radio Rivers.

Once we had accepted the suggestion that we hold a church service and visit Birabi's tomb, we made contact with the Venerable Archdeacon Ntor, a fine man whom I had known as a child when he worked in the Civil Service. He had later taken Holy Orders and was, at the time, in charge of the Anglican Church in the Ogoni area. He was based at Yeghe, next door to Bori, whose St Peter's Church building is probably the best in Ogoni. Yeghe was also the birthplace of T. N. Paul Birabi and his tomb lay next to the church. St Peter's was therefore an obvious choice for the inter-denominational service. The Venerable Ntor did not have any hesitation organizing the church service.

The Birabi family, once they heard that we were going to

visit the tomb of the great man, asked for financial assistance to keep the area around it clean and tidy. We provided that assistance.

On the morning of Sunday, 3 January, I was up early and set off for Yeghe immediately after breakfast in the company of Alfred Ilenre, General Secretary of EMIROAF, who had come to witness the march, and my young friend Hauwa Madugu.

A word need be said here of Alfred, who was to help immensely in the Ogoni struggle. Of Ishan extraction, he had taken to journalism immediately upon leaving school in 1958 or thereabouts, and had worked on several Nigerian newspapers and subsequently in the Angolan Embassy in Lagos when that country was involved in its struggle for independence. He was introduced to me by another friend, Tam Fiofori, when I was casting about for a journalist to help me promote *On a Darkling Plain*. He read the book and thought it would prove very influential in the future. From that moment developed a friendship which I will always treasure. A wise man, he had a thorough knowledge of Nigerian politics and had met and interviewed some of the best-known Nigerian politicians, including Obafemi Awolowo. I was to benefit a lot from his deep insights into Nigerian life.

When we arrived at Yeghe that morning, only Venerable Ntor and a few choristers were around. My heart fell. I had expected that the people of Yeghe, if no one else, would have milled around the church. One hour later, at about ten o'clock, there were still only a few people around. We waited until eleven o'clock and still there were not enough worshippers. Venerable Ntor at that point decided that we would have to commence the service. My disappointment was real, but I found comfort in the fact that Dr Leton and Edward Kobani had arrived along with Bishop J. B. Poromon of the Methodist Church who was to preach the sermon.

I need not have worried. By the time the service had gone some way, the church was full to bursting and more worshippers had milled outside. By the offertory, when worshippers were expected to dance their way to the altar to offer gifts to God, it became clear that if we did not curtail that aspect of the service, we wouldn't be able to return to our homes early. Chiefs, women, men and children from all parts of Ogoni, including Eleme, which was far away, turned up to worship God and to pray for the success of our protest march.

What I remember best of that service was the lesson read by Ledum Mitee, who had lately begun to play a prominent role in the affairs of the MOSOP. The passage had been well-chosen by Venerable Ntor, from the Lamentations of Jeremiah, and I will beg the indulgence of the reader to reproduce it in full:

Remember, O Lord, what has befallen us; behold, and see our disgrace! Our inheritance has been turned over to strangers, our homes to aliens. We have become orphans, fatherless; our mothers are like widows. We must pay for the water we drink, the wood we get must be bought. With a yoke on our necks, we are hard driven; we are weary, we are given no rest. We have given the land to Egypt, and to Assyria, to get bread enough. Our fathers sinned, and are no more; and we bear their iniquities. Slaves rule over us; there is none to deliver us from their hand. We get our bread at the peril of our lives, because of the sword in the wilderness. Our skin is as hot as an oven with the burning heat of famine. Women are ravished in Zion, virgins in the towns of Judah. Princes are hung up by their hands; no respect is shown to the elders. Young men are compelled to grind at the mill; and boys stagger under loads of wood. The old men have quit the city gate, the young men their music. The joy of our hearts has ceased; our dancing has been turned to mourning. The

crown has fallen from our head; woe to us, for we have
sinned! For this our heart has become sick, for these things
our eyes have grown dim, for Mount Zion which lies deso-
late; jackals prowl over it. But thou, O Lord, dost reign for
ever; thy throne endures to all generations. Why dost thou
forget us for ever, why dost thou so long forsake us? Restore
us to thyself, O Lord, that we may be restored! Renew our
days as of old! Or hast thou utterly rejected us? Art thou
exceedingly angry with us?

I doubt that we could have found a passage of literature
more apt for the Ogoni situation. And I was certainly not
the only one in the Church that day who received the true
tenor of the message. I could feel a slight tremor pass
through the pews when Ledum finished reading.

Equally interesting was Bishop Poromon's (a Gokana
man) sermon delivered in flawless Khana. By the end of the
service, I found myself greatly encouraged and imbued with
a new energy and faith.

When we finally trooped to Birabi's grave, the crowd had
become virtually unmanageable, but I got introduced to the
tremendous discipline of the Ogoni people which was to be
shown the next day. At the first greeting hailing everyone,
silence reigned and all movement stopped.

There were several speeches, Dr Leton, Edward Kobani
and I speaking in that order. Garrick Leton is not a platform
performer, being rather shy and speaking with a slight stut-
ter, but Edward was a real gem when he got to the podium.
'Do not be afraid,' he urged the audience. 'Nothing will
happen to you on this land which God gave us!' Great stuff,
meant to convince everyone to confront the authorities and
the oil companies bravely. It even served to bring out one
of the best speeches I have ever made extempore. I have
since seen part of it on videotape and liked it. I stressed the

fact that we were out on a non-violent struggle for our rights; that I wouldn't want any blood spilled in that struggle, and that we would no longer allow what happened to the Amerindians, the Australian Aborigines and the New Zealand Maoris to happen to us. I assured the Ogoni people of eventual victory.

The speech was meant to challenge the Nigerian system and to encourage the Ogoni people to resist their denigration. A short speech, but effective, I should think. And I was pleased when I observed that the Lagos press had sent its representatives to follow the event.

As we left Birabi's tomb, I noticed what had become a regular event: the crowd of cheering children, women and youths that would follow me wherever I went, who would want to shake hands with me, or touch me, and who would deprive me of all privacy. They ran after my car, raising a cloud of dust, and as I left the church premises I knew that something different had happened to the Ogoni people.

My only and greatest sadness was the conspicuous absence of Bennet Birabi from both the church and his late father's tomb. It was a betrayal which I knew would haunt the fellow for ever. And I knew that the Ogoni people would never forget it.

The meeting scheduled to be held at Beeri after the church service was well attended, far more so than that of the previous day. It was held in the residence of Chief Ema Apenu, an engineer, and a cousin of Dr Leton. There being so much enthusiasm around, all we had to do was put final touches to the arrangements we had on the ground.

Each Ogoni kingdom had six co-ordinators and each village four, to plan and streamline activities and movement. As indicated earlier, we decided to put some entertainment into our activities to eliminate the possibility of violence.

We had detailed the making of posters, banners and placards to various youths.

The main protest was to take place at Bori, the head-quarters of the Ogoni nation, and the activity there was expected to be well organized. We had found some of the most trustworthy men to entrust with that responsibility. One of them was Theophilus Tornwini, who had been my teacher at the Native Authority School, Bori, and had become a civil servant in the service of the Rivers State government and a respected friend through the years. He was not much older than me, and I was unhappy that he had had to leave the Civil Service quite early in life when he had so much more to contribute to Ogoni and Nigeria.

We found, on a thorough check, that all was going as well as could be expected in the circumstances, and that there was nothing to worry about. I had to trust to luck that everything would go well the following day. I returned to Port Harcourt in good heart.

Ordinarily, the ride to Port Harcourt should take no more than thirty minutes. There isn't a single hill on the way. But the road was in such terrible disrepair that going on it was like an obstacle course. The journey time tripled. It hurt sorely to think how much money Ogoni was belching forth and how such a short stretch of road could not be made motorable. In Abuja, the new Nigerian capital, oil money was being used to blast stones, break hills and build roads which were hardly in use.

Arriving in Port Harcourt, I had a quick dinner and re-paired to my office to prepare the address I was to make at Bori the following morning. We had arranged that in addition to Dr Leton's speech as President, other speeches would be made by me, Ledum Mitee representing the youth of Ogoni and by a woman who was yet to be identified. I had

asked Joy Nunieh, the lovely, humorous, young lawyer, to prepare a draft address on behalf of Ogoni women.

All that night I spent either writing my speech or editing
the other speeches. My staff were on leave, besides its
being a Sunday, and I had to work alone on the computer
in the office. Alfred Ilenre was around to keep me company and to encourage me whenever I showed signs of
wilting.

The speeches were ready by four that morning and I retired to bed quite exhausted. But by six o'clock I was up
again. I had no appetite for breakfast and tended to be at the
very short end of a fuse, being brusque with all those who
were unfortunate enough to be around me. Most of them
probably understood how I felt and made allowance for it.

We set off for Bori shortly after seven o' clock. My intent
was to stop at the headquarters of all the six Ogoni kingdoms but it was necessary to have all the Ogoni leaders
together. I therefore decided to drive directly to Beeri to see
Dr Leton and hand over his speech to him.

The road was remarkably quiet. It was Monday morning,
the first working day of the year after the Christmas and
New Year festivities. Ordinarily, a lot of people should have
been returning to Port Harcourt, and not only from the
Ogoni area, but also from Opobo, Andoni and Ibibioland.
But we did not pass a single vehicle until we got to Bori.

There were a few banners along the road, proclaiming the
day as 'Ogoni Day in the International Year of the World's
Indigenous People'. Shortly before Bori, at Yeghe, we began
to see signs of the readiness of the people to march. A
number of youths, men and women were already forming
groups, holding twigs, the symbol of the environment which
we had chosen. My brother Owens was already on the road,
in his ambulance, monitoring what was going on.

I drove into Beeri and handed over Dr Leton's speech to

him. He had been waiting for me and told me his cousin, Engineer Apenu, had already left for Tabangh, the headquarters of Nyo-Khana kingdom, on foot!

Thereafter, I drove to Mogho, at the centre of Gokana kingdom, where I was to meet the first glorious sight of that day. It was a little past nine o'clock. Tim Lambon, the Greenpeace photographer, and Shelley Braithwaite of the Rainforest Action Group, who was my guest in Port Harcourt, had begun photographing in the area, as was their wont, well before seven o'clock.

As I drove up, a huge crowd, the largest I had seen in my life up to that moment, emerged from the different roads which led to the primary school at Mogho, whose football field was to be the venue for the rally. They had apparently been at work since seven o'clock and had gone to K. Dere, the site of the Bomu oilfield, to symbolically take over the oilfield with its flaming gas flare. All the Shell workers had abandoned the area the previous day.

They bore down, these poor, denigrated Ogoni people, green twigs, banners or placards in their hands, songs on their lips, and anger in their legs and faces, moving in an endless stream to the Mogho playground. But there was also pride in their faces, and I felt incredibly proud with them. It was with a lot of effort that I stopped the tears which welled up in me from streaming down my face. The empowerment which had enabled them to stand up to their oppressors at long last was the issue of the day.

The youths would not allow me to walk from my car to the venue of the rally. They insisted on carrying me shoulder-high to the rostrum, where I was expected to address the teeming and excited crowd.

On arrival at the rostrum, another problem reared its head: crowd control. There was a real possibility that the rostrum might collapse, or that the crowd pressing forward to get a glimpse or to be close to the centre of action might crush me and others.

In the event; none of that happened. I was able to silence the crowd after hailing them with the traditional 'M kana mon Gokana!'('I salute all Gokana!'), to which they replied fulsomely, 'E zira!' ('We return your salute'). Edward Kobani spoke, congratulating them on having taken over the oilfields symbolically. He himself had been at the head of the action, which was a great thing for a man his age. And he asked, 'Did not the thieves run away the moment, we, the owners of the property, showed up to reclaim it?' 'They did!' replied the crowd enthusiastically, and the arena was drowned in cheers and handclaps. I felt ever so proud of my friend, the great Ogoni patriot he has always been.

I then spoke briefly in the Gokana tongue, outlining the reason we were marching, and assuring them that no matter how long the battle lasted, we should all be ready to fight because there was no alternative to struggle. I congratulated them on the achievement of the day, assuring them that victory would assuredly be ours in the long term.

I had to save myself for the speeches I would be making at the other centres. The sun had already risen high in the sky and the air was thick with humidity. Sweat glistened on all faces and the dust rose into the air, adding to our discomfort.

I was carried from the rostrum on the shoulders of Ogoni youths back to my waiting car in a very slow procession. It was by no means a comfortable way of travelling and I was not without anxiety for my safety. I got to the car eventually, but then the youths would not let the car move, insisting on sitting on the bonnet, blocking the view of my chauffeur as he tried to move off.

As we inched forward, a helicopter flew over the rally ground and a solitary policeman walked towards us in a friendly sort of way. I was quite worried for him, as I was for the pick-up van with a number of police personnel that drove past us in the opposite direction towards the local police station. I knew that the place was crawling with over a thousand policemen; I was later to learn that they had not been paid a salary or out-of-station allowances. In any case, they kept out of sight that whole day; those who showed up fraternized openly with the marchers.

We were able, eventually, to leave the Mogho area steaming with sweat. We headed towards Tai kingdom. There were now several people on the road, headed towards the different rally venues. When we got to Kira where the Tai kingdom rally was to be held, the venue was also full of people who were drumming, singing and dancing.

Dr Leton had now joined up, and he addressed the crowd briefly, after Mr Noble Obani-Nwibari, the foremost Tai activist, had introduced him. I spoke thereafter, in my Khana mother-tongue, drawing enthusiastic cheers. Noble took the rostrum after me, and when he was done we left for Bori, where the biggest rally was scheduled to take place.

The ride into Bori was a pleasurable one, that stretch of road being quite smooth and short. The road was chock-a-block with people, old and young, moving on foot towards Bori. As we got close to the venue of the rally, the Birabi Memorial Grammar School playground, the crowd thickened. It was, of course, a much bigger crowd than that at Gokana, and you would have thought that all of Ogoni was present on the field that day. And yet there were still people waiting for me at two other centres – at Baen in Ken-Khana kingdom and Tabangh in Nyo-Khana kingdom.

It was well nigh impossible to find a way through the crowd, which raised an enormous amount of dust, and since my car was not air-conditioned the discomfort was high. We rolled up the car windows and steamed in the car as we inched forward. We finally got to the VIP area and I alighted to the delirious cries of the marchers. The cream of Ogoni society, less the government-paid traditional rulers and party politicians, was present and the atmosphere was euphoric.

Drummers thumped away at the far end of the arena and dance troupes performed skilfully. I shook hands with the chiefs and other leaders present. The crowd milled towards the VIP stand and we were at pains to keep the canopies standing. Controlling the crowd was becoming a problem. I guessed that the sooner we got started, the sooner we would be done and so prevent any accidents or incidents. I motioned to the appointed Master of Ceremonies to get started.

Chiefs Gbarazian of Bori, Gbaranee of Yeghe and Apere of Kaani jointly poured libation in the traditional Ogoni manner, calling on the gods of the land to bless our endeavour.

Thereafter, Dr Leton was introduced and he read his speech, which reminded the government that the Ogoni people were not asking for the moon but for their rights, including the right to the modern amenities of life and to survival.

Miss Joy Nunieh followed him, outlining the considerable difficulties the women faced in a situation of environmental disaster and economic strangulation.

Speaking after her, Mr Ledum Mitee, representing the youth of Ogoni, assured the crowd that the youth were out to defend their patrimony and that no prison could stop them from pressing home their claim.

I noticed that the press were fully represented. I had seen the team from *Newswatch* magazine, consisting of a reporter and a photographer, at Yeghe the previous day. Here, there were others from various newspapers and radio. We had commissioned a team of videotape photographers and they were also at work. Someone whom I did not know at the time but whom I was to know better thereafter, Mr Meshack Karanwi of Baen, a lecturer in Communication Arts at the University of Port Harcourt, had turned up with the most eloquent statement at the rally – a burnt Nigerian flag – which he held on a pole over the heads of all the speakers.

When it was my turn to speak, I mounted the rostrum and sized up the crowd. From a vantage point above everyone, I saw a new profile of the Ogoni people, a profile I had not identified. I saw eagerness, determination and joy on the young faces that looked up to the men on the rostrum. And I knew that a new seed had germinated and everything would have to be done to water, nurture, grow and harvest it. Ogoni would surely not be the same again. And I also felt that I must not let them down ever, or they would be right to lynch me!

The dust in the arena was incredible, as dancers, masqueraders and revellers continued their celebration through other speeches. I wanted and demanded silence and got it. When the arena was absolutely still, I sized up the crowd and their mood and decided not to speak in English as the previous speakers had all done, but in Khana. I spoke to the prepared script, however, and went even further on the spur of the moment, starting with our solidarity song 'Aaken, aaken, pya Ogoni aaken!' ('Arise, arise, Ogoni people arise!'). I had written the song in the days of the civil war in 1968/9 and used it to mobilize the Ogoni people at that time. It had come in quite handy in the new Ogoni movement and was sung with the right fist clenched and punching the air at shoulder level. It called the Ogoni people to work, to study, to struggle, vowing that they would no longer tolerate oppression. Later, an Ogoni activist added the notion of joy to it. It never failed to call the faithful to their new responsibilities.

The prepared speech which I spoke to was as follows:

Your Royal Highnesses, Respected Chiefs and Elders,
President of the Movement for the Survival of the Ogoni
People, Ladies and Gentlemen,

I wish to thank you all for giving me the opportunity to
speak on this occasion. I speak in a dual capacity, as President of the Ethnic Minority Rights Organization of Africa
(EMIROAF), which promotes the human and environmental rights of indigenous and tribal peoples and ethnic
minorities in Africa, and as Spokesman of the Ogoni People.

The year 1993 has been formally declared the International
Year of the World's Indigenous People as directed by the
General Assembly of the United Nations under resolution
46/128. The opening ceremonies took place in New York on
10 December 1992, International Human Rights Day. The
event was co-sponsored by the Centre for Human Rights, the
International Labour Office, United Nations Development
Programme, United Nations Environment Programme,
United Nations Children's Fund and Unesco.

The declaration of the Year signifies the interest which the
fate of indigenous people is receiving in the international
community. Although the case of indigenous people in America, Australia and New Zealand is well known, indigenous
people in Africa have received scant attention. EMIROAF
hopes to fill this vacuum and it is to this end that we have
given full support to the efforts of the Ogoni people to draw
attention to their plight. We intend to organize further activities during this year.

Contrary to the belief that there are no indigenous people
in black Africa, our research has shown that the fate of such
groups as the Zangon Kataf and Ogoni in Nigeria are, in
essence, no different from those of the Aborigines of Australia, the Maori of New Zealand and the Indians of North

and South America. Their common history is of the usurpation of their land and resources, the destruction of their culture and the eventual decimation of the people. Indigenous people often do not realize what is happening to them until it is too late. More often than not, they are the victims of the actions of greedy outsiders. EMIROAF will continue to mobilize and represent the interest of all indigenous people on the African continent. It is in this regard that we have undertaken to publicize the fate of the Ogoni people in Nigeria.

The Ogoni are embattled and imperilled. Since oil was discovered in the area in 1958, they have been the victims of a deadly ecological war in which no blood is spilled, no bones are broken and no one is maimed. But people die all the time. Men, women and children are at risk; plants, wild life and fish are destroyed, the air and water are poisoned, and finally the land dies. Today Ogoni has been reduced to a waste land.

Unfortunately, the international community has not yet awakened fully to the grim nature of this sophisticated, if unconventional battle. For a multinational oil company, Shell, to take over US thirty billion dollars from the small, defenceless Ogoni people and put nothing back but degradation and death is a betrayal of all humanity.

For the Nigerian government to usurp the resources of the Ogoni and legalize such theft by military decree is armed robbery.

To deny the Ogoni the right to self-determination and impose on them the status of slaves in their country is morally indefensible.

The stunning silence and insensitivity, the primitive harassment and intimidation which the looters of Lagos and the bandits of Abuja have visited on the Ogoni people since they began to demand their rights peacefully indicate that the

Nigerian government lacks the ability or will to solve the problem and that only the international community can help the Ogoni people.

I therefore call upon that community once again to come to the aid of the Ogoni before they are driven to extinction by the combined activity of the multinational oil companies, and the oppressive, greedy rulers of Nigeria.

Oil has been mined in Ogoni since 1958. It is a wasting asset. When the oil finally runs out in ten years or so, what will the Ogoni people do? Who will come to their aid? Something must be done NOW to save Ogoni.

I congratulate the Ogoni people on their taking upon themselves the historic responsibility for saving themselves, their land and their environment, late in the day as this may have been.

I call upon you, my brothers and sisters, to fight relentlessly for your rights. As our cause is just, and God being our helper, we shall emerge victorious over the forces of greed, wickedness and obduracy.

God bless you all.

My speech must have been quite rousing, if not entertaining, as it was greeted with cheers, handclaps and laughter all the way. The Ogoni penchant for humour and satire is well known, at least to the Ogoni themselves. I am always struck by the ready response to taunts, jokes, innuendo and other tricks of satire which are displayed even on the most serious occasions.

The tenor of my extempore speech was that we would have to face both the rulers of Nigeria and Shell which had denigrated us and laid great burdens on individual Ogoni people. I declared Shell *persona non grata* and challenged them to kill off all Ogoni men, women and children before taking any more oil from Ogoni. I ended with a call upon all other oil-producing areas in the country to follow the Ogoni example. 'Rise up now and fight for your rights!' I urged.

By the time I was done, I was virtually wilting. It had been a particularly hot and humid day, and there wasn't a drop of anything – cold water or soft drink – in sight. I returned to my seat, heard one or two other speeches, and, almost fainting, made for my car.

Again, moving out of the arena proved quite a feat as children milled all over my car, chanting in Khana, 'Iyaa gbin emue ye! Iyaa gbin emue ye!' ('We want to see him! We want to see him!') in unison as if they had been rehearsed to do so. They raised quite a lot of dust too, and it was a very tired man indeed who finally found the gate of the school compound and, turning right, headed back to Port Harcourt. I had had to scuttle the planned addresses in the two Khana kingdoms.

I returned to Port Harcourt, the press corps following closely on my heels, so to speak. Arriving home, I ordered and drank a full and welcome bottle of beer, granted a few interviews to the pressmen and then retired to bed. It was about four o'clock, but I had had enough for one day.

Memories of the march were to linger in my mind for a long time. Almost two thirds of the Ogoni population had marched peacefully. Those who could not go to the central venues had marched in their village squares. It was a great dance of the anger of the people. Not a stone was thrown and no one was hurt. Some of the youths, out of misguided enthusiasm, did stop travellers going to Port Harcourt to work. But apart from that, there were no incidents whatsoever.

Now when I look back upon the day, I feel very proud of being an Ogoni man. Ours was a great feat, even if I say so.

The 4th of January was truly a liberation day: a day on which young and old, able and disabled, rich and poor, all of Ogoni came out to reassert themselves and to give notice that the nation had come of age and that it would not accept its destruction passively. We had surmounted the psychological barrier of fear. Ogoni would never be the same again.

And I thought how wonderful it would be for Nigeria, for Africa, if the various ethnic nations that make it up could assert themselves in similar ways. We would be heading for a more democratic system, far from the dictatorships which have ruined the continent, and we might succeed in reordering our societies, undoing Berlin of 1884 (see p. 183), so that there would not be so much exploitation at all levels in all parts of the continent.

Somewhere deep down in my heart, I hoped that I had started a movement which might transform Africa. Would the Ogoni revolution be a model for other small, deprived, dispossessed and disappearing peoples? If only we could make it! A large number of communities ready to take their fate into their hands and practise self-reliance, demanding their rights non-violently, would conduce to democracy and more politically developed peoples. The leaders of such peoples would no longer be able to take them for granted and cheat and oppress them without remorse.

CHAPTER SIX

The protest march out of the way, I waited to see what would happen next. I called Mr Terebor, the SSS man, and he told me he had been all over Ogoni on the 4th and could attest to the peaceful nature of the march. Dr Leton, Edward Kobani and I called on Governor Ada George and found barely disguised hostility. It was clear that he had not taken kindly to our action. There was not much we could do about that. But I guess there was a lot for him to do, such is the power of government, and in Nigeria, it almost always is used to discomfit those with whom there is some disagreement. Ada George probably thought that we were out to get him out of his gubernatorial position. Rivers State could easily become a dangerous area, a State of Emergency would be declared by Babangida, and our man would be shorn of power. He was not likely to accept that.

Five days after the march, on 9 January, I was in my office working on the film of the protest when a journalist came in excitedly to ask me to find my way out of town.

'Why?' I asked.

'The police are after you.'

'Are they?'

'Yes. I was at the police headquarters and overheard them say the Inspector-General of Police has sent the Deputy Inspector-General in charge of Zone 5 to arrest you. A team of policemen has been sent to search for you.'

'So where should I hide? And why?'

'Go to the village or some place. You know it's the week-end. Once you're arrested, there'll be no one to bail you out until Monday. You'll be in police hands for three days at least. You know what that means.'

'I see,' I said. I thanked him for his trouble. He was on the *Nigerian Tide*, the newspaper of the Rivers State government which I had set up in 1971 as Commissioner for Information and Home Affairs and which had since been misused by successive administrations and was now more or less useless. I had noticed that the newspaper was not represented at Bori during the protest march, even though I had specifically invited the journalist who had now turned up to give me information.

I asked my assistant to find me a fair sum of money and, putting it into my briefcase, returned to my work. I had no reason to worry about an arrest. I was well prepared to take the consequences of my action.

The police did turn up to ask after me but my staff informed them that I was not available and they went off. I continued to work in my office till late, as was my wont. When I repaired home at about eight o'clock at night, I found three policemen in plain clothes waiting at the gates of my residence. They calmly informed me that they had instructions to bring me along. I asked to be allowed to have my dinner as I was extremely hungry. They obliged me, and sat in my lounge while I dined.

I set off with them in their car – they insisted that I ride with them – and instructed my car to follow after us. We drove to the police guest house and I was ushered into the presence of the Deputy Inspector-General of Police in charge of Zone 5. He was a genial, smiling man, a Tiv, by the name of Malherbe. I found him very well spoken and courteous to a fault. He offered me a cognac and turned to the Commissioner of Police, whom I had met earlier at Government

House when Ada George was trying to dissuade me from organizing the march. The Commissioner had impressed me at that time because I found that he was a polyglot, speaking Hausa, Fulfulde (the Fulani tongue), Arabic, French and English. He was on the point of retirement in a matter of days and seemed glad to be so.

After Mr Malherbe had finished with his subordinate, he informed me that he had asked after me, Dr Leton and Edward Kobani because we would have to be leaving town the following morning by presidential jet. He did not appear sure where we would be going. None of the others had turned up and he wondered if I would be able to get them and give them the information. I offered to do so and we parted for the night after a light banter.

By the following morning, I had located the other two and when Dr Bennet Birabi heard that we were due to travel, he decided to accompany us. The presidential jet arrived after noon and soon winged its way to Lagos. Indeed, we did not know precisely where we were headed until after take-off. It would be either Abuja or Lagos, depending on where the Inspector-General of Police happened to be. Ever since Babangida had decided to move the capital of Nigeria post-haste to Abuja, which was still in the process of construction, civil servants and other government functionaries had been hopping wastefully between the old capital, Lagos, and the new one. The cost of all this was enormous, but the nation was floating on borrowed money, petrodollars and plain bad sense, so there was no need to worry.

We finally arrived at Lagos airport and were driven to Kam Selem House, the headquarters of the Nigerian police force. There, the Inspector-General of Police, Mr Aliyu Atta, was waiting for us. He was well known to everyone there except myself and shared a particular friendship, it would appear, with Bennet Birabi. He had been Commissioner of Police in Port Harcourt years earlier.

He received us warmly and said he would like to know what was our problem. All four of us spoke of the agony of the Ogoni, each stressing his particular angle of the tragedy. Having heard us out, he thought we should go back to our hotel and submit, the following morning, what we thought should be done. We thanked him and departed.

The police checked each of us into a suite at the swank Sheraton Hotel in the Lagos suburb of Ikeja. I agreed to stay there only because we needed to meet late and prepare a memorandum for the following morning.

As we drove from Lagos to the hotel, Mr Malherbe thought that we should ask for things that could be done in the short term such as the provision of amenities. We thought otherwise. The struggle was for something far more fundamental than that.

The memorandum which we prepared that night remained faithful to the central tenets of the Ogoni Bill of Rights. We asked for an Ogoni state in order to give power to the Ogoni people to do things for themselves, and we asked for a proper share of oil money. We asked, in short, for our rights.

In speaking to us, Aliyu Attah had assured us that he would reply to us within ten days. He did not, and we did not hear from him until he left his job with the disgraced dictator, Babangida, in August 1993.

Mr Malherbe turned up the following morning to send everyone back to Port Harcourt, this time not by presidential jet but by normal flight. I elected to remain behind in Lagos to follow the publicity arising from the march.

I realized quite early the value of publicity to the protest march, and, indeed, to the entire Ogoni movement. I had, as I have already indicated, learnt quite a bit about how to promote an idea or a product during my television production days. The lesson came in very handy now. Television production had made me the darling, so to speak, of the Nigerian media, including the junk press. And I had learnt how to use the print media, in particular, to promote my product. In Nigeria the electronic media are solidly in the hands of the government and are used for the purposes of oppressing the people and hiding information from them. Not so the print media. There are several widely read newspapers and magazines; since they offer alternate views to the tired, tedious and false news which all government-controlled media offer, they are extremely useful to the health of the nation.

I had written columns in Nigerian newspapers and was a regular contributor of essays and letters to the editor. As a prolific new writer of novels and other books, I was constantly on the book review pages of newspapers and magazines and was well known by publishers, editors, reporters, correspondents and photographers.

Now as I tried to promote Ogoni, all the foregoing came together and made my work not only easy but also inexpensive. I am quite convinced that if we had hired a public relations firm to promote our cause, it would have cost us millions of dollars and we would not have achieved the success we did, a success which proved a nightmare to our opponents.

The trick was the detailed attention which we paid the newspaper houses. I was constantly at the doors of publishers, editors, columnists, news editors and reporters. We inundated them with position papers, press releases and photographs. And I was always ready to give interviews. I had my facts at my fingertips, and because of the variety of my interests I presume that I may well have been good copy. Moreover, since the argument was about politics, the economy and the environment, we fitted into a wide variety of publications. Even the junk press found something of interest in a television comedy producer turning his pen from the comic to the serious. I must have cut quite a comic and, therefore, entertaining figure.

Nor was my influence limited to the Nigerian media. I was already a regular at Bush House, London, where I was interviewed on my books, had my stories and plays broadcast, and had also judged some short stories on the very popular African Service. So that when I began to push the Ogoni story, the BBC African Service became an ally. The producers and broadcasters on the Service did not ever fail to warn me of the dangers of my cause. But I wasn't daunted.

The week I spent in Lagos was useful, publicity-wise. The respectable magazine *Newswatch* had sent one of its reporters and a photographer to Ogoni during the protest march, and the newspaper later came out with a cover story of the event. Those news magazines and newspapers which did not do a cover story of the historic event or did not carry it prominently gave me extended interviews and published feature articles.

I regret that radio and television were not available to us throughout our campaign. If this had been the case, we should certainly have captured the entire Nigerian public faster than we eventually did. I had purchased a good still camera and one of the new, small, technically competent video cameras and ensured that our important events were covered filmicly. The problem was that we could not show the films to the public! And that was a decided loss.

Our publicity effort turned the Ogoni people into avid readers of newspapers. Where previously they had not warmed up to newspapers, they now not only read newspapers but filed cuttings. As the newspapers or magazines reported Ogoni stories or wrote editorials or feature articles, intrepid Ogonis made photocopied cuttings and sold them throughout the land. Thus, there was proper information to the grassroots on all the arguments surrounding our cause. And it was truly surprising how fast the information flowed, considering that radio and television were not available to us and did not carry our news. The Ogoni bush radio proved as effective, if not more effective, than the conventional media.

By May 1993, we had started a four-page monthly newsletter, *Ogoni Review*, edited by my nephew Barika Idamkue. He had edited a university newspaper in his days at the University of Port Harcourt, and had worked with me while we promoted the television series *Basi & Co*. He had also proofread and copyedited most of my books and was certainly a very good editor of the *Ogoni Review*. The review was sold at all rallies in Ogoni and was distributed free to those on our mailing list. Since I had a desk-top publishing system in my office, producing the review came as inexpensively as possible. Again, my career as a publisher was aiding the Ogoni movement tremendously.

CHAPTER SEVEN

If I thought that there would be no answer to the march by those we had challenged, I was greatly mistaken. And, as usual, the first persons to be used were the Ogoni people themselves. A few of them were very close to Governor Ada George and were benefiting by his being in power. And it was to them he turned for assistance to wreak his revenge on the Ogoni people.

Their agreeing to do his dirty job for him was no surprise. The other man who joined them was unexpected, but should have been no surprise. The late Albert Badey, the son of a Methodist priest, a fine man whom I knew well as a child, had studied at the Methodist College, Uzuakoli, where he was something of a great success, scoring well in the Higher School Certificate examinations in 1958, thereby securing a competitive scholarship to University College, Ibadan, where he read English. He thereafter joined the administrative service of the former Eastern Region and was well set to rise to the top of it. The civil war, in which he was on the Biafran side, sent him back to the Rivers State Civil Service in January 1970. I remember having to send one of my private trucks to bring his personal effects back from the Igbo heartland at the end of the war. And of ensuring that he got back his rightful place in the Civil Service. He did Ogoni proud in the service.

The problem with Albert Badey was that he was a dyed-in-the-wool gerontocrat. The older a man is, the wiser. And he did not believe in the masses. A few people could always take decisions for the latter and all would be well. The latter derived, I think, from his training as a civil servant. For Albert was a superb bureaucrat, dedicated to his career, and anxious not to rock the boat, any boat.

He rose steadily to the position of Permanent Secretary, the top of the Civil Service, and following the topsy-turvy methods of the military government, became Chairman of the Public Service Commission, then a commissioner and, by the time we started the Ogoni movement in 1990, was Secretary to the Rivers State government, the highest position anyone could achieve in the Civil Service. In short, Albert had achieved everything a man could achieve at the local level. He hungered for more, I think, and was young and talented enough to expect more. Had he been from anywhere else but Ogoni, he would have gone much further. Being an Ogoni, he was merely left to fester at the local level.

By 1993 when we intensified the Ogoni struggle, he was out of government. He was a great example of how the individual success of an Ogoni man could not make a difference to the generality of the Ogoni people. Albert, it would seem, did not understand that.

As we were being flown to Lagos, the Ogoni friends of Governor Ada George were assembled at Kono Beach on Saturday, 9 January, to react to the protest march. I had been invited to the meeting, along with Dr Leton and Edward Kobani. Our absence did not stop them from holding the meeting. Albert, who, until then, had stayed resolutely away from the movement, was among them, along with a gaggle of government chiefs who had signed the Ogoni Bill of Rights but had stayed away from the march of 4 January. The communiqué which they issued at the end of their meeting in Kono appeared to take the side of the government against the Ogoni people.

*Communiqué issued at the end of a representative meeting
of the Ogoni people held on Saturday, 9 January 1993*

At a fully representative meeting of the Ogoni people held
today, Saturday, 9 January 1993, the events of the past days
relating to the welfare of the people as a distinct ethnic entity
contributing immensely to the growth of Nigeria were re-
viewed in detail. At the end of the meeting, it was resolved as
follows:

1. That the Ogoni people retain their position that they
desire and are entitled to the attention and special treatment
by the government of the Federal Republic of Nigeria.

2. That the Ogoni people remain united and indivisible to
a man in these matters.

3. That in seeking for their right and appropriate treatment by the Government, they reaffirm their faith in the Federal Republic of Nigeria and reconfirm their commitment to
peaceful pursuit of their grievances as the demonstration of
Monday, 4 January 1993 fully proved.

4. That the Ogoni people are aware of the recent encouraging actions of the Federal government in establishing the Oil
Mineral Producing Areas Development Commission and
they express their happiness about this development. In view
of this, it is their expectation that our President and
Commander-in-Chief of the Armed Forces of the Federal
Republic will grant the Ogoni people audience for a reasoned
presentation of their demand. Consequently, no further
demonstration will be held in expectations of the positive
reaction of government to their cry.

Signed:
1. HRH Chief W. Z. P. Nziidee (Gbenemene Nyo-
Khana)

2. HRH Chief J. P. Bagia (Gbenemene Gokana)
3. HRH Chief M. S. N. Eguru (Gbenemene Ken-Khana)
4. HRH Chief Mark Tsaro-Igbara (Gbenemene Babbe)
5. HRH Chief G. N. K. Gininwa (Gbenemene Tua-Tua Tai)
6. HRH Chief C. B. S. Nwikina Ewah III (Menebua Bom).

Those of us who had travelled to Lagos were shocked to find the communiqué advertised in the rag of a government newspaper, *Nigerian Tide*. Considering that the men who signed the paper would not have had the funds to take a full-page advertisement in any newspaper, unless it was on the pain of death, we knew who was behind it all.

On 17 January we quickly called another meeting of all the signatories of the Ogoni Bill of Rights at the Beeri residence of Engineer Apenu. And everyone recommitted themselves to the movement and reaffirmed that MOSOP was the only organization responsible for the well-being of the Ogoni people and therefore authorized to speak and act on their behalf.

The day after this declaration was signed, I left for The Hague to attend a meeting of UNPO. The Ogoni people were admitted to the organization by the Third General Assembly and I was elected Vice-Chairman of the Assembly. UNPO gave us the opportunity to appear on the world scene and CNN, the American world-wide television network, showed a slice of the Ogoni march, which Nigerians had not been able to see on their own television screens. And, for the first time, Ogoni appeared in *Time* magazine.

At the meeting I attended a workshop on non-violent struggle. I recall that one of our lecturers, a Palestinian, after hearing the Ogoni story from me, felt better about the fate of the Palestinians. He had not ever thought that any group of people could be worse treated than his own people. I also introduced him to another type of violence: environmental degradation and I did ask whether there was anything in the books as to how it could be confronted in a non-violent manner. No one, it appeared, had ever thought of it.

I also met an official of Shell at the assembly and in a private discussion with him suggested that Shell would do well to ally itself with the owners of the land on which it operates rather than seek the co-operation of bandit governments. I doubted that the message sank in. Indeed, it did not.

Shortly after that meeting, Shell International's Public Affairs Department summoned to London and to The Hague two of its top Nigerian managers, Nnaemeka Achebe, General Manager, Business, and a Mr Okonkwo of the Health and Safety Department, where they devised plans for dealing with the menace of Ken Saro-Wiwa and the Ogoni people. They had not forgotten that I had called their environmental record in Ogoni into question in the documentary *The Heat of the Moment*, which, as I have indicated, was screened in London in October 1992. The minutes of their meeting which came into my hands subsequently indicated that 'key players' such as myself were to be closely watched, our movements and actions followed closely throughout the world to ensure that we did not 'embarrass' Shell. I knew that Shell would revert to its usual acceptance of the government apparatus being used against us while stating that it knew nothing whatever about what was happening.

I began to think my life was seriously at risk. I was, however, ready for such a development, and wrote my will and informed my family, that they should prepare for the worst. Nor did I ever fail, in my public speeches to the Ogoni people to warn them to expect unsavoury developments from the Nigerian government. Later events were to prove me dead right.

On my return to Nigeria from The Hague via London, Dr Leton, Edward Kobani and I were summoned to Abuja on 14 February to meet the Director-General of the State Security Service, Mr Peter Ndiokwu. Glittering in lovely robes in the newly constructed ornate office of the service in Abuja, he read us the riot act. He particularly warned me in regard of my writings and press interviews. I assured him that I was merely drawing government attention to certain of its responsibilities and, as to his warning of the possibility of detention, I was quite ready to face the consequences of my actions. It was Valentine's Day and I confess to having had a dinner date at government expense at the swank Sheraton Hotel in Abuja.

When I returned to Ogoni the next week, it was to launch the One Naira Ogoni Survival Fund (ONOSUF) by which we sought to commit all Ogoni men, women and children to the struggle. At the launch at Bori, on 27 February 1993, I gave the following address:

A Call to Commitment

Distinguished President of the Movement for the Survival
of the Ogoni People (MOSOP), Your Royal Highnesses,
Citizens of the United Kingdom of Ogoni, Brothers, Sisters
and Friends,

It gives me great pleasure to address you this afternoon on the occasion of the formal launch of the One Naira Ogoni Survival Fund (ONOSUF), and I thank you, Mr President, for calling upon me to formally launch the Fund.

Almost three years ago, the chiefs and people of this blessed land took the first steps of a historic journey when, here in Bori, we formally established the Movement for the Survival of the Ogoni People (MOSOP) with the aim of extricating all Ogoni people from the shackles of indigenous colonialism and environmental strangulation, and of challenging the obnoxious, disgraceful and oppressive system imposed by successive military regimes on the peoples of Nigeria.

Since that day three years ago, the Ogoni people have established their identity as a distinct and unique people, reclaimed their right to freedom and independence, successfully placed their case before the international community, and put past and present rulers of Nigeria before the bar of world opinion, where judges do not take bribes and rulers cannot enact obnoxious decrees to imprison justice.

Today, the Ogoni people are involved in two grim wars. The first is the 35-year-old ecological war waged by the multinational oil companies, Shell and Chevron. In this most sophisticated and unconventional war, no bones are broken, no blood is spilled and no one is maimed. Yet, men, women and children die; flora and fauna perish, the air and water are poisoned, and finally, the land dies.

The second war is a political war of tyranny, oppression and greed designed to dispossess the Ogoni people of their rights and their wealth and subject them to abject poverty, slavery, dehumanization and extinction.

Taken together, both wars, waged against a defenceless and small people, amount to genocide and are a grave crime against humanity.

Pitted against two deadly, greedy, insensitive and powerful enemies, the Ogoni people have refused to yield and are fighting doggedly and heroically for survival. And the war must be won, for the alternative to victory is extinction.

Our goal has been set out in the Ogoni Bill of Rights, where we underlined our determination to achieve political autonomy, the right to use our economic resources for our development, the right to protect the Ogoni environment and ecology from further degradation and the right to adequate and direct representation AS OF RIGHT in all Nigerian national institutions.

For the avoidance of all doubt, let me reiterate that this last item underlines our desire to remain within the Nigerian nation-state. This decision has been taken, not because we think that secession is wrong, not for fear that the Nigerian constitution regards secession as treason (we are quite prepared to defy that constitution when necessary and to face the consequences of such defiance), but because we firmly believe in the brotherhood of black people world-wide and in sharing the blessings of God on an equitable basis with all.

MOSOP has an underlying social philosophy: ERECTISM, an acronym for Ethnic Autonomy, Resource and Environmental Control. We believe that under this umbrella, there will not only be self-reliance, democracy, social justice, healthy competition and progress, but that the Nigerian confederation which it proposes can be widened to embrace other African peoples in unity, peace and prosperity based on hard work.

The alternative to ERECTISM is dictatorship, retrogression and disintegration of the Nigerian nation-state. Those who therefore cling dishonestly to the frightening failures which characterize today's Nigeria because it works for them are riding the horse of disaster. In the event of the disintegration of Nigeria, they will suffer the most.

In pursuance of the laudable goals of ERECTISM, we in Ogoni are reconstructing our society even as we fight the grim war of genocide. We aim to (a) rehabilitate and reconstruct our proud heritage – the Ogoni nation – which has suffered enormous setbacks in the course of the life of this country (b) ensure our cultural survival by regenerating our traditional means of securing happiness, social interaction and well-being (c) re-emphasize the practice of self-reliance

149

for which our forebears were noted and (d) ensure the study of our languages, Eleme, Gokana and Khana.

One of the first steps to this end is the establishment of ONOSUF. Why one naira we might ask?

The Ogoni people are an extremely rich but dispossessed people. In establishing this fund, we want to emphasize not money but the symbols of togetherness, of comradeship, of unity of endeavour, of the total commitment of young and old. Money cannot win the war of genocide against the Ogoni people. God Himself will win the war for us. But all Ogoni men, women and children, including newborn babies, will contribute to ONOSUF as a statement of their will to survive as individuals and as one indivisible nation.

The cost of reconstruction and recovery of the Ogoni nation is estimated to exceed US fifteen billion dollars. We will have to find that money. In accordance with the political will of our people and in total condemnation of the deliberate and wicked exploitation of the Ogoni by the Nigerian nation-state and her agents, ONOSUF will not accept donations from any government in Nigeria. However, our friends at home and abroad are welcome to contribute towards the reconstruction and rehabilitation process in Ogoni.

Mr President, we have noticed over the last three years that the Nigerian government has shown a remarkable lack of will to do anything to mitigate the agony of the Ogoni. A government which routinely doles out millions of naira to minor social organizations and girlfriends has foundit easy to ignore the death of thousands of Ogoni children whose heritage it is dissipating recklessly. Certainly, the problems which the rulers of Nigeria have inflicted on the Ogoni people are so monumental and daunting that the Nigerian nation-state cannot even contemplate them. Therefore, only the international community working through the United Nationscan stop this genocide, this savagery so unworthy of the twenty-first century.

I call upon the United Nations to intervene now to save human lives. I thank the only Nigerian organization (Campaign for Democracy) which has openly fraternized with the Ogoni people. I thank the Unrepresented Nations and Peoples Organizations, the European Community, the Parliamentary Human Rights Group of the British House of Lords, Cultural Survival of America, Greenpeace, the Rainforest Action Group and other non-governmental organizations which have shown understanding of the Ogoni situation and are working to stave off another African tragedy.

Mr President, distinguished guests, I am pleased to launch ONOSUF with the sum of one naira, and I appeal to you all to contribute to the fund not only the sum of one naira but, much more importantly, your total commitment and dedication. For we are witnessing the birth of a new phenomenon, the decision by a small group of people that they will not tolerate their dehumanization even by people of the same colour of skin. And that all the guns of the world, the casuistry of dictatorship and the threat of death and imprisonment cannot deter a people determined to secure their God-given rights and protect their inheritance.

Thank you.

At meetings of the Steering Committee there were some who had thought that the effort would be wasted. But when we got down to it, it proved quite successful. The amount we had chosen was small and everyone felt that they should pay voluntarily. A total sum of about 700,000 naira was realized in a very short time – an unprecedented feat.

The following month we held a night vigil throughout the Ogoni nation. The Christian Church, as I have said, has a powerful hold in Ogoni, and the arrival of the Pentecostal Churches at a time of serious economic difficulties had led to even more people seeking solace in religion. I did not like the development at all, for it was making the people not seek answers to their many problems but to rely on divine intervention. Besides, the Pentecostal Churches tend to be one-man outfits out to exploit the people. They lack the strength of the organized Churches, which I definitely admire. Anyway, we had to use whatever instruments could sell our movement to the generality of our people and the Churches proved most important. The vigil was duly held on 13 March.

I drove into Bori at six o'clock that evening, and already Ogoni youths had massed up at the Birabi Memorial Grammar School playground. As the sun dipped in the west, a candle-lit procession took off. In an orderly single file, the youths marched through the length of Bori chanting: 'Go down, go down, go down to Abuja/And tell government, government let Ogoni go!' They ended up at the Suanu Finimale Nwika Conference Hall at the other end of town, where the Bori vigil took place. For reasons of crowd control, we had decided to keep the Bori crowd small and had instructed that the vigil take place in all Ogoni villages and towns simultaneously.

It was a very successful night, and as many of the Ogoni elite as possible were present at Bori. It was perhaps the last thing on which the pitiable group were agreed, it being harmless. The one thing I remember of it is that my 89-year-old father was with us until four o'clock the next morning. Most of the elite stole away at midnight. The rest of us continued until daybreak.

On the ides of March, the sad news came of the sudden death of my youngest son, Tedum, on the playing fields of Britain's Eton College. I had to go to England to complete the funeral obsequies of my lovely, fourteen-year-old boy, whose soul, please God, may find eternal, peaceful rest. I wish to thank the Provost and Headmaster of Eton College, the Housemaster of Waynfleet House, the Headmaster of Cheam School, Headley, Newbury, and the Headmistress of Roedean School, Brighton, as well as a large number of friends in London for the support they gave my family in our bereavement.

I had a commitment to lecture Itsekiri students in Warri on 3 April, and in spite of the pain I had in my heart, I returned from London and drove to Warri to keep the appointment. I arrived to find twenty policemen waiting to throw me out of town like some vermin. As I have said, they actually deported me from Delta State, seeing me across the Niger at the Patani Bridge and back into Rivers State. My first arrest.

From that moment onwards, I was in real trouble with Babangida's bloodhounds. When the Federal government sent a team to Port Harcourt ostensibly to dialogue with people from the oil-producing areas, I was not allowed to speak on behalf of the Ogoni people. I had a chance to say all that was in my mind later that night when Governor Ada George invited me to a dinner at which the then Minister of Petroleum, Mr Asiodu, and other representatives of the NNPC and the government would be present.

I was happy to be able to confront Mr Asiodu, whose statement about the marginalization of the ethnic minorities in the oil-bearing delta is the most insensitive, callous and provocative statement on record. Given, however, the small size and population of the oil-producing areas, it is not cynical to observe that even if the resentments of oil-producing states continue, they cannot threaten the stability of the country or affect its continued economic development. He argued that he had not meant what he said. I disputed him, stressing that by no analysis whatsoever could any positive construction be put on the words by which he posited that the people of the Niger River Delta could be exploited and denigrated. I promised, however, to report him faithfully in my next book – the one which I have now done.

Not allowing me to speak to the public appeared to be the ploy of government. I was, in short, being denied my right to freedom of expression. But the ideas were abroad, and I did not see how they could be stanched. The government had other ideas.

On 18 April I was returning from a trip to Lagos when the security agents came tapping my shoulder at the Port Harcourt Airport. They took me away to their shabby head-quarters, searched my offices and home, including my bed-room and toilet, seized a mass of documents and tapes and released me eighteen hours later, having afforded me only a wretched meal in that time. My second arrest.

Five days later, they returned to my office and seized me at about noon. My third arrest. Mr Terebor, the Director, no, misdirector, of the SSS in Rivers State queried and questioned me about an Ogoni flag, an Ogoni National Anthem, the UNPO, and so on and so forth. He was obviously trying to establish a case for treason, secession being treasonable under Nigerian law.

Of course, there was nothing treasonable in the Ogoni demands. The Ogoni Bill of Rights had expressly stated as follows: 'now, therefore, while reaffirming our wish to remain a part of the Federal Republic of Nigeria, we make demand upon the republic as follows . . .' Only an idiot or a man fishing for trouble could ever construct those words as secessionist. Mr Terebor was no idiot and his subordinates were quite intelligent, as my conversation with them showed. So, what dirty job were they up to?

I was kept in their office for hours and questioned end-lessly. Having not had a meal all day, I collapsed shortly after seven o'clock in the evening. When I began to feel bad, I asked for a doctor but they could not produce one. Only after I had collapsed did they let me go, but with instructions that I not leave Port Harcourt. In short, I was under town arrest.

That incensed the Ogoni people. Ogoni youths in Port Harcourt decided to stage a peaceful protest against the authorities and made arrangements to present a petition to the Rivers State House of Assembly. As I came to know later, they had planned to march from my Aggrey Road office to the Rivers State Government Secretariat about two miles away, where the House of Assembly normally convened. By the night of 28 April, they had all their placards ready at the MOSOP office, which was in the flat directly above my office.

At about six o'clock in the morning of the 29th one of my relatives came to my residence to inform me that the Police Mobile Force had surrounded my office and that it was advisable that I keep out of the area that day. I thanked him for his advice and remained in bed that morning till late.

In spite of the blandishments of the security agencies, who also mounted guard at the entrance to the House of Assembly, the march went on as planned. Alerted by the new security measures, the youths quickly changed plans. They abandoned the placards at the MOSOP office and quickly wrote new ones. Then large numbers of them slipped into the premises of the secretariat pretending to be government clerks and workers.

By the time the assembly went into session, a rousing song rent the quiet air and protesters marched into the entrance of the assembly. Employees in the secretariat were taken by surprise and rushed to see what was happening.

Ogoni youths were making their protest heard as the assembly speaker came forward to receive the Ogoni petition demanding that their leaders be no longer harassed. Thereafter, they marched in a peaceful procession, holding aloft their Bibles, along the streets of Port Harcourt to the motor park on the Port Harcourt–Aba Expressway.

The march showed the remarkable organizing ability of Ogoni youths and their determination to use all the instruments of non-violent struggle in the demand for Ogoni rights. Their placards showed their faith in me and expressed their concern that I was being continually harassed by security agencies.

The message must have fallen on deaf ears. In any case, the battle was already joined, and we were probably no longer in control of whatever happened or was to happen. We were, from that day, largely reacting to what our opponents did, except for the decision to boycott the presidential elections of 12 June (as we shall see later).

The very next day, on 30 April, disaster struck. Shell had been dualizing the Trans-Niger pipeline, which carries oil from most parts of the delta through Ogoni territory to the export terminal at Bonny. They had not carried out an environmental impact assessment study. They had not negotiated with the landlords whose land they were using and/or desecrating. They simply got soldiers of the Nigerian army to guard them, who then bribed their way through any complaining villagers.

The soldiers had gone through a number of Ogoni villages, but when they got to Biara, where a major oil spill had polluted streams and the land two years earlier, incensed villagers, mostly women, turned out to question them. The women held twigs as they had been advised to do to indicate that they were protesting peacefully. The soldiers emptied their live ammunition on them. Eleven people were wounded, among them Mrs Karalole Korgbara, a mother of five children who was shot in the left arm – it was subsequently amputated.

If the powers that be thought that this would scare the Ogoni people, they were mistaken. The next day thousands of unarmed Ogoni people poured into the site, daring the soldiers to shoot. This was a bit too much for the stomachs of the American engineers who were working for the American pipeline contractor firm, Wilbros, which subsequently withdrew from the site. But not before the soldiers had murdered another man, Agbarator Otu, who was in a group of protesters at the nearby village of Nonwa. MOSOP was left to bury the dead and provide medicine for the wounded, including Mrs Korgbara.

The Ogoni people were very traumatized by this event, and they protested on 30 April and the next day by massing on the roads and disrupting the movement of commuters. Some hoodlums attempted to vandalize Wilbros equipment.

The MOSOP Steering Committee was upset by this development and Mr Ledum Mitee, Edward Kobani and I were delegated to tour Ogoni to calm the people. Denied access to government radio, we sent letters appealing for calm to all villages through the chiefs. We followed that up the next day with visits to the two sensitive kingdoms of Gokan and Tai, and the headquarters at Bori, where we spoke to large crowds, asking everyone to keep calm and maintain the peace. We received an immediate response which was very satisfying indeed. Calm was quickly restored.

In the face of this tragedy, some Ogoni politicians and traditional rulers, the friends of Governor Ada George, issued another press release which was given wide coverage in the newspaper and radio, castigating MOSOP and its leaders over the shooting, and inviting the government to do whatever they wished in order to establish law and order in Ogoni. Their release read:

The Activities of the Movement for the Survival of Ogoni People (MOSOP)

We, a very substantial section of the Ogoni leadership, in our meeting held on 4 May 1993, have decided to register our anger and complete disapproval of the lawless activities of certain elements in Ogoni who claim to be operating under MOSOP, or the Movement for the Survival of the Ogoni people.

We wish to state that the Ogoni people have not mandated any person or group of persons to coerce the public, cause bodily harm and threaten life and property. Specifically the Ogoni people have not mandated any person or group of persons to obstruct the legitimate operation of any normal business operations in the area or to interfere with government security men who are carrying out their duty of maintaining law and order.

We wish to apologize to all non-indigenes of Ogoni who have been assaulted, molested or had their goods seized or destroyed by this violent group of irresponsible persons.

Ourselves, and on behalf of the entire Ogoni people, wish to apologize to our Governor Chief Rufus Ada George for the insults and disrespect organized and insinuated on him. We also wish to apologize to the government of Rivers State and the entire Rivers people, particularly our neighbours, for any embarrassment this development might have caused them.

We wish to state that we agree with the basic issues raised by MOSOP by highlighting the neglect of Ogoni land over the years in terms of development, and we hope a correct atmosphere of peace and friendship can be created so that dialogue with government with a view to correcting the age-long neglect can start.

We also apologize to the Federal government for any embarrassment caused the nation and wish to state that we appreciate the steps now being taken by the Federal government to address the issues of the development of oil-producing areas in general and Ogoni in particular. We therefore appeal to the agencies who have been given this assignment to expedite action towards this goal.

We wish to appeal to the leadership of MOSOP and the youths of Ogoni to be calm, because only in an atmosphere of peace can our grievances be attended.

Finally, may we state that no government will allow a break-down of law and order which will result in a state of anarchy. And we associate ourselves with any action by government to protect life and property of innocent citizens.

Signed:

(1) Mr S. I. Kogbara
(2) Chief S. N. Orage
(3) Chief Hon. Kemte Giadom
(4) Chief J. K. Kponi
(5) HRH W. Z. P. Nziidee (Gbenemene Nyo-Khana)
(6) HRH J. P. Bagia (Gbenemene Gokana)
(7) HRH M. S. H. Eguru (Gbenemene Ken-Khana)
(8) HRH M. T. Igbara (Gbenemene Babbe)
(9) HRH G. N. K. Giniwa (Gbenemene Tua-Tua)
(10) Dr N. A. Ndegwe
(11) Elder Lekue Lah-Loolo

The stipulated cost of the advertisement showed that the advertisers were sponsored by the state government, which simply allowed them free services on the state media. Shell was later to use this advertisement in international circles in a vain attempt to show that MOSOP was working at cross-purposes with the Ogoni people, and that I, in particular, did not have the support of the Ogoni people.

Indeed, ever since February, when it was decided to monitor my activities, Shell had been working extraordinarily hard to destroy all my efforts. Now, do not ask me for hard evidence. These things are never done in writing, and even if it were done, neither of the parties would make the letters available to me. But Shell has accepted publicly that whenever it feels threatened in its operations, it appeals to the Federal authorities. At about this time Shell had decided not to work any more in Ogoni and had placed all its flow stations on automatic. The area, it claimed, was not safe for Shell staff.

I have to state that MOSOP did not stop Shell, although we did let it be known that the company was *persona non grata* in our land because of its destruction of the environment, its uncaring exploitation of the community, and its refusal to make any restitution whatsoever for the great harm it had done to the Ogoni people and environment.

In that sense, the Ogoni people will have lost nothing should Shell pull out of the area for ever. The company having taken over nine hundred million barrels of crude oil from the area in thirty-five years and put absolutely nothing back but death and degradation, the Ogoni people would be very foolish indeed to welcome it back without a full agreement carefully worked out and signed as to adequate compensation, rents and royalties, employment opportunities, rate of exploitation of oil, and other aspects of the day-to-day operations of the company as they affect the Ogoni people. The serious questions of shortage of land and of sustainable development and the propensity of Federal Nigeria to exploit the Ogoni people in conjunction with the oil companies mean that the Ogoni people and their leaders must receive cast-iron guarantees before oil and gas can be mined in the area again. If this is not done, the Ogoni people will become extinct. And it will be their fault.

Shell feels affronted that a black man, a black community, has dared to challenge it; and it has shown the world that the company is an environmental threat in Nigeria, but not in Europe or America. For this reason, it is determined to humiliate me publicly and to discredit the Ogoni people. It is, perhaps, a question of time and methods for them. Whatever does happen, I am pleased that the Ogoni people have been able to stand up to their denigration at the hands of Shell.

As to the advertisement by the self-proclaimed 'very substantial section of the Ogoni leadership', it has to be said that it annoyed the Ogoni people to a very high degree. The advertisement was meant to incite the government against the MOSOP'. The MOSOP had not invited the people to protest against Wilbros and Shell. Women farmers had acted on their own, in response to a particular situation.

The sycophantic so-called leaders had libelled MOSOP and they knew it. They were deliberately using the government and its coercive instruments against the MOSOP, its leaders and the Ogoni people. This led Edward Kobani to characterize them as 'vultures', a term which stuck for all time. Their action was in contradiction of the agreement reached at Beeri on 17 January 1993 after the first advertisement by the government-paid chiefs. They had succeeded in creating a breach between themselves (a tiny group) and the masses of the Ogoni people led by the MOSOP. This breach was duly exploited by both the government and Shell.

By this time, Babangida and his cronies were churning out a decree, the infamous Treason and Treasonable Felony Decree 1993, which stipulated the death penalty for anyone who 'conspires with himself' to 'utter' the words 'ethnic autonomy' or plans secession or seeks to alter the boundaries of any local government or state previously decreed by the military authorities.

There was no doubt at whom the decree was aimed.

Curiously, Shell's 'Briefing Note' issued at about the same time and accusing me of seeking 'political self-determination' for the Ogoni people (as if that a crime), agreed entirely with Babangida's law:

SHELL BRIEFING NOTE

Tensions in Nigeria

Oil companies are being singled out for attention by activists because of increasing internal tensions in Nigeria. Local community concerns are being taken up by international human rights groups and receiving media attention.

Shell has been active in Nigeria for more than half a century. As operator for a joint venture in which it has a 30 per cent interest, Shell Petroleum Development Company (SPDC) has made a substantial contribution to the economic development of this large and complex African country. It has also contributed to community development.

This Briefing Note explains the background to the current situation and puts the allegations against Shell and other oil companies into perspective.

Background

Nigeria is more than one and a half times the size of France, with a population of more than eighty-eight million. One out of every four Africans south of the Sahara is a Nigerian.

Its government faces great challenges in providing employment and basic services for the thousands of communities which make up the country.

The oil industry generates over 90 per cent of the country's foreign exchange and over 50 per cent of the Federal government's revenue.

Shell has been operating in Nigeria for more than fifty years. SPDC is the largest company in oil and gas exploration and production. It provides about half of the country's oil.

Most of the oil and gas is in small, scattered fields in the Niger River Delta. It is a difficult operating environment, much of it swamps, and the network of pipelines linking the fields would stretch from London to New York in one line.

Tensions

Oil, as Nigeria's main source of revenue, is a highly political subject. The country has suffered serious economic difficulties since the oil price collapse of the mid 1980s.

Unemployment is high among the rural communities in Nigeria, which includes most of the oil-producing areas. Young people, often highly educated, and other groups are frustrated, believing that these oil-producing areas in particular are not getting a fair share of the oil revenues, and are challenging traditional local leadership and government.

SPDC has sympathy for some of their concerns and played its part in persuading the Federal government to double the special fund for the development of the oil-producing areas from 1.5 to 3 per cent.

There is considerable doubt, however, as to how much, if any, of this money reached the people it was intended to help. New, more radical community leaders are emerging who, prevented by law from openly criticizing the government, are targeting Shell.

Some demonstrators have been orderly, but others have been violent. In at least two incidents, protests led to police action which resulted in fatalities.

Shell, as by far the largest international oil company in Nigeria, is a convenient target for those seeking to internationalize the problem. A representative of the Ogoni people, Ken Saro-Wiwa, has been travelling abroad extensively. He has raised the profile of the issue with a number of activist groups, particularly in the Netherlands. Though he is attempting to single out the Ogonis for particular attention, their situation is no different from that of other oil-producing communities in Nigeria.

The case of the Ogonis has been taken up by one of these groups, the Unrepresented Nations and Peoples Organization (UNPO – not a United Nations body).

Allegations

In his public statements Mr Saro-Wiwa accuses Shell of 'waging an ecological war against the Ogonis'. He claims SPDC does not carry out environmental impact studies, does nothing for local communities and refuses to talk with the Ogonis. None of these allegations is true.

SPDC has conducted environmental impact studies on new developments in recent years, and has in place a five-year environmental plan for improving earlier and older installations.

Although community development is a government responsibility, SPDC has been running formal community assistance programmes for more than twenty-five years. These are carried out in consultation with the communities. They include building roads, providing water and health facilities, assisting with agricultural development and offering education scholarships.

Despite the problems of recognizing which claimants are community leaders in times of change, SPDC is involved in discussions with Federal and state authorities and oil-producing and community leaders, including the Ogonis and Mr Saro-Wiwa.

However, Mr Saro-Wiwa has made his ultimate aims clear. He is seeking political 'self-determination' for the Ogoni people, for whom he says he is spokesman. Other Ogonis refute his claim and some only recently have resigned from his movement. Their claim for political self-determination and demands for US ten billion dollars in royalties and reparation have been stated in his correspondence with overseas non-governmental organizations, Nigerian press reports and recently directly with SPDC.

Shell position

The reasons for Mr Saro-Wiwa's attacks on SPDC are therefore clear. He is attempting to use SPDC in his efforts to raise the international profile of his concerns for the Ogoni people and to meet his objective of their political self-determination. At no time has he acknowledged the positive contribution SPDC has made to Nigeria in its many forms. By involving SPDC in his emotive and exaggerated attacks, he wishes to gain the support of international pressure group, whom he is personally visiting in many countries outside Nigeria with the objective of raising pressure on the Federal government of Nigeria.

Despite this, SPDC does sympathize with community concerns and continues to try in every possible way to help promote harmony between the communities, local and Federal government and the oil companies working in these areas.

However, Shell believes that these are Nigerian problems. They should be resolved in Nigeria by agreement between Nigerian people.

SPDC has a programme of continuing improvement to facilities and environmental performance, and of community assistance in infrastructure, health, agriculture and education. This commitment is not cosmetic or token – it is something which has been established over many years.

Further details are available in the leaflet *Nigeria and Shell: Partners in Progress*.

Most of Shell's claims in this 'Briefing Note' as they concern me and the Ogoni people are spurious and undignified. Shell's contribution to community development in Ogoni is negligible and is most insulting when quantified and placed side by side with what the company has taken out of the area or the harm it has caused the environment.

The roads allegedly built by Shell are often to its various locations, through farmland. They have the effect of depriving the Ogoni of much needed farmland and, this may sound funny, force the poor farmers to wear shoes to their farms – a thing they can hardly afford. These so-called roads would not answer such exalted names in Europe.

In Ogoni, Shell locations lie pat in the middle of villages, in front and back gardens – that should lay a particular responsibility on Shell to be absolutely cautious in its operations. The company remains negligent and wilful. In the years from 1958 until MOSOP swung into action in 1993, Shell had had no trouble whatsoever from the Ogoni people. But that is because the people were not organized, not because Shell was acting correctly. When the MOSOP gave voice to the voiceless, Shell persisted in its perverse ways, which had by then become habit. The double standards which the company operated could be easily shown up. There were enough films, magazines and books to show how environmentally conscious Shell was in Europe and America. The story in Nigeria was entirely different.

I agree that Shell's behaviour in Europe and America was dictated by the pressure of environmental groups and the governments of the countries concerned. Given that experience, why did Shell take such great exception to my work and that of the MOSOP? I can only attribute it to the fact that Shell knows that the military dictatorships which have ruled or misruled Nigeria over the years have depended almost entirely on the revenue which Shell generates and are therefore beholden to the company in a very crucial manner. The company therefore adopts a godlike 'we can do no wrong' attitude.

To say that a community leader in Nigeria is prevented by law from openly criticizing the government and therefore targets Shell is not true. Anyone who reads the newspapers in Nigeria will attest to the fact that no matter what laws are enacted, informed Nigerians openly criticize the government. In my case, any of my books or numerous newspaper essays will bear testimony to my wide-ranging, strident and scathing criticism of government. My criticism of Shell was also in the same tradition. Nor was I ever unreasonable.

Indeed, most of the top Nigerian employees of Shell happen to have been my contemporaries at school and university. Some of them have told me privately that they agree with most of the points I have made and that they have raised the same points only to find that they cannot influence company policy, which is invariably dictated from The Hague or London.

I challenge Shell to show the public what environmental impact assessment studies it conducted in Nigeria prior to 1993. To accuse me of 'emotive and exaggerated attacks' is to attempt to deflect attention from my well-laid criticisms of Shell's environmental record. It is cheap propaganda and deserves to be dismissed contemptuously.

It is well known that a boil on one's nose is more painful to the afflicted than an earthquake which happens thousands of miles away killing thousands of people. I am inclined to think that this is why the Ogoni environment must matter more to me than to Shell International ensconced in its ornate offices on the banks of the Thames in London. But I cannot allow the company its smugness because its London comfort spells death to my Ogoni children and compatriots.

I am flattered that Shell should find me deserving of so

much attention. However, they are going after the messenger instead of the message. And there is no doubt in my mind at all that they are on the wrong path and that they will finally admit the truth and thank me for enabling them to create a healthy operational environment in which they can reap the profits which I do not begrudge them. I can only hope that they will not have entirely ruined the Ogoni people by their present obtuseness before that time comes.

I should stress that Shell either completely and deliberately misunderstands my intentions or puts a wrong construction on them for its own mischievous purposes. Let me state here for the avoidance of all doubt that my overall concern is for the fragile ecosystem of the Niger River Delta – one of the richest areas on earth. I am appalled that this rich company, with the abundance of knowledge and material resources available to it, should treat the area with such callous indifference. I consider the loss of the Niger River Delta a loss to all mankind and therefore regard Shell's despoliation of the area as a crime to all humanity.

Ogoni is but a thousand of the 70,000 kilometres of the Niger River Delta. If I have predicated my struggle for the delta environment on Ogoni and the Ogoni people, it is only because I recognize that the argument is an arduous, dangerous and expensive one. Ogoni is a good laboratory to make the experiments which will apply to the delta as a whole. My methodology is scientific. Besides, my political argument is predicated on ethnic self-reliance. The delta is host to about twenty different people and cultures. The success of the Ogoni is bound to influence all the others positively in the same direction – and, by implication, the rest of Nigeria. Thus, Shell errs and misunderstands me woefully when it seeks to categorize my endeavours as some localized action by a self-proclaimed 'Spokesman' of the Ogoni People.

If, indeed, Shell thinks of me as not representing Ogoni

interests, why does ɪ
I agree that I did have
eral Manager, Eastern Dɪ
Udofia. At that meeting I prᴇ
and urged the company to looᴋ
know which of the demands it cᴏ
the future or not at all. I had one oᴛ
Wnaemeka Achebe, the General Manaᵍ
Lagos office. I have known Mr Achebe for　　　　　　ᵈ
have the highest regard for him. Regrettably, tɪ　　　ᵈ did
not bear much fruit because, I suspect, company ᵧ ᴄy dictated from London and The Hague was that MOSOP and
myself should be regarded as pariahs and treated as such.

I am aware that Shell often prefers to deal with its problems secretly and outside of public purview. Unfortunately,
where the Niger River Delta (and Ogoni) environment is
concerned, the issue is public because the neglect of the past
is of enormous proportions and remediation will be expensive. Shell's shareholders might well need to know in advance
what their Nigerian operations are going to cost their
pocketbooks.

I should also state that I have the support of at least 98
per cent of the Ogoni people in the struggle for Ogoni survival. To them, their environment is their first right and the
struggle for it takes precedence over all else. And that puts
Shell on the first firing line, even before the Nigerian military
dictators.

The amount of compensation demanded by the Ogoni
people is peanuts and this shall be proved when an environmental audit is done to determine how much damage Shell
has done. If one spill from the *Exxon Valdez* could cost
Exxon five billion dollars in punitive damages, Shell must
pay more than the four billion dollars which the Ogoni
have demanded in reparation for the ecological damage to

...nd over a 35-year period in which there
...s, blow-outs and continual gas flaring.

...es, Shell knows that royalty is, by definition, what is
paid to a landlord for mineral extracted from his land. When
Shell pays 20 per cent in royalties and rents to the Nigerian
government, and turns round to thump its chest because it
has encouraged the government to pay the landlords 3 per
cent instead of 20, then there must be something really
wrong with the policy of the company.

Shell knows, for instance, how much it pays the Shetlands
Council in the UK annually in taxes, just for siting oil tanks
in Sullum Voe. Knowing how much it pays, by comparison,
to the Ogoni local government councils, the company should
be ashamed to join issues with the Ogoni people on this
matter.

The good thing is that the Ogoni people now know and
will no longer be taken on a ride by Shell. No matter how
hard the company tries to wriggle out of it, they will have to
confront the truth of their Ogoni operations soon. And then
they will find that indifference and double standards are
expensive items for a multinational interested in world-wide
operations. Shell must compensate the Ogoni people fully
for their losses.

Shell should adopt the path of dialogue. MOSOP has left
its doors open for such dialogue. In the interest of both
parties.

But to return to my story, I do not, as a rule, watch Nigerian
television. I find it boring and its news programme too time-
consuming, lasting almost a full hour while delivering little.
But on the night of 4 May I did tune in, fortuitously, to the
eleven o'clock news summary. And I heard the Federal
Attorney-General and Minister of Justice Mr Clement Ak-
pamgbo say in reply to a question as to whether the decree

was aimed at me and the Ogoni people, that if the cap fitted, we should wear it. I was quite unperturbed. In the quest for justice for my people, neither prison nor the threat of death nor death itself could ever deter me. A few days later we received a call to make another visit to Abuja.

On the first occasion, as I have related, Dr Leton, Edward Kobani and I had been asked to see the newly appointed Director-General of the SSS, Mr Peter Ndiokwu. A personable, impeccably dressed young man seated in a glittering office in the outsized SSS headquarters building structured in the wasteful fashion of the new offices of Abuja, he had read us the riot act, and we had asked for justice and understanding.

When next we visited, he asked, at the prompting of his subordinate, Mr Terebor, that we should allow Shell to lay its pipeline in Ogoni. We could not promise that. When he mentioned that my writing could get me into detention, although he personally did not like to apply such measures, I assured him that all my writings were usually carefully considered, that I took full responsibility for them and that I would accept all consequences resulting therefrom. I told him that detention only makes writers stronger.

On the occasion of our third visit in early May, we were accompanied by Albert Badey, who had begun to attend the meetings of the Steering Committee of the MOSOP. The first man to raise doubts as to his presence at our meetings was Edward Kobani, who expressed reservations privately to me of Albert's good faith. He said that he knew for a fact that Albert was meeting regularly with the group that had denounced MOSOP publicly after the shootings at the end of April.

But I assured him that I thought Albert's talents would be very useful to the committee. I truly thought that Edward was merely transferring the rivalry of Bodo, their common homeplace, where divisions were deep and complicated, to the committee. And I was not going to allow that to happen. With the twenty-twenty vision of hindsight, I now realize that I was wrong. Albert's mission was to disrupt the MOSOP. Who sent him remains a mystery to me.

Our third trip to Abuja brought us face to face with the power behind the throne: Brigadier-General Halilu Akilu, head of the National Intelligence Agency, Major-General Aliyu Mohammed, National Security Adviser, and Alhaji Aliyu Mohammed, Secretary to the Federal military government. Speaking with them at the glittering presidential palace, I had the feeling that Big Brother was listening in on a hidden television screen.

The discussion went quite well. Major-General Aliyu Mohammed is a very genial man, and we shared a common friend in Colonel Sani Bello, whom I had met in Bonny during the civil war and who became a family friend. General Aliyu showed sympathy for our case, as did Akilu, whom I had also known before then. They expressed surprise when we showed them the ethnic make-up of Rivers State. It became clear to them that we were also being oppressed at state level. I believe that they had initially thought that all people from Rivers State were one.

They gave the impression that they wanted to do something and did ask that we provide a list of all unemployed Ogoni youths and information on how oil-bearing areas in other parts of the country are treated by their governments. They also asked that we indicate once again in writing precisely what we wanted. We parted on joking terms, General Aliyu assuring us that our next meeting would depend on receipt of the information they had demanded.

When we returned to Port Harcourt, a delegation was sent by the MOSOP Steering Committee to Governor Ada

George to complain about the silence of his government on the shootings that had occurred in Biara. The delegation consisted of the elderly members of the committee along with Ledum Mitee.

The delegation returned to inform us that upon the pleas of Governor Ada George, who apparently went on his knees to them, they had agreed to allow Shell to lay its pipelines and to accept compensation for the wounded and the dead of the Biara incident.

The steering committee members were angry at this, as the delegation did not have a mandate to come to a decision on its behalf or on behalf of the Ogoni people. The deal was rejected outright. And the gerontocrats were furious. Their reputations, they argued, were at stake. Whose fault we might ask? Here was another sign of trouble.

The first sign had occurred when Babangida in one of his famous U-turns suddenly lifted the ban on old politicians and both Edward Kobani and Dr Leton became free to take part in party politics. We had agreed that in the interest of the MOSOP, none of its top officials should do so, as that would leave them open to partisanship and divide the members of the movement.

In defiance of the agreement, Edward Kobani decided to contest the post of Chairman of the Rivers State branch of the Social Democratic Party. Luckily for us, he crashed, beaten by a chap young enough to be his son. It was a disgrace which he might have avoided.

Then, Dr Leton, also in defiance of our agreement, decided that he would become a delegate to the National Convention of the Social Democratic Party. He had already won a delegate seat before we became aware of what he was up to. At a meeting of the steering committee, the danger to MOSOP of what this meant was brought to his notice. He gave the impression that he would comply with our wishes and stand down. He reneged on his word and duly attended the convention.

At this stage, our advice was to get both of them voted out of their positions as Vice-President and President respectively, which the steering committee would surely have done. But on consideration of the danger of tearing the movement apart, we decided to leave them in their positions. This was an error. Both men were becoming a liability, and their decision to allow the construction of the Shell pipeline against the desire of the steering committee was adding to our burdens.

I had to travel to London for family reasons and went off in the middle of May. My passport was confiscated at the airport, and I missed the flight on which I had been booked. A midnight phone call to Major-General Aliyu Mohammed, the National Security Adviser, ensured that I retrieved the passport and enabled me to travel the following night.

On arrival in London, the Secretariat of UNPO at The Hague felt that in view of the Treason and Treasonable Felony Decree 1993 which hung on my neck like a millstone, I should travel to make objections to the decree known in Europe. I did meet with Foreign Office desk officers in the Netherlands, Switzerland and Britain, and with officials of the United Nations Human Rights Commission and the International Commission of Jurists in Geneva. This was, as expected, transmitted to Abuja. The men in power did not like it. I also gave an interview to CNN which, I guess, did not please Abuja either.

Before I could return to Nigeria, news came that Dr Leton, Edward Kobani and Albert Badey were doing all in their power to convince the Ogoni people to allow the construction of the Shell pipeline to proceed. I made my objections known to them, sending an emissary from my Lagos office to deliver a personal message to them. As fate would have it, the local people would not hear of the completion of the pipeline either.

I returned to Port Harcourt at the beginning of June, ten or so days before the presidential elections scheduled for 12 June. As early as February I had mooted the idea of our having to boycott the elections in pursuance of the non-violent struggle for our rights. The idea had been well received by several members of the steering committee, the party politicians excepted. Dr Bennet Birabi had spent almost an hour on the telephone from Abuja to me in London on 29 May to convince me that an election boycott would not be in HIS political interests. I advised him to come to the next MOSOP Steering Committee meeting, where the matter would be discussed.

A meeting of the committee was scheduled for 2 June, the day after my arrival. Both 1 and 2 June were Muslim holidays and I did not meet any of the members of the committee before the meeting, which took place as usual in the residence of Dr Leton.

I placed before the meeting a motion that we boycott the elections. The motion was hotly debated, and in the end Dr Leton as Chairman decided, after pressure by Edward Kobani, to put it to the vote. The boycotters won by eleven votes to six. Kobani immediately gave notice that he would not accept the majority decision, even if he had to resign as Vice-President. He had become Vice-President some time in February (at a meeting which I did not attend, being away in Europe or Lagos) in place of Mr L. L. Lah-Loolo, who had refused to take the position or even join the MOSOP Steering Committee.

Two days later I was in my Aggrey Road office in the morning when in trooped Dr Leton, Edward Kobani, Albert Badey, Titus Nwieke, who was Treasurer of MOSOP, and Engineer Apenu. Their purpose was to convince me to rescind the decision of the steering committee to boycott the elections. I did not see my way through that and told them so. A democratic decision had been taken and it was our responsibility to carry it out. They left my office after a hot exchange, as angry as they could be. Both Dr Leton and Edward Kobani informed me that they would be resigning. It was up to them, I said, and there rested the matter.

I was due to travel to Vienna to attend the United Nations World Conference on Human Rights scheduled for 11 June. Before leaving for Lagos en route to Vienna, I travelled through Ogoni to place before the people the decision of the steering committee to boycott the presidential elections. Everywhere I went, the decision was applauded and upheld. At each place I advised that there was to be no violence on election day, and that those who wanted to vote should not be obstructed from doing so. I expected that the turn-out for the election would help us decide the popularity or otherwise of MOSOP.

I held a press conference as 'spokesman' of the Ogoni People to explain to the nation why we would be boycotting the elections:

Gentlemen of the Press,

I have called you here this morning to inform you of the decision of the Ogoni people to boycott the presidential election of 12 June, in confirmation of the non-violent struggle launched by the Ogoni people on 4 January 1993 against the planned genocide of the Ogoni by the Nigerian nation-state.

The decision is informed by the fact that section 42(3) of the constitution of the Federal Republic of Nigeria (1989) discriminates against the Ogoni people as an oil-producing section of the country, expropriates their land and resources, does not protect them as a minority of 500,000 people in a country of eighty million, and consigns them to extinction. Secondly, the political structure designed by the departing military and inserted by them into the said constitution condemns the Ogoni to second-class citizenship and denies them their fundamental human rights to self-determination, which rights are enjoyed by other Nigerians.

As you are all aware, the 1989 constitution was not subjected to a referendum and the methods of the constituent assembly were, to say the least, inimical to democracy.

Since the election of 12 June will produce a President who will swear to protect the diseased and undemocratic constitution of 1989, the Ogoni have decided that to vote in that election will be to vote for slavery, genocide and extinction.

The Ogoni boycott is also meant to emphasize the demands of the Ogoni people on the government and people of Nigeria as detailed in the Ogoni Bill of Rights of 1990 for (a) the right to political control of Ogoni affairs by Ogoni people (b) the right to the control and use of Ogoni economic resources for Ogoni development (c) the right to protect the Ogoni environment and ecology from further degradation and (d) adequate and direct representation as of right in all Nigerian national institutions including the armed forces.

The Ogoni people demand the immediate convening of a sovereign national conference to discuss reforms of the existing political and constitutional system and to redress the balance of power in the country so that ethnic minorities in the nation-state can exercise all those rights conferred by the African Charter of Human and Peoples Rights and the United Nations Bill of Rights to which Nigeria is a signatory.

I wish also to inform you that these views have been presented to the international community, which has expressed its concern and its support for the Ogoni people.

I went off to Lagos on 7 June to complete arrangements to

enable me to travel to Vienna. Delay in receipt of my airline ticket kept me in Lagos longer than expected. During that time I got a telephone call informing me that the radio in Port Harcourt had been announcing, in my name, that the Ogoni people would vote in the elections, contrary to the decisions that had been taken by the MOSOP Steering Committee and approved by the people. I issued a prompt denial.

In any case, the activists on the ground had not been deceived by the announcement, which they knew to be a dirty trick. They therefore went into action in Ogoni to ensure that the trick did not succeed and that the people were not deceived.

I was to come to learn later while in police custody at Owerri that the Ogoni party politicians, including Dr Leton, Edward Kobani and Bennet Birabi, had met and resolved to make the public announcement in my name. It was essentially a forgery. And believe it or not, Dr Leton told me about it with a straight face, in the presence of an inspector of police, Mr Ledum Mitee, Dr Birabi and Mr Simeon Idemyor, my cousin. Dr Birabi had written my name in his own hand beneath the announcement.

I have to state that I was shocked beyond belief by Dr Leton's revelation of the dirty trick. I had a very high opinion of him. I had met him first at the University of Nigeria, where he was lecturing in chemistry in 1967 when I went there as a graduate assistant a few months before the outbreak of the Nigerian civil war. A big man, handsome, well built and highly intelligent, he struck me at the time as the quintessential Ogoni man. He had studied at the Methodist Boys High School, Oron, and the Hope Waddell Training Institute before he proceeded to the University of London to take a first and a doctorate in chemistry.

For all his education, he was very much wedded to Ogoni culture. He could sing and dance to traditional Ogoni songs in a way which few of the educated elite in Ogoni could ever equal. And he won my heart.

During my seven-month stay at Nsukka, he subsidized my meals at his house on the campus. At the outbreak of the civil war, he got involved in the Biafran war effort on the scientific side. When the war ended, he returned to Port Harcourt and, as he had indicated that he did not wish to return to academia, I began to involve him in the affairs of the Rivers State government, appointing him Chairman of a committee which studied the establishment of the state's first tertiary educational institution. I also helped him get a loan from the Rivers State Rehabilitation Committee, which he use to set up a furniture factory.

Garrick Leton would shine wherever he might be. He had shown much brilliance through secondary school and University, and in Rivers State; he soon became a Commissioner (Minister) and was later appointed to the Federal Cabinet as Federal Commissioner for Education and later, Commissioner for Establishment Matters in the Obasanjo regime.

In the following civilian regime of Alhaji Shehu Shagari, he held office as Chairman of the National Fertilizer Company of Nigeria when the fertilizer plant was being set up in Ogoni. He often joked that he was not a politician, but liked to profit by politics.

For all that, I did feel that he was politically naïve. An honest man, he was not one to tamper with funds, but I often thought that he was not in tune with the Nigerian politics with which he toyed, and that he was probably not meant for it. I often wished that he had remained within academia. The generality of the Ogoni were not happy with him, thinking that in all of the positions which he held, he had not been helpful to them. In short, he had not behaved like the Nigerian politician who would always use public office to help his kith and kin.

I was personally not worried about that, my only doubt about him being that if he weren't part of the leadership of an Ogoni outfit, he was wont to destroy it. Indeed, this was the reason I prayed that he would lead MOSOP once we had set it up. What I did not count on was that his political education, or the lack of it, would force him and us into errors along the way, and that he would then look for a way to ruin the movement. This Mr Lah-Loolo had predicted and given as a reason for not assuming the vice-presidency of the organization.

As he confirmed the dirty trick that had been played on the Ogoni people that day, I wept inwardly for him, and for Bennet Birabi on whom I had invested so much emotion and my lean resources at an earlier time.

But to get back to my story, on the night of 11 June I was on my way to Vienna to attend the United Nations Human Rights Conference when my passport was again confiscated at the airport and I was not able to travel. I was the only Nigerian barred from the conference. I had, however, sent the materials for a planned photographic exhibition of the environmental degradation of Ogoni in advance and other Ogoni activists including Ledum Mitee did travel to Vienna. So all was well from an Ogoni point of view. I resented the denial of my rights, of course, but that could wait. The Vienna Conference was useful to the Ogoni because Ledum Mitee met Anita Roddick there, thanks to the UNPO. Anita Roddick and her organization, Bodyshop, were later to play a very important role in the Ogoni struggle.

I was in Lagos on 12 June and was by the television at night to hear of the boycott of the elections in Ogoni and of a minor fracas in the town of Yeghe involving Dr Bennet Birabi.

Apparently, as I was to learn when I got back to Port Harcourt and investigated the fracas, on the morning of the elections, finding that even the people in his hometown, Yeghe, had resolved not to vote, Bennet summoned them to the town square and publicly berated them. The answer of the people was that he hadn't spoken to them since he won his last election. And they wondered why he would get them together only because an election from which he hoped to benefit was due. In effect, they gave him notice that they were not prepared to be exploited politically, not even by a local politician. The meeting ended in a public disgrace for Bennet, who was, at the time, the Senate Minority Leader. But the people weren't finished with him. Just in case in the usual dishonest manner of the Nigerian politician ballot boxes were being stuffed in his house, some of his own relations went to his home to check. And that is where one of his aides sustained a minor injury.

I also learnt that Ogoni youths in various locations physically stopped the movement of ballot boxes, and also of some politicians such as Edward Kobani, who was forced to remain indoors throughout the period of voting. Some young men even stopped election materials from being delivered by the Electoral Commission, turning back vehicles which carried such materials.

All of which I very much regret, since this is not the sort of boycott we had envisaged. But the fault must be put squarely at the door of Dr Bennet Birabi, Dr Leton, Edward Kobani and all those other politicians who conspired to forge my signature on a document to which I was not privy, hoping thus to use the great confidence which the Ogoni people have in my leadership for their own benefit. I have sued the radio station and all those involved in that forgery, since the police have refused to act on the complaints made to them about it. I must also say that the refusal of the Ogoni people to be exploited by their politicians indicates the success of our mobilization efforts and the political education of the Ogoni people. The Ogoni people have always known what was right, but sometimes lacked the leadership that would encourage them to stick by that. What MOSOP had done was to empower them.

The next day, Sunday, 13 June, Nigeria's national newspapers were full of the news of the Ogoni boycott. The Ogoni had made the point that they would not accept slavery and extinction, or for that matter the legalization of the expropriation of their resources, which is what the constitution (under which the elections were being held) stipulated.

I was as proud as a peacock that Sunday. I felt that no matter what happened, the Ogoni people had redeemed themselves. At long last!

CHAPTER EIGHT

The success, so far, of the non-violent struggle of the Ogoni people led me, invariably, to think of the possible implications for the rest of Nigeria and, indeed for black Africa. For the continent is made up of nation-states conceived in the European colonialist interest for European imperial or commercial purposes. In virtually every nation-state are several 'Ogonis' – despairing and disappearing peoples suffering the yoke of political marginalization, economic strangulation or environmental degradation, or a combination of these, unable to lift a finger to save themselves. What is their future?

In 1884 European powers had gathered in Berlin to carve up the African continent along water courses and lines of longitude and latitude on a map. I have often pictured to myself the scene at the conference table where it all happened and ground my teeth at the little realized consequences of the actions of the conferees on unsuspecting African peoples and nations, the victims of that exercise. Peoples got separated willy-nilly, coming under the different administrations of different European nations; old African empires were destroyed in the new structures which resulted from the misadventure, and several cultures were thenceforth forced to live under the same roof, so to speak.

The partition of Africa was to be followed by the pacification of peoples who either dared to protest the new imposition or had to be brought under the new colonial administration. In the heyday of the idea of the nation-state in Europe, new African nation-states came into being. European will, European desires were always the underlying factors. The pacification exercise meant the destruction of peoples, of ways of life, and it took different forms in different regions of black Africa.

The resultant effect on various peoples and cultures is a subject well deserving of study but this is not the place for it.

I do not suggest that the colonial experience was only destructive. It may well have enhanced and improved some peoples, freeing them from local tyrannies and offering them new opportunities. However, the overall effect is there for us to see today, as African nation-states reel under seemingly insoluble social, political and economic burdens.

The African nation-state owed its continued existence under colonial rule to the coercion of the colonizing power. In the case of Nigeria, about 200 different peoples and cultures whose major link is skin colour were brought together under a single administration for the first time in 1914. Under colonial rule, the clash of peoples was controlled by administrative fiat. Well, not quite: the clash of cultures remained an undercurrent while colonial rule lasted and afterwards. With the advent of political independence in the 1960s, the clash of peoples and cultures moved into a more prominent position. It could only be controlled by the use of coercive force, which the new elite which inherited the colonial mantle readily used. This explains the prevalence on the continent of military dictatorships or civilian dictatorships bolstered by armies bequeathed by the departing European colonialists.

I have outlined elsewhere (in my book *Genocide in Nigeria: The Ogoni Tragedy*) the experience of the Ogoni people in the twentieth century. Briefly put, it is a tale of administrative neglect, of exploitation and slavery in which the British colonial administration, the newly emergent Nigerian nation-state, the rulers thereof and, signally, the multi-national oil giant Shell have had a role to play. The Ogoni have, themselves, unwittingly lent a hand to their denigration, as is usual among indigenous peoples on the way to extinction.

The Ogoni first came into contact with the British in 1901. A column of armed African men under the command of a young British officer raiding Ogoni villages sporadically between 1908 and 1913 was enough to 'pacify' the Ogoni and to destroy the social fabric of their society. The Ogoni were absorbed into the Nigerian nation-state in 1914. Thereafter, the British administrator billeted hundreds of miles away did not bother to establish anything whatsoever in Ogoni, except that an Irish missionary, belonging to the Primitive Methodist Mission, began to work among the Ogoni and was soon followed by African missionaries of other religious denominations.

Twenty-five years after their first arrival, the local British administrators were conscience-stricken by their neglect of 'this large tribe' and sent in the lone British administrator (District Officer) who began to get the Ogoni to cut roads, build court houses and pay their taxes to a central, local administration. Even then, the effort was half-hearted. The Ogoni did not benefit from any infusion of funds from outside, and it was to take all of nearly fifty years before the Ogoni, in 1947, were able to get an administration called 'Native Authority' devoted entirely to their own affairs. Thenceforth, their taxes could be devoted solely to their development, overseen by their chiefs and leaders. Alas, too late! Constitutional developments in the wider Nigerian nation of which they were only a nominal part had left them far behind. They found themselves in an administrative set-up, a 'region', called Eastern Nigeria – one of the three regions into which Nigeria had been carved in 1951. By 1956 the

Native Authority system was duly scrapped and the Ogoni had had less than ten years of some form of limited autonomy in which they could do things for themselves.

The important thing in the foregoing is that things were happening to the Ogoni. Everything happened to them: colonization, pacification, absorption into Nigeria, allocation into Eastern Nigeria. And more was to come, none more important than the arrival of the drilling rigs of Shell in 1956 and the commencement of oil production and pollution in 1958. Then, in 1960, Nigerian independence.

As Nigeria celebrated independence, the Ogoni were consigned to political slavery at the hands of the new black colonialists wearing the mask of Nigerianism. The new Nigerian masquerade was in the public arena, leashed to a rope held by an unseen hand, and steadied by the oil of the Ogoni and other peoples in the Niger River Delta. In effect, the producers of that oil, the multinational oil giants, truly controlled the masquerade in the arena. And if any child dared do more than enjoy the dance of the masquerade, it was liable to be frightened to death by it.

The image of the masquerade dancing in a public arena is one which an African can relate to quite easily. In the masquerade is a man, an ordinary human being subject to the usual humours which afflict humanity. Yet, once he wears a mask, he is transformed into something else, something dangerous. The masquerade can perpetrate evil, hurt spectators. And that is why when a masquerade engages in more than its share of evil, brave spectators are allowed to disrobe it. The mask falls from its wearer and the puny man in the masquerade is seen for what he truly is: all flesh and blood, the son of so-and-so. This unmasking of the cruel masquerader is very important. But it is a difficult task.

By 1966, six years after the attainment of independence, the Nigerian masquerade was running amok in the public arena. The clash of cultures and peoples which I alluded to earlier was leading to catastrophe. The three biggest ethnic groups in Nigeria, the Hausa, the Igbo and the Yoruba, were at each other's throats. The oil of the Ogoni and other small ethnic nations in the Niger River Delta fuelled the feud and, predictably, the Ogoni were to suffer as grass in the fight of the elephants. In the civil war which raged between 1967 and 1970, an estimated 30,000 Ogoni people, about 10 per cent of the population, died, most of them in the refugee camps in the Igbo heartland to which they had been forcibly evacuated on the orders of Ojukwu, the Igbo warlord.

One result of the war for the Ogoni is that they were now grouped into a Rivers State (Nigeria having been split into twelve states as a way to blunt the Biafran secessionist threat). Within the context of Rivers State, the Ogoni could make much more progress than was possible in an asphyxiating Eastern Nigeria, with its massive, all-powerful Igbo majority. Some Ogoni did manage to acquire an education and to begin to function within the Nigerian nation in a limited way. But Nigeria was headed in the wrong direction. The nation was not about to care for its minority ethnic groups or to allow the producers of oil to enjoy the benefits thereof. It was to remain a slave society in which jungle law predominated, allowing survival only to the fittest, the more numerous ethnic groups. And the men who controlled the means of violence, the military bosses, were headed for the spoils of war: the rich oil-find in the Niger River Delta.

By 1990 the Nigerian masquerade had become a real pain to the Ogoni, the more painful because Ogoni resources had gone to dress it up. And in the masquerade were bungling soldiers who mouthed platitudes about Nigerian unity and all such while they purloined the Ogoni and others.

It had become painfully clear, after thirty years of independence, that the main thing which bound the various ethnic groups constituting the Nigerian nation was skin colour, apart from the commercial interests of the erstwhile colonial master. And skin colour is not strong enough to stop the oppression of one group by another. Sometimes it reinforces oppression because it makes it less obvious. White people oppressing blacks in South Africa draws instant condemnation because it is seen to be racial. But black upon black oppression merely makes people shrug and say, 'Well, it's their business, isn't it?'

No one could hope to disrobe the masquerade without finding out the views of those who held its leash. Accordingly, I found time to brief the British High Commissioner in Lagos on my views and on what I purposed to do. Shell in Nigeria is controlled by the British arm of the multinational, although it is not really as simple as that; Shell's organization is as complex and convoluted as they come. But it is enough that some recent Managing Directors of Shell Nigeria have risen to become Managing Director and Chief Executive of Shell International based in London. Nigeria produces 14 per cent of Shell's total oil output. Shell's profit from its Nigerian operations is said to be on the very high side. Which should surprise no one. Shell does not spend as much on environmental protection, salaries and health care as it does in other countries where the company operates. So, indeed, Shell matters a great deal to the British government. And Shell's Nigerian operations tie in neatly with the British government's overwhelming interest in Africa's largest nation and market, its former colony.

My contact with the British High Commission and subsequently with the Foreign and Commonwealth Office in London was minimal, exploratory, and in the case of the Foreign and Commonwealth Office, at low level, but it was enough to enable me to form the impression that there was a mind-set about Nigeria. Stability seemed to be their credo, stability to ensure continued economic 'co-operation', for which read exploitation. In that sense, an Ogoni argument was a minor irritant. Nor did it have a chance of success unless it was backed by, wait for it, Shell. But in fairness to those I met, I should say that they listened patiently, and pointed me to that other great institution of the British: the liberal lobby. Which was how I came into contact with the Parliamentary Human Rights Group headed by Lord Avebury, and thence to other non-governmental organizations interested in human rights.

As with the British, so with the Dutch and the Swiss whom I had the opportunity to meet on one or two occasions in their home offices. They were even further removed from the problem, the Dutch interest being pre-eminently connected with Shell. In effect, the problems of Nigeria, of Africa, were not really on the table. The tribal problems that were important were those of the disintegrated Soviet Union or of Yugoslavia. Europe itself had sorted out its tribal problems much earlier and was now dedicated to supervising other peoples, ensuring that there was enough stability all round to allow the business of economic exploitation for greater European comfort to proceed apace.

No, there would not be help for the Ogoni from European officialdom until there was a radical change of government policy. The danger was that a change of policy might move in a direction opposite to what I was proposing, based on my experience of Nigerian life. As William Ptaff asserts, it is now the convention in right-thinking Western circles that Africa's tribes and ethnic groups are repressive colonial inventions and that nothing significant distinguishes Zulu from Xhosa, Masai from Kikuyu, or Tutsi from Hutu, notwithstanding the reactionary western sciences of ethnology and anthropology. Right thinking! What absolute balderdash. Even more unforgivable is Ali Mazrui, whose very sharp intellect lets him down when he proposes the re-establishment of the old League of Nations trusteeship system, with African and Asian nations among those appointed by the United Nations to govern certain countries under the guidance of a council of major African states which would possess a peace-keeping army. Again, an army. And 'major African states' such as Nigeria, no doubt. Perish the thought.

Robert Heilbroner, in *The Future as History: The Historic Currents of Our Time and the Direction in which They are Taking America (1960)*, says

> imperialism imposed on its colonies the raw economic drive of capitalism without the social and political underpinnings and protections which blunted that drive at home ... Into [the] primitive circulation of life a powerful and dangerous virus was injected with terrible effect. It turned millions of traditionally self-sufficient peasants into rubber-tappers, coffee-growers, tin miners, tea-pickers – and then subjected this new agricultural and mining proletariat to the incomprehensible vagaries of world commodity fluctuations. It uprooted ancient laws and gave in exchange Western justice, whose ideas disrupted the local culture by striking at the roots of time-honoured traditions and customs ... Colonialism, even in its most missionary moments, never succeeded in seeing the 'natives' as equals, and it usually simply took for granted their irremediable inferiority.

Well said, in general. Applied to the Ogoni, we should say British imperialism imposed on them oil exploitation and the Nigerian nation-state, both powerful and dangerous forces which together spelt omnicide in Ogoni.

Unlike William Ptaff and Ali Mazrui, I do not think that the remedy for what Robert Heilbroner describes is a return to European or United Nations colonialism. Based on my experience of Ogoni life, I can confidently say that it is still possible to return to 'the local culture', to 'time-honoured traditions and customs', in short, to re-create societies which have been destroyed by European colonialism, neo-colonialism, or the newly inspired and even more destructive 'black colonialism'. And that what we needs must do is examine each society critically, identify the motive spirit of its being and mobilize its people to new horizons.

I do not think that there is any ethnic group in Nigeria which cannot survive on its own. Far from being 'repressive colonial inventions', Africa's tribes and ethnic groups are ancient and enduring social organizations complete with their own mores and visions, which no colonialism has been able to destroy over the centuries. The African nation-state as presently conceived has only succeeded in stultifying them, in denying them their vital force and limiting their capacity for self-reliance.

The men who argued for Nigerian independence, and particularly Obafemi Awolowo, clearly knew the foregoing and argued convincingly that the only way forward for Nigeria was to allow each ethnic group to exercise autonomy and grow at its own pace using its genius and its political system. The British colonialist, rather than allow this, created a federation of 'regions', each region being run as a unitary state. Thus, there was 'unitarism' at regional level and 'federalism' at the centre. This predictably came to grief, because in the regions there were ethnic groups struggling for autonomy, while at the centre the regions fought each other for control of the commonwealth of Nigeria. When this resulted in disastrous civil war, an attempt was made, through the creation of states, to return to a proper federation of ethnic groups. Had this process been carried to its logical conclusion, Nigeria might have seen progress. However, the Nigerian military foolishly turned back the hands of the clock and returned Nigeria to a *de facto* unitary state, while proclaiming the nation still a federation. The state creation exercise was soon turned into an instrument of internal colonialism. The Hausa got split into eight states, the Yoruba into six, and the Igbo into four. Meanwhile, the smaller ethnic groups were herded into unitary states, where they continue to suffer political and social discrimination. Thus, a group like the Ogoni, rich and viable as a unit, capable of practising self-reliance, find themselves in Rivers State, where they have to scramble for survival with nine other ethnic groups who are together marginalized by the Nigerian centre.

When I started the MOSOP one of my purposes was to draw attention to this unholy alliance between oil interests and the Nigerian military, which enforces military or even civilian dictatorship over Nigerian democracy as well as the vital force of Nigerian federalism and individual Nigerian ethnic groups.

I was aware of the success, in the past, of the mobilization movements which had been based on the ethnic group. In the fifties, Dr Nnamdi Azikiwe had successfully mobilized the Igbo, Chief Obafemi Awolowo the Yoruba, Ahmadu Bello the Hausa-Fulani and Tarka the Tiv. This mobilization effort had not been stopped by the British. It had, indeed, brought Nigerian independence sooner rather than later.

Unfortunately for the Ogoni, their mobilization was being opposed by the military dictatorship in Nigeria and their allies. Whether we would succeed was still to be seen.

I think that should the Ogoni movement succeed, it will point a way to the rest of Nigeria, if not Africa. While I agree that the borders imposed by 1884 Berlin are not perfect, I am not anxious at this time to re-draw them. I believe that the nation-states as they currently stand can be allowed to exist, but within them there must be the practice of federalism based on the ethnic groups. Each ethnic group must be mobilized and taught to be self-reliant. And each must be allowed to grow at its own pace, politically and economically. Each must be allowed to control its environment and economy. Hence, as I have said previously, I call for the practice of ERECTISM – Ethnic Autonomy, Resource and Environmental Control – within each nation-state which must be run as a federation. This is the way forward for Africa. But will Europe and the multinationals who control Africa's wealth allow it? Because that would mean progress for Africa and I am still to be convinced that the West and their multinational corporations do not want African progress. They want Africa to remain at their feet. It seems to me that only the liberals in the West want African progress, and they aren't in power.

It has been asked in Nigeria if we could have successfully mobilized the Ogoni if there had not been oil, a devastated environment which would win world attention, and a small, easily organized population, quite apart from the factor of my presence as a writer, and a highly committed one with some financial independence. My answer is that where there is a will, there is a way. Indeed, the presence of oil and a devastated environment have made the task of mobilization even more difficult. These twin evils have drawn the ire of the Nigerian military dictatorship upon the Ogoni. Dividing the Ogoni, overtly and covertly, the better to be able to rule them, has become a credo. And this is what threatens to destroy the Ogoni movement. Had these elements been absent, mobilization would have been much easier, more effective. All it would have needed is a leader (who will always emerge) capable of pointing a people to their ability to survive in the past, and the need for survival in the future. Oil pointed to the possibility of economic viability but we were always aware that brains are more important than mineral resources, and that is why one of the slogans I devised for MOSOP is 'We must use our brains!'

Certainly, what we have done for the Ogoni can be done for other groups in Nigeria, in Africa. Its importance lies in the fact that a small ethnic group has not only been prepared psychologically to confront its history and take its fortune into its hands, but is prepared to take on its oppressors in the form of the nation-state and a multinational oil giant.

It is also very important that we have chosen the path of non-violent struggle. Our opponents are given to violence and we cannot meet them on their turf, even if we wanted to. Non-violent struggle offers weak people the strength which they otherwise would not have. The spirit becomes important, and no gun can silence that. I am aware, though, that non-violent struggle occasions more death than armed struggle. And that remains a cause for worry at all times. Whether the Ogoni people will be able to withstand the rigours of the struggle is yet to be seen. Again, their ability to do so will point the way of peaceful struggle to other peoples on the African continent. It is therefore not to be underrated.

CHAPTER NINE

So much for the thoughts which ran through my mind as I waited in the detention cell (for cell I must call it) of the Nigerian police at Owerri. One week had gone and our captors had still not returned, nor was there word as to what would happen to us.

I had instructed Barry Kumbe to go to court to demand our release. He went to work immediately but was not making progress. No judge in Rivers State was willing to sign the writs. Wherever Barry went in the state, he was told that there had been a red alert on me and all cases related to me. Of course, we might have pursued the case which we had filed in Lagos. But the Lagos courts were not sitting, since all Lagos lawyers had decided that they would boycott the law courts in protest against the annulment of the 12 June selections. What to do?

Barry decided to file the case in Owerri where we were being held. There, he had no problems whatsoever and the hearing was fixed for early July, by which time we would have been in detention for almost ten days. At this time, Ledum Mitee was away in Vienna, where he had gone to attend the United Nations World Human Rights Conference.

Our captors returned a week and a day after we had been in Owerri. The presence of Mr Ogbeifun and his man Friday had not yet started to give me a running stomach. When he came in that afternoon, I still thought that he was doing a job for which he had some distaste. At that moment, I had in the cell Bishop Poromon, the Methodist Bishop of Port Harcourt, an Ogoni man. There were others with him, including Mina, my friend, who had brought me food, and my personal assistant, Mr Deebii Nwiado, who had come to brief me on his journey to Vienna.

No sooner did Mr Ogbeifun come in than he started to bully me. Why were there others in the cell? Well, he could tolerate the presence of the man of God, but the rest, goodness, he could not, would not tolerate. I seemed to be asking that I be sent to where I really belonged: the cramped guardroom downstairs where all suspects were meant to be kept. And dehumanized, I thought. He went on and on.

Bishop Poromon, a man of few words and great courtesy, was astounded. He offered to say a prayer. Mr Ogbeifun gruffly allowed him to do so. And he prayed for me, my fellow captives and our captors. And then he graciously withdrew.

When we were left alone, Mr Ogbeifun grabbed all the papers I had on the writing-table and went through them. Among them was a diary of my first week in detention, some papers from the Vienna Conference, and poems which I had begun to write. He warned that I did not have the right to write, and that if I was not on good behaviour, he would have no option but to treat me according to the book.

To bring the enormity of my crime to me, he ordered that Dube and Nwiee be sent to the guardroom downstairs. He had me cheap there, because I would rather have gone down with them than allow them to go there alone. For my peace of mind and against all my instincts, I had to appeal to him to let us stay together in the wretched room to which we had been consigned.

Having thus humiliated me, he now casually informed me that he still had no further orders from his superiors and that he would have to return to Lagos. We would have to wait in Owerri.

I raised the matter of my health with him, arguing that I ought really to be in hospital, if my condition was not to further deteriorate. I asked him to have word with Dr Idoko, if he wanted to have confirmation. I was to learn later that Mr Ogbeifun could not do anything without the approval of his superior in Lagos, the Deputy Inspector-General of Police in charge of the FIIB.

As I watched Mr Ogbeifun and his man Friday walk off that evening – it was about 6.30 pm – I remembered what my brother had told me at the Central Police Station in Port Harcourt: that I would be away for a long time. It didn't sound funny this time.

Once I accepted that I might be in detention for an indefinite period, I ceased to worry about what orders came from Lagos or not. Mr Ogbeifun and his superiors could go hang. And as for the man with the ultimate responsibility for our detention, General Ibrahim Babangida, I reserved for him that contempt which I normally accord to vermin. I settled into my new life in a proper frame of mind. The only worry I had was my health, about which I could do precious little anyway.

The days were not particularly dull, come to face it. I had the use of my transistor radio and bought newspapers daily, so I was well informed. I was also able to read whatever book I wanted, and since I was expected to feed myself, I did have the sort of food that suited me, even though it cost me a fortune and a great deal of trouble in a town where I could only rely on friends.

I have to state that the police officers and men at the station were kind and polite to us. There was absolutely no hostility towards me, Dube and Nwiee, and where we needed anything, they exerted themselves to help.

One of the senior police officers had served with an Ogoni man in his early days in the force, and he had not forgotten what times they shared. On that score alone, he became a frequent visitor to our cell and was quite solicitous of our comfort. He made sure that my supply of pipe tobacco did not run out.

Journalists also kept me somewhat occupied. They would come into the cell by hook or by crook, or with the permission of the police authorities, ask me questions on any developments in the country and give me the news behind the headlines. I treasured the moments I shared with them, for I knew that whatever they were able to publish would keep a large number of people informed of my whereabouts and my state of mind.

But above all, I had a constant stream of Ogoni visitors. It isn't necessary to detail all those who came calling, as every day they came in batches from all parts of Ogoni and beyond, offering us solidarity, comfort and, wait for it, money! If there was anything which buoyed me up, it was this show of loyalty and solidarity from the Ogoni people. From far away Lagos, the Ogoni community sent a delegation with words of comfort and 2,000 naira which I requested them to pay to MOSOP, as I did not need the money. I imagined to what length they would have gone to collect the money. And I was touched, deeply touched. Some weren't allowed to see me, as Mr Ilozuoke had to use his discretion, and if he was not around, no one could take decisions on his behalf. He was not averse to visitors but had to ensure that the cell wasn't crowded, and that visits were kept as short as possible. Those who couldn't see me on any one day repeated the visit on another one.

The youth of Ogoni and the women were my most frequent visitors. My detention had the potential of destabilizing the MOSOP, more so as Dr Leton and Edward Kobani had resigned their positions, ineffective as they had become. But once the remaining members of the steering committee had heard from me that the work of the movement must proceed apace, they got together, formally elected a new executive and got down to business. I was elected President, in absentia, Ledum Mitee became Deputy President, Father Kabari, an Oxford University-trained Catholic priest, was elected Treasurer and Simeon Idemyor was made Financial Secretary. Dr Ben Naanen, bright and up-coming historian of the University of Port Harcourt, remained Secretary. There were also six Vice-Presidents, all of them much younger than me, representing each of the six Ogoni kingdoms. This was definitely a much stronger team than we had had in the past, and infinitely more committed. There was no room for wafflers and fifth columnists. That was the message the steering committee had sent to the Ogoni people.

I also came to learn that certain people who were seen as traitors to the Ogoni cause had found it quite difficult to remain in Ogoni and had taken refuge in Port Harcourt as guests of Governor Ada George. This group consisted largely of four of the six government-appointed chiefs in Ogoni. There were others too.

The most important of them was Edward Kobani. He too came to see me with his wife, the gentle and beautiful Rose. I saw Edward regard the cell in which we were kept with some satisfaction. And when he opened his mouth to speak, it was to remind me that I had once said, at a steering committee meeting, that the revolution would invariably claim its victims. The implication was that I was its first victim. I did not mind that, I thought. But when he began to whine about his inability to get to his hometown, Bodo, because of fear of reprisals from the youth of the place, I knew that he needed a discussion with me.

*

I have known Edward Kobani since childhood. He grew up in Bori where his father was a court clerk, and attended the Native Authority School there as did the rest of us, children of what was then the Ogoni elite. By the time I started school in 1947, he had left or was about to leave the school. One of the earliest memories I have of him was his father, who was a large, tall man with a deep voice, shouting himself hoarse at something that had happened to Edward. I did not know what it was all about at the time, but much later in life I was to learn that the young Edward had got himself rusticated from the Okrika Grammar School for some offence or other.

When I next heard of Edward, he was a student at the University College, Ibadan, and we often met at annual meetings of the Ogoni Students Union. It was not a very successful organization, but it served to keep Ogoni students in touch with one another, and for those of us who were in secondary school the contact with university undergraduates was inspiring

By 1961, when I began to cast about to form the Ogoni Divisional Union, Edward had graduated from University. He flirted for a while with doing a post-graduate diploma in librarianship, could not sustain it, and began to teach in a number of private, poorly financed and equipped schools in Onitsha. There he became an official of one of the fringe political parties in Nigeria at the time, the Dynamic Party, formed and headed by the mathematician Professor Chike Obi. I believe that Edward contested an election in Ogoni on the platform of the party and failed, although he would have been a better candidate than the winner of the election. In Eastern Nigeria at the time you would have to have been exceptionally strong to have won an election against the government party, the National Council of Nigeria and the Cameroons (NCNC).

By 1962, when I got to the University of Ibadan, Edward was teaching in another private secondary school in Port Harcourt, Niger Grammar School, owned by a would-be politician, Mr Frank Opigo. In my first long vacation in June of 1963, I found a job in Port Harcourt and, having nowhere to stay in the town, was offered a room in the flat which Edward was occupying with his young Ogoni bride, Rose. I also spent the 1964 long vacation as his guest, and when I graduated in 1965, before I rented a flat while I taught at Stella Maris College in Port Harcourt, I was also his guest. I was never to forget this kindness, which Edward had offered me when it mattered most.

I learnt a lot in his company, meeting a great number of young graduates who were his contemporaries at the University of Ibadan and who now occupied various positions in the country. One of the people to whom Edward introduced me was the late Dr Obi Wali, who was to become a close friend and a mentor. Edward was also endowed, in the best traditions of the Ogoni, with wit, humour and *bonhomie*. He also had a knack for putting the right English word in the right place. At that time in my life, these things mattered, and I was suitably impressed with my friend.

We discussed politics, both national and local, and worked at the Ogoni Divisional Union of which he was President and I, Secretary. He was anti-establishment, a fact which I liked at that time of my life, more so as the establishment was seen as inept and corrupt, and definitely oppressive of the Ogoni people. We often dreamt of transforming Nigerian society for the better.

When the opportunity came in 1966 for us to initiate that transformation, Edward and I were at the meetings of the Rivers Leaders of Thought at Port Harcourt, where we took the decision to ask for the creation of Rivers State by decree. I was expected to sign the memorandum making this demand, having served as Secretary of the committee which drafted the memorandum. For reasons of my health, I was absent at the signature session and Edward signed on behalf of the Ogoni. This was right, anyway, since he was much better known than I was.

When war broke out in 1967 and I decided to cross the fighting lines to identify with the Federal government, Edward was one of the few whom I took into confidence. He played a minor role in the Biafran venture, as a member of its Propaganda Directorate, while I was on the Federal side as Administrator for Bonny and subsequently Commissioner and member of the Executive Council of the newly formed Rivers State. These positions, were, for me, an opportunity to give service to the country and the local community and I was quite oblivious of the power and prestige which they conferred. I had, indeed, had to scuttle the academic career which I had mapped out for myself in order to serve and that was a constant source of worry. What I also didn't count on was that my new profile would be envied by close associates. But more of that later.

At the end of the civil war, I was on hand to get Edward and his family out of the refugee camp at Etche, and I regarded it as my responsibility to ensure that he was properly rehabilitated. I introduced him to the new administration of which I was a part, and before long Edward had become a Commissioner and member of the Executive Council of Rivers State.

For doing this, I was to receive a lot of flak from his erstwhile Ogoni colleagues in the Biafran venture, including most prominently, Dr Leton. They never tired of telling me what a dishonourable fellow Edward was, and they considered that my putting him on a pedestal was a fatal flaw in my make-up. I didn't believe them.

However, I was soon to get evidence that the Ogoni elite

who had returned from Biafra resented me. I put it all down to the gerontocratic nature of Ogoni society which decrees that age is synonymous with wisdom and that no son should be greater than his father. For the Ogoni who were older than me, my 'rise' wasn't acceptable. I should have learnt to take my place in the queue behind them.

Being in government was no big deal, as far as I was concerned, and being away from it would only free me to do all those things which I really wanted to do but couldn't find time for.

In the meantime, I had a lot to be dissatisfied with in the administration: the inefficiency, the dictatorial nature of decision-making, the corruption, the tribalism which again placed the Ogoni people at a clear disadvantage. I wanted to resign the job. Pressure was brought upon me not to do so by a large number of Ogoni people whose interest and protection my presence in government served. And so I remained as a historian of the system. But it couldn't be sustained. I became more strident in my criticisms and was appropriately given the boot unceremoniously in March of 1973.

By then I had come to the conclusion that there was need to split Rivers State, as the interests of the ten-odd ethnic groups in it could not be meaningfully reconciled. Along with my colleagues in the Cabinet, notably Dr Obi Wali and Mr Nwobidike Nwanodi, I began, in 1974, the argument for the creation of a Port Harcourt State which would include all the non-Ijaws in Rivers State who happened to live on the plains north of the Niger River Delta proper. Edward Kobani lent his full weight to the argument.

When the state government was dismissed following the military coup of 1975, all of us became private citizens but we continued to put our argument. By 1977 arrangements were being made for a constituent assembly and I decided to contest a seat in it. To cut a long story short, Edward Kobani led the effort to ensure that I didn't get there. Dirty tricks eventually won the day and even when I went on appeal, the judge told me his hands were tied and he could not but dismiss the appeal.

Shortly thereafter, I met, in Lagos a notable journalist, Uche Chukwumerije, who, by the time this book opens, was playing a prominent role in the Babangida maladministration. He had been a contemporary of Edward's at University College, Ibadan. As I rode with him in his car, he told me stories of Edward's life at Ibadan: how he had planned with other students a fence-breaking riot but chickened out on D-day; how he had secured for himself a trip to Switzerland offered by Amorc, the private society, at the expense of another student; and so on and so forth.

Thereafter, I didn't have to be told that I needed to give Ogoni politics a wide berth. Which I did. Having decided that I wouldn't involve myself in politics local or national, until I had developed myself properly, this didn't prove difficult at all.

What returned me to Ogoni politics again was the quest for Ogoni identity and the survival of the Ogoni people. There was need to take everyone on board, and particularly the spoilers among the Ogoni elite. I also knew that whatever the case, Edward would always stand for the interest of the Ogoni people. But would he be able to sustain it, especially if his personal interests were compromised? That was the question.

As he sat before me in long robes that dismal afternoon, complaining that Ogoni youths would not allow him into his hometown, Bodo, I got upset. There was I, unable to take a walk outside of my detention cell without an armed guard following me, in a place 150 kilometres from my hometown, and unsure what the next day would bring, with a draconian law prescribing death hanging round my neck, being asked to feel pity for a man who was free to do everything else but face the anger of young men whose future they thought he had mortgaged. I gave him the length of my tongue. I reminded him how he and the others had conspired to issue an announcement in my name. He denied having been a part of the plot. I assured him that it was that action which loused up all the arrangements I had made to ensure that the elections went on smoothly, with all those who wanted to vote being allowed to do so. There were some more arguments.

Edward and I often disagreed, but we always got together again. I was close to some of his children and to his wife, Rose. Indeed, one of his children, Tombari, had designed the MOSOP flag. Edward's visit worsened my ill health, which was my main worry at the time. He was plain bad news that day.

In detention, the restriction of movement didn't bother me much. I was quite used to a sedentary life, and even when free would sit at my desk in my office from nine in the morning until ten at night. And back at home, after dinner, I would go into my study after a brief rest and work until two in the morning before I would have my usual four-hour sleep.

At Owerri, I and Dube and Nwiee would wake up at six o'clock to perform our ablutions. I would get dressed, go downstairs into the courtyard, take a walk the length of the open courtyard several times, counting the number of paces, and then return to the cell, have a breakfast of fruit and whatever, then wait to receive visitors. By evening, when the visitors would have thinned out, I would again do a turn in the yard before returning to the cell to prepare for a long night, reading, listening to the radio, and chatting with Dube.

I had known Dube for quite a while. He had come to me

years back, having just completed his studies in printing at Manchester University. He needed office space to carry on his private business, but had no money. I offered him one of the spare rooms below my office and he set up in business there. He often came to talk with me, and I found him quite engaging and energetic. Watching his seriousness of purpose, I often did regret what few openings there were for him, merely because he was Ogoni. In Hausaland, he would have held the exalted post of Government Printer. But here he was, scrounging around for a living. When we started MOSOP, he threw his boundless energy into it without invitation and became virtually indispensable to the steering committee.

Kabari Nwiee, the other detainee, I had never seen in all my life until that night when we fetched him from the police cell at Abagana. It transpired that he was a father of nine children from two wives. He had been chairman of NYCOP in his village of Opuoko. My childhood friend, Mr Lah-Loolo, had taken exception to something he did or did not do and had reported him to the police. Which was how he ended up in illegal detention. Just that. He was a small fry, given to few words, or so I thought, until, one day, he had a drop of alcohol, or what Nigerians call 'hot drink', and then the words came tumbling out of him like water from a spigot.

My discussions with Dube invariably centred around the Ogoni and their problems. We analysed and thought about the struggles of MOSOP, the future of the struggle and what else we might expect. And it was comforting that there was someone to share these thoughts with.

In such times, poetry comes handy. And I did write poems for my late son, Tedum, which I somehow lost, and the single anthem for Ogoni which appeared first in my Khana mother-tongue:

Yoor Zaansin Ogoni

Bari a dem Ogoni
Le buen ka le zor
Fo efeloo le wereloo
Doo kor zian aa I le yee
Ne i o suanu le ekpo
E ema ba pya baa

Bari a dem Ogoni
Le buen ka le zor
Ne i o leelee denden son
Kwa dee ne pya Gokana
Khana, Eleme, Tai le Babbe
Doo lo Ogoni lu ka

which, translated into English, reads:

Creator of Ogoni
Land of glory and wealth
Grant us thy peace and lasting love
Plant justice over our land
Give us thy wisdom and the strength
To shame our enemies

Creator of Ogoni
Land of glory and wealth
Grant everlasting blessings Lord
To people of Gokana
Khana, Eleme, Tai and Babbe
Glorious Ogoni land

And so the days passed. We were now waiting for the hearing of the action we had instituted, which was fixed for 10 July.

Before that event, Claude Ake came calling. His visit was

very important to me, psychologically. It was the first time a prominent non-Ogoni person would be visiting us. I had noted that so far, not one person from other parts of Rivers State, including those with whom I had worked in the Rivers State Study Group where we examined the problems which assailed the peoples of the State, had come to visit with us in solidarity.

Claude was entirely of a different breed. A political scientist, he was educated at King's College, Lagos, the University of Ibadan and Columbia University, where he taught before proceeding to the Chair of Political Economy at universities in Canada, Dar es Salaam and Nairobi. In 1977 he took up the Chair of Political Economy at the University of Port Harcourt and became Dean of the Faculty of Social Sciences there. Highly respected in academic circles world-wide, he had won the Nigerian National Merit Award in 1992, in addition to being the only black man in the American Social Science Academy. He was later made a member of the New York Academy of Sciences.

I had only started to associate with him in about 1989. I met him in Washington, DC in 1990 when I was touring as a Distinguished Visiting Fellow of the United States Information Agency. He was then at the Brookings Institution. In October 1991, as I have said, he graciously agreed to travel all the way to Lagos to my fiftieth birthday book launch. He had set up the Centre for Advanced Social Studies, an independent think-tank, in 1991 in Port Harcourt, and was clearly a very valuable man to have around.

He had been abroad at the time of my arrest, and only came to know about it when he read Tony Daniels's piece on it in *The Times Literary Supplement*. He returned to Nigeria on the Tuesday and the very next day, Wednesday, 6 July, spent five hours with us at Owerri. In that time, we analysed,

discussed, X-rayed and thought of my situation. He did everything to comfort me, and showed intense concern for Dube
and Nwiee, feeling happy that I was sharing a cell with them.
It was from him I gathered that interest in my arrest had
been aroused in Britain in particular, but also elsewhere.
When he eventually left in mid afternoon, I felt relieved,
grateful, joyful and even fulfilled.

I had been impressing on the Owerri police the need to let
me have proper medical attention. Dr Idoko was around on
a daily basis to check my blood pressure and to do whatever
he could to reassure me. He had recommended that I be
transferred to a clinic, but the decision rested with his superiors and they were taking their time over it. They probably
had to refer the case to Lagos for a decision. Which meant
that if I had to die, Lagos would determine it. They were
surely playing God!

A bit of drama was not lacking either. On the Thursday
afternoon a man with a briefcase came barging into the cell.
He looked scruffy and ungainly.

'Do you need any help?' he asked.

'What sort of help?' I demanded.

'Bail. Or something like that.'

'Our lawyer is arranging for bail.'

'Then you will never leave here.'

'Why not?'

'Lawyers are no use. They only complicate things for
people in police custody. They complicate things.' He shook
his head in commiseration of people who are in police custody and seek the assistance of lawyers.

'I don't understand,' I said.

'You see, today is Thursday. Tomorrow is Friday. On Fri-
days, the senior officers who give approval are in meetings
the whole day. There is no one to sign the bail. Lawyers
cannot get into the meeting. They are too big. Besides, they

have to go to court. I can wait all day for the senior officers to finish their meeting and have the papers signed. And, you know, if you don't get bailed on Friday, you have to stay in the cell until Monday. That's not good.'

I thanked the 'bail expert' for the information, and he left, a trifle disappointed. And I was left to ponder what men often do to earn a living!

CHAPTER TEN

The approval for me to move to the police clinic had come that Thursday, 8 July. I expected to be produced in court the next day, but that did not materialize because the summons had not been served on the police, or they so claimed. The judge ordered that we be produced on 13 July.

The 'O/C Admin' was a very important man in police headquarters, and you felt it at every point. The incumbent was a tall, black man with a developing paunch. If I had to move to the clinic, only he could sanction it and make arrangements for me to move. All day Thursday, he found it impossible to conclude arrangements for a vehicle that would drive me to my new abode, which was no more than a mile away. Not all the pressure in the world would move him from his accustomed speed of action. There were just too many obstacles in the way. The papers he had to sign, the orders he had to give, the myriad things he had to supervise. The 'O/C Admin' was a man of power in an inefficient place.

When everything official failed, he had to do me a favour, the next day. He took me in his personal car to the clinic. I sat between two armed police guards for the ten-minute drive through dirt roads, farm-patches and ill-constructed, ugly houses. Dr Idoko was not immediately available to receive me upon arrival, but he soon showed up and made me welcome. The clinic itself was a new one, and I was the first patient to use it. That is not to say that it was spick and span and everything in place or in good working order. Far from it. It had been constructed in the usual splash and dash manner of Nigerian official contract jobs, no doubt at ten times the normal cost, and opened with fanfare by the wife of no less a personality than the Inspector-General of Police, after whom (the wife, I mean) it was appropriately named.

It was only after I had been officially admitted that curtains of some sort were crudely hung on the front windows whose louvred shutters would not open. I had to buy a bedsheet for the other long window which gave out on to a corridor separating the ward from the bathroom and toilet.

The ward itself had four beds on which no one had slept so far. All in all, it was much better than my previous cell. There was absolute quiet all around, the building being far apart from other buildings in the area and separated, as it was, from them by farm patches. I had to arrange to purchase a table fan in order to live in some comfort. The toilet was working, and with an electric coil, which I also purchased, found warm water in which to bathe. I had my first bath in two weeks! While in the cell at the police head-quarters, I had contented myself with towelling myself down each morning and night.

Before leaving for the clinic, I had worried myself to no end as to what would happen to Dube and Nwiee. I had pleaded with Assistant Commissioner of Police Ilozuoke to leave them in the room we had been using and desist from sending them into the guardroom. He was not forthcoming in this regard. It continued to be a point of anxiety. Separated from both of them, I was quite anxious for their welfare. I had left them with some money for their food, although Dube's staff and family often made the long journey from Port Harcourt to bring him food which he shared with Nwiee, whom no one came to see.

On hand to guard me at the clinic were six armed men of

the Police Mobile Force, who were there twenty-four hours a day. Each watch lasted twelve hours, sometimes twenty-four. I noticed that they were not fed throughout, and often had to find them funds to assist with their meals.

It was not so funny, this detention, in which I had to feed myself, buy my own medicine, feed my guards, and hope for the best. I often wondered how easy it would be for one of the guards to move into my room, shoot me through the head, and that would be that. I was quite sure that they would let it be known to the world that I was trying to escape when I was gunned down.

Mercifully, nothing of that sort happened. The guards proved quite friendly. Each change of duty was reported to me, and their leader would introduce himself politely. Most were familiar with my struggle, had heard of me, and were quite sympathetic. They were only doing their duty, I had to understand.

The days were full, as usual. Delegations upon delegations of Ogoni people came calling each day, and we had a lot to discuss. Always, my advice to them was 'Get organized in your villages and your various kingdoms, along the lines established by MOSOP. Your strength lies in organization. Avoid violence!'

We were still at the seminal level of organization, but we had done quite well, the Ogoni being quick on the up-take, and most being imbued with a sense of urgency, having realized that we were facing the possibility of extinction.

I believed that if we had the opportunity, we would be able, relying upon ourselves and our genius, to re-create Ogoni society. Enthusiasm was very high, most had given their time and money freely, and hopes were equally high. What I did not count on was that all this would raise the profile of the Ogoni and engineer the envy of others. So that instead of its being a model, it would be seen as something to be crushed. Even at that, I felt that the Ogoni were being forced into a struggle, and that the process would strengthen them eventually. The price might well be worth it.

In the end, the real difficulty was having to cope with the debilitating poverty of the people. It stymied organization, and stopped people from doing what they would like to. Casting my mind back on the mobilization efforts which had succeeded somewhat in Nigeria, I noticed that they were all carried out against a backdrop of the possession of some measure of power and under the nose of a colonial government which was not murderous, but was guided by the rule of law. In any case, the people being mobilized were numerous enough. The Hausa-Fulani, the Igbo and the Yoruba were among the biggest nations on earth, and although the Tiv, the other group which had been mobilized by their leaders, were not that numerous, they were still the fifth largest ethnic group in the country, and therefore had more resources upon which to call.

All the same, the sacrifice of the youth and women of Ogoni was most encouraging. Everyone had volunteered their services and time freely and without complaint. They took whatever tribulation that came stoically, finding instances in the Bible of similar events. Mostly, they relied on the journey of the Israelites from Egypt to the Promised Land, and in many cases, I received homilies on the life of Moses, who, they insisted, was my model.

Apart from the Ogoni people, I also had a few other visitors, particularly the writer Charry Ada Onwu, an energetic and powerful lady if ever there was one, who came in the company of another member of the Imo branch of the Association of Nigerian Authors, of which I was President, to offer me humorous and entertaining stories.

But it was not to last. The next Monday, barely three days after I had arrived at the clinic, Olu Onagoruwa, my lawyer, came in from Lagos to appear in court the following day. He and a junior from his chambers chatted me up for about an hour or so, and then went to their hotel.

'I'll see you in court tomorrow,' he said.

'That's if the police agree to produce me.'

'They will this time. They've run out of excuses. You'll have to be granted bail.'

Cheering news, no doubt. But no sooner had he left than the Coffin arrived, bearing Mr Inah at his most lugubrious. He must have felt bad that I was in a clinic. I think he would have preferred my being in the dank, over-populated guard-room at the police headquarters or in the mortuary.

After he had exchanged a few words of greeting, he took yet another statement from me. The import of this did not strike me immediately. It was only after they had left and another police officer came to ask after them that I knew something was brewing.

The police officer in question had always been polite and extremely helpful. But that afternoon, he was not smiling. He appeared anxious. He wanted to know if Mr Inah had come to see me. I confirmed that he had.

'Where is he now?'

'I don't know. I think I overheard him say he would be leaving for Port Harcourt.'

'Port Harcourt?' There was consternation in his voice.

'Yes,' I answered. 'Is there a problem?'

'No. No. It's O K.'

'Are you coming to take me to court tomorrow? The judge ordered you to produce me.'

'That's not in my hands. Stay well. Goodbye.'

And he left, taking long and urgent strides. I watched from the window as he drove off.

I slept well that night, giving no thought to the oppressive ways of the Babangida regime. I may have taken false comfort in the reassuring presence of Olu Onagoruwa or in the court order. And it was just as well that I had some relaxed sleep.

At five o'clock the next morning, the sound of the Coffin driving into the compound woke me up from sleep. The sound of the mobile police guard saluting smartly indicated that a superior officer was around. The sound of boots on the staircase. The harsh knock on the door of the ward. Mr Inah's familiar outline in the long caftan. Behind him, another man in flowing robes who always accompanied him, but often remained in the Coffin.

'Get ready, sir, you are due to travel.'

'Where to?'

'I don't know.'

'But I'm not well.'

'I have my orders.'

'I'm not well enough to travel.'

'We have to go. Time is not on our side. Get ready, sir.'

'I have to see the police doctor.'

'You're only wasting time. You've always co-operated with us. Please co-operate.'

'I can't leave the clinic without the permission of the doctor.'

'You don't need his permission.'

'I do. I'm his patient. He has to confirm to me that I'm in a position to undertake a road journey in a coffin.'

'Coffin? Which coffin?'

'Your J5 bus.' I couldn't see his face in the darkness.

'We have to leave immediately. I don't want to use force.'

'Get the doctor to certify that I can leave his clinic.'

Mr Inah turned on his heels and left. While he was gone, my car, which always waited on me, turned up. The chauffeur slept in town in a friend's house. He had turned up earlier than usual. One of the guards came up to tell me that he had information that I was being taken to Port Harcourt to appear in court on a criminal charge. 'Don't agree to go with them, sir.'

I sent my chauffeur to inform Olu Onagoruwa of the latest development. He was no sooner gone than Dr Idoko turned up with Mr Inah. He went through the motion of checking my temperature and blood pressure. He said there was nothing he could do to stop the police officer from taking me away. I thanked him for his trouble and bade him goodbye.

I asked Mr Inah to allow me bathe and get dressed. He agreed. I went through my morning ablutions deliberately, hoping that I would get word back from Olu Onagoruwa. No dice.

Before long I had dressed up, packed my personal items and left them aside to be conveyed by my chauffeur back to Port Harcourt. I walked downstairs, bade the guards goodbye and climbed into the front seat of the Coffin. Mr Inah got in after me and we drove out of the compound. There were six or so armed policemen in the back of the Coffin.

As we drove out, it struck me that in the four days I had stayed there, I had not once stepped out of doors. I had only gone downstairs once, and that was to see off Baridon and Rose Konya, possibly the most outstanding and exemplary Ogoni couple of our time, who had spent a good part of the Sunday with me.

The Coffin threaded its way back to the police head-quarters and came to a stop in front of the building which I had left four days earlier. There, Dube and Nwiee joined us and we headed out of Owerri town.

The morning was bright and the air which rushed into the Coffin quite refreshing. As we drove past the Concorde Hotel, where Olu Onagoruwa was lodged, I wondered if he had got my message at all. Anyway, it didn't matter any more.

We drove the distance to Port Harcourt, stopping only once when one of the policemen wished to answer the call of nature and was allowed to do so in a nearby bush. As we got close to the Port Harcourt International Airport, Mr Inah began to wonder where his boss might be. The latter was supposed to have arrived by air, and Mr Inah had a mind for the Coffin to get to the airport to see if he had done so. So to the airport we went. Mr Ogbeifun was not to be found. We headed towards Port Harcourt.

I did wonder for a while where we were going. I found out soon enough as we drove into the high court premises in the centre of the town. Ready to receive us was a unit of the Police Mobile Force in glittering riot gear which seemed to have been purchased that very morning. They surrounded the magistrates' court, to which we were driven and offloaded.

I thought wistfully of the comic half of the event. As we drove from Owerri, we passed several cars and buses carrying hundreds of Ogoni people to the high court in Owerri, where I was to have been produced by the order of the judge. Ogoni men, women and youths had been there in their hundreds the previous week, and had gone home frustrated because the case had been adjourned. But that hadn't stopped them from making the long journey once again. However, whereas they were in Owerri, here were we, in Port Harcourt where no one, not even my lawyer, Ledum Mitee, knew that we would be. And in all that calm, there was a riot squad waiting for a riot they knew would not be.

We sat in court and waited while the magistrate, who I later knew to be a Mrs D, famous as a government hang-woman, if such a term exists, cleared her desk, so to speak.

Within five minutes, she had adjourned the case that was before her, and she then called our case.

We stepped into the box. I was quite familiar with the court and with the procedure. I waited with bated breath for the charge to be read. I could have laughed my scorn to the roof of the grimy court hall if that would not have been regarded as being disrespectful to the court. I heard it said that we had assembled at an Ogoni village which I had not visited all my life, there to plan I know not what. That we had designed a flag and written an anthem, and planned I know not what against the government of Nigeria or some place like that. All this amounted to a six-count charge of sedition and unlawful assembly. Did we agree to be tried in that particular court? The answer was merely perfunctory. The magistrate wrote in her book. Were we guilty or not guilty? There was no reason to answer. The magistrate, Mrs D, wrote in her book.

Then she wrote in her book, and wrote in her book, the skinny young woman behind a pair of glasses. And she lifted up her face after she had written in her book, and decided that we had a case to answer. How she came to that marvellous conclusion, I don't know. She was committing us to prison custody. That was the long and short of it. It wasn't that simple, though. We had no counsel, but there were lawyers in court, all of whom said they were appearing for us, on a sympathy basis, I presume. The lawyer who demanded bail for us, since the offence was bailable, later came to the prison to see me. He was a Mr Briggs, who had taught at the Birabi Memorial Grammar School in Bori, my home town.

Well, Mrs D was not disposed to grant us bail since, in the opinion of the prosecuting sergeant, we would be raising hell and disturbing the peace of a whole lot of well-fed people. So to prison custody we would have to go. And, by the way,

Mrs D would be going on leave shortly after turning her fine legal mind to our case. And after that, the courts would be on their annual recess, and then, and then, well, she would be disposed to hear the case again on 21 September. By which time, I quickly calculated, I would have been held for three months, which was close to the prison term of six months laid down for the offence of sedition.

I had been dragged out of a police clinic which was less than the hospital bed which I needed. Was there a chance Her Worship (Worship!) would give an order that I be sent to hospital? That was not her business, her sole business being to send us to prison custody. As Her Worship pleased.

No, I was not upset with Mrs D. I felt sorry for her, and for Mr Ogbeifun and for Mr Inah, and for all those men and women who were being forced by the system to subvert the law, tell lies, play dirty tricks, in order to earn their monthly pay. I also felt terrible when I thought that the three players I have mentioned above were from ethnic minority areas, and were acting for the Hausa bandit, if Hausa he is, called Babangida, who should have been before a firing squad for treason against his country. But that momentary feeling only evoked in me a determination to pour all my resources, intellectual and otherwise, into creating a society where such things would not be. It brought forth the beginnings of a song which I completed in prison a week later:

The True Prison

It is not the leaking roof
Nor the singing mosquitoes
In the damp, wretched cell.
It is not the clank of the key
As the warder locks you in.
It is not the measly rations
Unfit for man or beast

220

Nor yet the emptiness of day
Dipping into the blankness of night
It is not
It is not
It is not.
It is the lies that have been drummed
Into your ears for one generation
It is the security agent running amok
Executing callous calamitous orders
In exchange for a wretched meal a day
The magistrate writing in her book
Punishment she knows is undeserved
The moral decrepitude
Mental ineptitude
Lending dictatorship spurious legitimacy
Cowardice masked as obedience
Lurking in our denigrated souls
It is fear damping trousers
We dare not wash off our urine
It is this
It is this
It is this
Dear friend, turns our free world
Into a dreary prison.

Yes, we, the MOSOP Three, were headed for the Port Harcourt Prison. The police had prepared everything. As we stepped out of the magistrates' court into the Coffin, a siren wailed a shrill cry of terror, injustice and temporary triumph. A truckload of armed police followed the car blowing the siren, another Peugeot pick-up van carrying more armed men followed the Coffin, and in another five minutes we were before the gate of Port Harcourt Prison. We got down from the Coffin, and the gate opened to let us in.

The night of 13 June, as the presidential election results were being announced, I had gone with Alfred Ilenre to see Lateef Jakande, sometime Governor of Lagos State. My passport had just been seized by the security agencies. And he had said, to my startled ears, 'As the prison doors open to let you in, so they will open to let you out.'

As I stepped into Port Harcourt Prison, a.k.a. Alabama City, I recalled Jakande's words gladly.

CHAPTER ELEVEN

Port Harcourt Prison lies but a stone's throw from my 24 Aggrey Road office and was there before I began to know Port Harcourt in 1954. It is equally a stone's throw from Stella Maris College where I had taught after graduating from university in 1965. I ought to agree that it is a shame that I had never visited it. It was there, at the back of Port Harcourt, close to the marshy swamps, solid, grey, forbidding from the outside. It was always a place to be avoided.

I cast my mind back now, and think that in Ogoni society prisons did not exist. Wrongdoers were killed, fined, sent into exile or made to swear an oath. Thus, when the colonialists introduced the idea of a prison, a place of correction where wrongdoers spent time, it was novel, and has not sat well with our psyche. A prison was always a place to be avoided. Murderers and thieves were there together. No one had reason to be there. If you were there, you had to be an outcast.

Since our denigration as a people was unprotested, no one had ever been held on his conscience. So that the fact that an innocent man could be sent to prison was unthinkable.

It is true that we had read of the detention of people in Nigeria, but it was mostly a phenomenon of Lagos, where there were several human rights activists. That was until I told the Ogoni people that they were being cheated, denied of their rights to a healthy environment, and the resources of their land. Then almost the entire 51,000 Ogoni men, women and children became activists. Still, prison seemed far away. We could understand death at the hands of a murderous army or police, but I do not think that we could understand imprisonment. And yet I do remember that I kept warning the Ogoni people to prepare for harassment, imprisonment and death.

Altogether, it was fitting that I should be one of the first to be detained. It would show subsequent detainees that they were in good company.

There were all sorts of preliminaries to be endured before one became an inmate of the prison, such as handing over all cash and other belongings to the prison authorities and being inducted into the life of the prison community.

I suppose that I was treated as a Very Important Prisoner and therefore my story will not be as lurid as it should be. All the same, I did find the prison a very depressing place. If its exterior is solid, grey and forbidding, as I have said, its interior is grimy, squalid and dilapidated.

I must say that I find it very distasteful writing about Port Harcourt Prison. Given the way public buildings are kept throughout Nigeria, no one would be surprised to hear that the prison was in total disrepair and unfit for human habitation.

You can tell the state of a nation by the way it keeps its prisons, prisoners being mostly out of sight. Going by this criterion, Nigeria was in a parlous state indeed.

The prison had been built in colonial times; it was, at that time, the largest prison in West Africa, and was well laid out, with plenty of open space for fresh air, and all educational facilities, such as workshops and library. It also had an infirmary. It had, and still has, a women's wing. But everything was in disrepair, everything was collapsing, everything was gone.

The administrative block itself had not been painted for ages; the room where the senior prison officers worked was stuffy and dirty, furnished with old chairs and tables, without fans or air-conditioners. There was no telephone, only one watercloset which was kept strictly for the boss of the prison, and no one there had a car. Oh, the wretchedness of it all is scandalous. And there are Nigerians who have been Ministers of Internal Affairs and supervised all this, and not said a word? More, there are prominent Nigerians who have been held under these conditions and have come out and done nothing about it.

I hadn't been in the prison for more than a day when I knew that the condition of Nigerian prisons and prisoners would be added to the long list of campaigns I had already accumulated.

After we had gone through the motion of being properly registered, our property logged, our weight and height recorded, and so on and so forth, we were invited upstairs to meet the boss of the establishment, a Mr Ikpatti. This was a special treatment, because as I have said, I was special. Mr Ikpatti, a short man with a developing paunch, well spoken and rather kindly looking, introduced me to the ways of 'Alabama City', the nickname of the place. How it got the name, I don't know. But from what I heard officially, I knew that I was in a different world indeed.

Theoretically, everything was being done to ensure that prisoners or those in prison custody had as proper a life as the deprivation of their liberty would allow. The constraints of space do not allow me to go into detail here. In practice, what we had in Port Harcourt Prison was a travesty. And that probably wasn't because the government had failed to put money into it. The negligence, callousness and incompetence of some thieving officials who had run the place over the years had a lot to do with it. To cut a long story short,

Mr Ikpatti welcomed me to 'Alabama City' and hoped that I would have a good time there.

I thanked him and, based on what he had told me, applied for and got permission to feed myself. I knew that Nigerian prison food was not edible; in any case, I need a special diet for survival, and only my family can provide that in Nigeria. And I obtained special permission to stay in the infirmary, since I needed medical care.

I got to the infirmary late that afternoon, the admission formalities having lasted four or five hours. A look at the infirmary and my heart fell. It was leaking like a sieve; there was no ceiling; the entire place was damp; there was only a bucket latrine; the narrow beds had rotten mattresses; and heavens, what else was there not, in that place?

It didn't come as a surprise, anyway. I asked that my office send three mattresses to us, along with bedding and a lot of cleansing material – detergents, disinfectants, insecticide, anything to help us clean the wretched place.

I hadn't eaten all day, and when dinner finally came from my house at about six thirty I found I had no appetite for it. It had to be tasted first by whoever brought it, in this case, my steward, and I had to eat it in the presence of the warders, in a dingy front cubicle. No, I needed to get into the rhythm of the prison. In my state of mind I could take anything for the cause I believed in, but I did need a certain acclimatization at every new turn of events.

Already a crowd of Ogoni people had begun to gather before the prison gates. One of the earliest callers was Mrs Z, a lawyer and first daughter of Mr Nunieh, the first Ogoni lawyer, who, I was later to learn, had gone to Owerri to represent me alongside Olu Onagoruwa, Ledum Mitee and Samuel Igbara (a childhood friend, and younger son of one of the landlords of Bori). About 800 Ogoni people had, indeed, gone to Owerri, only to learn that I had been sent to

Port Harcourt. A number of them now attempted to see me in the latter place. In the end, I reluctantly had to place a limit on the number of people I would see. I didn't do this in order to keep away from visitors. But each time a visitor came, I would have to be sent for from my cell some distance away. And I couldn't really cope with the continual coming and going.

I finally got my mattress and the other items I had ordered from my office at about nine o'clock, and went to bed thereafter. Next to me in the infirmary was a young Ogoni boy who had spent three years and more in the prison, waiting for someone to sign a bail bond of 5,000 naira on his behalf.

Apart from Dube and Nwiee who naturally stayed with me, there were three or four young men in the ward who introduced themselves to us. They gave us an idea of how the ward was run. We had to pay a levy of a hundred naira each, which was used for the upkeep of the ward: to replace electric bulbs, etc., etc. I knew it was illegal, but I didn't bother myself with that.

I slept well that night. The only problem I had was when the warder locked us in for the night. That was a novel experience, and I hated it thoroughly. What if I needed medical attention at night? There was no telephone, and no doctor either. Mercifully, the University of Port Harcourt Teaching Hospital was, literally, around the corner. But I would need to get there! I had to call on my store of humour to internalize the experience quickly and accept it as 'one of those things'.

I woke up after my usual four-hour sleep to analyse my new situation. What came to my mind was how often a prison had featured in my fiction. There were *Prisoners of Jebs* and its sequel, *Pita Dumbrok's Prison*. And in 1992 I had completed *Lemona*, my fifth novel, in longhand only to have it stolen along with my briefcase at Lagos Airport on my return from my trip to Geneva to present the Ogoni case before the United Nations Working Group on Indigenous Populations. I thought how much better the novels might have been if I had written them after my current experience. The loss of my last novel, whose heroine had spent twenty-five years in prison, had affected me badly, killing my desire to write fiction. I hoped that I would be able to find the will to rewrite the novel and that it would be much enriched by my experience of prison.

I thought too of the other harrowing discovery, that one third of the 1,200 inmates of that prison were Ogoni people. Most of them had just been dumped there on minor charges, forgotten by the police and the judicial system which sent them there, with no one to take up their cases and give them justice. My attention had been drawn to the fact by the fairly large number of the prison staff who happened to be Ogoni. Again, it was not surprising that that number of staff should be Ogoni. The conditions of service of prison staff were dismal, and the salary a mere pittance. Who wanted to work in the prison except the condemned of the earth?

My enemies were soon to capitalize on the fact of the number of Ogoni people on the staff. When day broke and the staff had their usual morning briefing, the Ogoni staff were told that they were not to get too close to me, as information had reached the authorities that there was a plan to storm the prison and effect my release. I had to work quickly to dispel that piece of blackmail. I had a press release issued to the effect that there was no need to seek my release from detention, as every day I spent there helped to advance my cause.

All that day I had a steady stream of visitors, some of whom I couldn't refuse to see, as they had travelled a long distance from Ogoni in order to meet me. My aged parents came calling also, and it was quite cheering to see them look so brave. I had initially asked my brother Owens not to allow them to come to Owerri. I had forewarned my father two years earlier that I might well end up in prison or in the grave for my endeavours, and he certainly seemed to take it well; but Owens had informed me how badly my father really felt, and I had then thought that he should not be made to suffer any more. At eighty-nine, he did not have to take the trouble to come to faraway Owerri. But when I read a brave interview which my mother gave to a national newspaper and heard her insist that I must carry on the struggle, I had no more worries about them coming to see me in detention.

And so they did come to Owerri. My father appeared quite calm, but my mother looked shaken. I had to assure her that I was perfectly all right, and that there was nothing to worry about. Like all mothers, she was quite solicitous of my well-being and had brought along a delicacy which I enjoyed in my youth: nutless palm fruit. I had quite forgotten it, not having had any for forty years or so. I was really thrilled to eat them. And after she had left, I was moved to song:

Mama Came Calling

She came visiting today
The lovely little lady
In her hand a dainty meal
Of nutless palm fruits
A long-forgotten delicacy
From my childhood days
Into which I dug my teeth
As my baby gums her breasts
And found therein once again
The milky sweet of a mother's blessings

On their visit to Port Harcourt Prison, the laugh was at the expense of my father. When he came to Owerri, he had not told me of the birth of his youngest son, my youngest half-brother, on the day of my arrest, 21 June. Indeed, everyone had forgotten to mention it to me; it came to me via a publication in a national newspaper. When my father came visiting, I teased him no end. The grand old man only smiled.

In the first two days in the prison, I worked very hard at adapting myself to the routine of the place. Because we were in prison custody, and also in the infirmary, we were not really subject to the full routine of a prison, although we had the rights to which prisoners were entitled. One major problem was again the toilet facility. My friend Mina, who was around most of the time, realizing my predicament, encouraged me to use what was available. The thought of it alone would kill the call. Eventually, on the morning of the third day, I was forced to use the bucket latrine, after ensuring that it was thoroughly disinfected and cleaned out. To urinate was to empty the bladder into a dirty little container whose contents were then poured through a hole in the wall out to the back of the building. Ugh! But having used it once, I learnt to endure it.

Company was not lacking in the prison. Perhaps the most celebrated man there was Major-General Lekwot, who had governed Rivers State between 1975 and 1979. He was the victim of one of the worst cases of political injustice – the well-known Zangon Kataf affair, in which a minority ethnic group, the Katafs, had risen against their Hausa-Fulani oppressors. The latter had taken heavy reprisals: a phoney tribunal had been set up, before which a group of hapless Katafs, most of whom had had nothing to do with the actual uprising, were arraigned and condemned to death. Babangida had granted them a reprieve, changing their sentences to various prison terms. The affair had aroused national and international furore, but injustice prevailed, and Lekwot and his kinsmen remained in jail.

I found them all, and Lekwot in particular, in a calm frame of mind. He did his exercises regularly, and I had to pass by his cell, a sort of VIP abode, each morning as I went to have my bath in a stone enclosure in the open air. We got talking, and analysed the national, Kataf and Ogoni situations.

Also in prison was Mr O. C. Nsirim, who was having to clear his name over the murder of my dear friend, the late Dr Obi Wali. I had a lot of difficulty talking with him, which is understandable. I had known him for a long time, and when he slumped on the Thursday or Friday morning in his cell, there was cause for concern. I called on him once to extend my sympathy. He recovered and left the prison before I did.

The prison day was quite long, starting at about six o'clock, when the nightsoil man came to clear the latrine bucket. Some of the longer-serving inmates engaged him in a humorous banter in Igbo. Then would follow the general cleaning and after that breakfast. I took a look once at the food that was being served and almost puked. It was fit neither for man nor beast. Thereafter, for me, it was a matter of receiving visitors, having read the newspapers which arrived with my breakfast. There was a bit of time to read, and I followed the news on my radio very keenly. The day ended at about seven o'clock when the warders locked us in. Quite dreary, I would think. And not meant to keep one in good health.

By the Friday my health had deteriorated. I still hadn't had the opportunity to see my doctor, even though I requested it the very day I got to the prison. Instead of my doctor, the Coffin turned up, bearing in its depths Mr Ogbeifun and his man Friday. We went through the process of my making another written statement and answering a few more silly questions from Mr Inah. I specifically asked Mr Ogbeifun if he meant to transfer me again to another prison. He lied to me and swore upon it that that was not the case.

That evening, it became imperative for me to consult a doctor. I sent for my brother Owens, who happened to be around, and asked him to get in touch by all means with Dr Ibiama, who had been looking after me. Bobo Ibiama, a consultant physician, had been my contemporary at Ibadan University and had spent all his working life in Rivers State, where he rose to become Director of Medical Services before retiring into private practice and consulting for the University of Port Harcourt Teaching Hospital. He had lately made an unexpected foray into party politics, contesting the position of Governor of Rivers State. He was too fine a man to win a Nigerian election and duly crashed out. Very well born to a Bonny family, he was a model of a gentleman, and came into the prison as soon as he heard of my condition.

Along with him came Professor Claude Ake, all anxious for me. Bobo took a look at me, applied his stethoscope and sphygmanometer and decided that I had to be moved to the teaching hospital. He gave orders to that effect.

Effecting the order was to take all of the time and patience of Professor Ake, my brother Owens, my friend, Alfred Ilenre, who had come down from Lagos to see me, and one of the prison officers, Mr Okpoko, who had gone out of his way to ensure that I was properly taken care of.

It transpired that because I was in prison custody, I remained the responsibility of the Nigerian police force and not of the Nigerian prison service, and that the permission of the Rivers State Commissioner of Police would have to be obtained before I could be released into hospital. When the Commissioner was contacted very late that night, he said we would require a court order from a high court judge. No judge could be contacted that night.

The following morning, Saturday, my brother was able to obtain the high court order, but when it was presented to the Commissioner of Police, a bovine-looking man called Bayo Balogun, he merely threw the court order to the floor. This took place before a journalist from the respected newspaper *The Times* of London. And there the matter might have ended.

All that Saturday I was in agony. Then came the Sunday. I met with the *Times* reporter, Mr Kyle, and came to learn that there had been quite some concern in Britain over my safety. Indeed, Claude Ake had given me that morning a copy of *The Times Literary Supplement* in which Tony Daniels had done a piece about my arrest.

I had met Tony, an exciting medical doctor whose wander-lust has carried him through most of Africa, in March at my Port Harcourt office, and swapped stories with him. He had such a fund of jokes on Africa, it was really most unbeliev-able. He had also written several travel books on Africa and I thought it really nice of him to have exposed my travails to the British public.

That Sunday night when my condition deteriorated fur-ther, I had to cry for help through the window of our ward. A helpless warder came round, and sent for the Superintend-ent; he turned up equally helpless, looked through my window and mumbled something really inane. I might just as well have died. But I was determined not to give my tormen-tors that comfort. The will to survive saw me through the crisis.

When morning came, I sent urgently to the boss of the prison and challenged him. I virtually called him an assas-sin before most of his senior staff whom he had invited along. I could not understand, I said, why he had refused to send me to hospital in spite of a consultant's order. I refused to accept that the police should determine what happens to me. The prison authorities and Mr Ikpatti himself, personally, would have a lot of accounting to do to my family and to the Ogoni people if anything should happen to me because they were dithering over who was to sign what paper or because they did not know what to do about simple matters of life and death. Somehow, it worked. After a six-hour wait, during which Mr Ikpatti must have consulted the gods and oracles of his native Ibibioland, he finally informed me that he had found a way round the regulations. He would send me to the hospital and inform the Divisional Police Officer, a minor official in the pecking order, about what he had done. It would be up to the DPO to send the information to his superiors.

Then another real problem cropped up. The prison had no writing-paper and all the shops had closed. Mr James Nwibana, a printer from Ogoni, had visited me the previous day and left me a ream of paper, just in case I wanted to write. I sent for the paper and offered to type the letter myself just in case the prison typist had gone home.

Mercifully, the typist was an Ogoni man who had refused to close for the day. He finally typed the letter without an error, and I was on my way to the University of Port Harcourt Teaching Hospital. The prison had no ambulance and no car, of course. I had to travel in a car provided by my office, in between two prison officers.

We drove past my office on Aggrey Road, and were, within a few minutes, at the blessed hospital. Mrs Beredugo, an experienced Matron and the wife of an old friend, was on duty, and took steps to ensure that I was safely installed in a private room in the hospital within a very short time indeed. Dr Ibiama had left orders to that effect, and I was under sedation before very long.

Believe it or not, fifteen minutes after I left 'Alabama City' for the hospital, an order signed by the Chief Judge of Rivers State arrived, asking that the MOSOP Three be transferred to different prisons. I was to be sent to Enugu, and Dube and Nwiee to Owerri Prison. Mr Inah was on hand to execute the order, and only waited until MIDNIGHT to commence operations.

He arrived at the prison with armed guards, ordered the hapless Dube and Nwiee to get ready, hurled them into the Coffin, and came to the teaching hospital to fetch me. I was rudely awakened out of deep sleep to see the unwelcome face of Mr Inah at the door.

'I have orders to take you away,' Mr Inah intoned coldly.

'Where to?'

'To Enugu.'

I looked at the time. It was thirty minutes past midnight.

'Sorry, I'm not well,' I said weakly.

'I have my orders.'

The Matron on duty came in to ask what was happening. Mr Inah reported his mission.

'Sorry, you can't take away the patient without the specific instructions of the Chief Medical Director.'

'I have my orders, madam,' Mr Inah emphasized.

'And I have my orders too!' The Matron was firm.

Mr Inah withdrew. I could hear the rain pouring down.

'Don't worry,' the Matron assured me, as she tucked me into my bed. 'Nobody will take you away from here.'

Later that night, Dr Longjohn, my contemporary at Ibadan University and a friend from those days, turned up. He woke me up and asked if I had been taken proper care of. I replied in the affirmative.

'That's fine. You can go back to sleep.'

I rolled over. Dr Longjohn had just saved me from the conspiracy which involved Governor Ada George, the

Commissioner of Police, Bayo Balogun, and other highly placed persons in the murderous Babangida regime.

Fate had played its own part. That night, Mr Ogbeifun and Bayo Balogun did their damnedest to find the leader of the police mobile squadron to organize men to storm the hospital and take me away. That man was not to be found. And they gave up, reluctantly.

According to Dube, who was in the Coffin while Mr Inah drove around looking for the Chief Medical Director of the teaching hospital, the Police Mobile Force leader, the Commissioner of Police and Mr Ogbeifun, they finally drove off when all else failed, at about two o'clock, in the direction of Owerri. Arriving at the Port Harcourt International Airport, Mr Inah decided that he needed some sleep and the Coffin stopped at the airport so he could do so. They arrived at Owerri Prison at nine o'clock the following morning. The prison authorities were not very willing to take them in, as the regulations had been breached. In the end, they were admitted.

That morning Dr Longjohn came to inform me, humorously, that he had been told that Ogoni warriors would be coming to storm the hospital. Was I assuring him that that would not happen? I gave him the undertaking. He laughed and went off.

Unknown to me, a great number of people and organizations in Nigeria and abroad had taken steps to save me from the fangs of Babangida, the Monster of Minna. Amnesty International, which had adopted the three of us as Prisoners of Conscience, The Times of London, the Observer, the Committee for Writers in Prison of International PEN, the BBC, Ken Jr, my first son, William Boyd, the peerless British novelist, the United Nations Working Group for Indigenous People, UNPO, Greenpeace, the Association of Nigerian Authors had all played a role in my release. Nor must I fail to mention the staff in my office at Port Harcourt and Lagos, Apollos Onwuasoaku, Innocent Iheme, Deebii Nwiado, Emeka Nwachukwu, Kweku Arthur, Sunday Dugbor and others. And, of course, the entire people of Ogoni, Olu Onagoruwa, Ledum Mitee and Barry Kumbe, Senator Cyrus Nunieh, Samuel Igbara and Mr Briggs, the lawyers who took up my cause free of charge. I must also thank the senior police officers at Owerri, including Mr Ilozuoke and Mr Ukah, the prison officers at Port Harcourt Prison, Dr I. I. Ibiama and the doctors and nurses at the University of Port Harcourt Teaching Hospital.

Release finally came on 22 July, when one of the police officers in mufti who had abducted me on the highway in June came to inform me that he had instruction to grant me bail. This instruction, it would appear, had come from someone called Aikhomu, who was said to be Vice-President of some place called Nigeria. Just where were the courts, you wonder? What of Mrs D, the magistrate who was busy writing in her book and sending us to prison custody? The court no longer mattered. A man called Aikhomu had decided. Shame on these men who subvert the law and morality! The bail bond, I was told, could only be signed by my 89-year-old father. I'm stumped if these guys haven't all gone crazy. I thanked the messenger for his troubles, anyway.

Meanwhile, in Owerri, by the crazed dance of the Nigerian masquerade, the good judge who sat over my suit, which we continued to press, had found that the state had held me illegally and ruled that I be paid some compensation and set free. The ruling did not matter to the Babangida government: it had already taken a decision unguided by the law which it was supposed to be obeying.

I had been detained for a month and a day, during which I had witnessed the efficiency of evil. In a country where virtually nothing worked, the security services, armed with all the gadgets of modern invention, made sure that all orders were carried out with military precision. And the men were marvellously faithful to their instructions.

When Mr Ogbeifun and Mr Inah turned up at my bedside in the hospital to say something about bail and whatnot, I could only offer them the scorn of stony silence, my eyes shut, so I wouldn't see their extraordinarily handsome faces.

Had I known what the conspiracy had in store for the Ogoni people, I might not have been so thankful that I had got off lightly. Notice had been given that on 15 July, 132 Ogoni men, women and children, returning from their abode in the Cameroons, had been waylaid on the Andoni River by an armed gang and cruelly murdered, leaving but two women to make a report.

The genocide of the Ogoni had taken on a new dimension. The manner of it I will narrate in my next book, if I live to tell the tale.

Port Harcourt
17 May 1994